Hippocrene Insiders Guide to
JAVA & BALI

ippocrene Insider's Guide to
JAVA & BALI

Jerry LeBlanc

HIPPOCRENE BOOKS
New York

Copyright © 1992 Jerry LeBlanc

All rights reserved.

For information, address:
Hippocrene Books, Inc.
171 Madison Avenue
New York, NY 10016

ISBN 0-7818-0037-4

Printed in the United States of America.

Contents

An Introduction to Java and Bali   9

About the People and the Places   13

The Travel Planner   23

Jakarta   37

Bogor and Bandung   75

Java's West Coast   87

Yogyakarta   99

East Java   117

Bali   129

Other Islands   183

Appendix   203

Index   219

Maps

Java   6

Bali   7

Jakarta   38

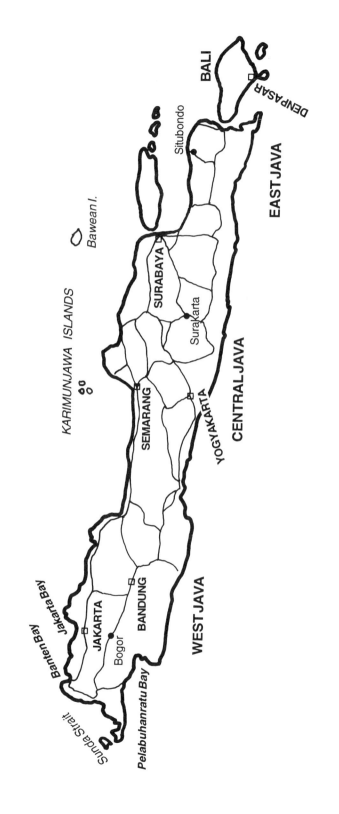

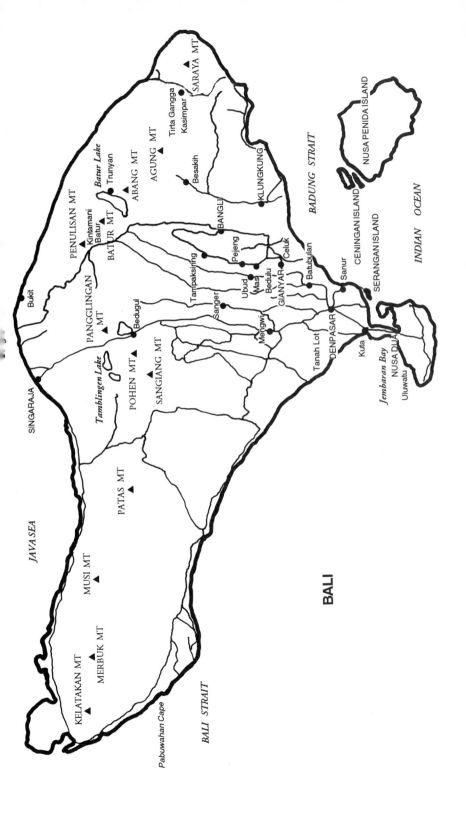

BALI

An Introduction to Java & Bali

When we dream of islands, of faraway places, we do not have to go much beyond the simple mental image of gleaming white sand, palm trees and water. Java and Bali have these, of course, in abundance.

If we set about to make our dream come true, to put ourselves in it, then we must endow our dream with a few requirements. Of course we want the place to be beautiful, and it should be exotic, intriguing, something really different. Then, too, we want a friendly place. A place that is safe and inviting. Java and Bali fill all of these needs superlatively.

Indonesia, the nation of which Java and Bali form the very heart, offers experiences that run the gamut from sophistication of modern resort life to, literally, *terra incognita*.

Consider this: for years all the tourist publications and reference works declared the number of individual islands in Indonesia as 13,677 precisely. In 1990, an official government publication hedged on the figure for the first time. It said, "Recent satellite pictures show there are more."

After the most recent count, dated 1991, government publications revised the figure upward to a staggering 17,508 islands. This shows that they have so many islands that they actually could not count them! Any nation that can misplace 3,800 or so islands has to be worth visiting!

The rich diversity of this vast, far-flung archipelago can be sampled in full on Java and Bali: storybook temples a thousand years old, villages where ancient lifestyles have been preserved since anno Domini one, the palaces of sultans and kings, colorful museums, spectacular local markets, accessible wild animal refuges, huge rain forests second only to those of Brazil, lush green parks, beaches bathed in warm sun, gleaming crater lakes and historic volcanos—not to mention a metropolis or two—all await the visitor.

The beauty of Java and Bali—dazzling, moving and memorable—is enhanced by a people so friendly and charming that they make their home yours; but the surroundings will never let you forget for a moment that you are in a different, exotic land. Unlike many parts of the world which are seething in political unrest today, Indonesia is at peace and eagerly welcomes Westerners, especially Americans and other English-speaking visitors, for English is a second language to Indonesians, taught in schools and recognized as the world language of the future. This is a safe place. The 1990s were launched with a "Visit Indonesia Campaign." You are invited. You are welcome here.

If you decide that you must see this very special place, you will find that you must travel almost half way around the world to get there, but when you immerse yourself in the serenity and splendor, the sights and sensations, you will believe that every mile was worth it; you will find yourself treasuring each day.

How many days can you give to Java and Bali? They deserve as much time as you can spare. Two weeks is considered the optimal minimum, and even in that time span hard choices will have to be made. You can travel east to west or west to east, schedule one or two main stops, or a half dozen. This book will help you make your choices, even if the only choice you make is leaving the decisions to others.

Some travel books will tell you how—often at great discomfort and through time-consuming effort—you can save a dollar or two a day. This book makes the assumption that your enjoyment and your general comfort are worth more than that, yet the information in these pages will save you handsful of money on the bigger things, without sacrifice.

After all, even if you travel on a tight budget and have scrimped and saved all year long for your trip, you did not endure frugality so that you could sweat through your underwear in a blind, dusty, noisy, three-wheel golf cart in life-threatening traffic far across the seas, or why would you leave home at all? Try instead the regularly scheduled morning traffic jam on the freeways of Los Angeles or the commuter highways of any major American city.

The three-wheel cart mentioned is a good example. It's called a *bajaj* and plies the streets of many Java cities. You can bargain for a really cheap ride in one of the things, which are kind of a cross between a rickshaw and a forklift, but since they are barred from major streets they take much longer to get anywhere and you end up saving little. So why waste your time and comfort, unless you crave new experience at any cost?

The view of this book is that one should throw away the coins treating oneself while ringing up major savings on the larger bills that really count. There is a theory of travel involved in the principle.

Tourism, or leisure travel, is a kind of imitation exploration. What the anthropologist Margaret Mead did a half-century ago in observing native tribes in their Bali village, we do by mini-bus, at an agreed rate, including lunch. Travel can be educational, to be sure, but the object of it all, not discounting the insight into other worlds and other lives, is enjoyment. And in that perhaps all travelers owe a debt of gratitude to the Australians, whose international reputation for fun-filled excursions have helped to reinforce the notion that what tourists really seek is a good time.

Even the impressive research of scientist Mead dealt more with the relationship of personality to culture than the ritual manifestations of culture. She cared more about the people and their lives than their ceremonies and art.

Think about it. You might learn more by taking a Javanese to lunch than by watching a staged presentation. Buy a Balinese a drink.

Travel should cater to your very own personal preferences. Do you go to Cape Cod to watch pilgrim pageants or for the cool breeze in summer? Do people race to the Miami sun in winter for the monuments there? Do they visit Las Vegas to see where the first casino was erected? Is the changing of the guard at Buckingham Palace after all more significant than the tradition of the neighborhood pub? Which practice brings the visitor closer to the people and their land?

So there are choices to make. There is so much to see and do that no single suggested route will be ideal for everyone. But even if you choose a different route than that suggested by the sequence of this guide, each section—Bali, Jakarta, etc.—stands on its own and can serve you as you require. Our Travel Planner section offers interesting suggestions for mapping your own, personalized tour.

If the author should occasionally point out potholes in paradise, this is done with love and not disparagingly. One can love life and still criticize the details. If levity sometimes enters the text, it is to be considered an effort to bring a measure of sanity to tourism, or the way we regard travel in general.

The author also pleads guilty to occasional blasphemy and sporadic irreverence in regard to some traditional aspects of tourism, but it should be known that this does not indicate any displeasure whatsoever with Java and Bali, which are so dearly loved, in fact, that a campaign of prayer and good works has been undertaken in order to press a suit for personal reincarnation there, if any openings should come up—above the level of a taxi driver, of course.

Read on. You are in for a wondrous experience.

CHAPTER ONE

About the People
and the Places

The people of Java and Bali are cheerful, friendly, proud, patriotic, religious but tolerant, pro-U.S.A., anti-communist, non-aggressive, curious, poor, generous, industrious, clean, attractive and extremely polite. These generalized traits have roots in the collective experience of the nation of Indonesia.

Their history was virtually predetermined by geography and geology, with major events hinging on the strategic location of the islands at the door of the South China Sea and Indian Ocean. The islands were encountered by outsiders as soon as man began seafaring excursions. Their location, plus the rich natural resources of the islands, made them a crossroads of shipping through the ages. Whatever nation dominated the waters of the region also tended to try to dominate Java and its neighboring islands.

Java and Bali are next-door neighbors, lying just below the equator, roughly 600 miles southeast of Singapore and 800 miles northwest of mainland Australia, separating the Pacific Ocean from the Indian Ocean, and bounding the South China Sea to their north. From the west coast of the United States, the islands sit about 7,500 miles away.

Bali, located off Java's eastern tip, is tiny. It is no bigger than Oahu in the Hawaiian Islands, to which it is often compared for its lush beaches and mountainous interior. Java, more than 700 miles long, ranks in size with Florida or Cuba. The two islands are closely linked by an efficient ferry system.

Both Java and Bali present a diverse topography. Plateaus and plains, rocky cliffs and flat shorelines, steaming jungles with swinging vines, and a line of volcanic mountains stretching uninterrupted, east-west, in mid-island as if the two islands were one, sharing the same backbone.

Because they are the most developed, the most populous of all the Indonesian islands, and because of their proximity to one another, they offer a practical capsule experience of all Indonesia in so far as is possible for a visitor without a lifetime to wander. Both Java and Bali offer accommodations and transportation at a level that foreign visitors are used to—unlike most of the other islands.

But for all their similarities, Java and Bali are different enough to be regarded almost as separate nations, miles apart from one another. Their history tells us why. On these neighboring islands until 500 or 600 years ago, the people lived very similar lives.

The fact that Bali was the more isolated, more distant from the shipping channels and lacking deep water ports (or any port facilities to speak of), plus the fact that Bali had few natural resources to invite robbery by the Western world, gave the smaller island a degree of peace and security that neighboring Java did not share once the colonial movement sent the gunboats of Europe far and wide.

Even before the European penetration of Java and the Spice Islands—of which Bali was not considered a prize member—the Muslim influence introduced to Java by Arab traders separated Java and Bali significantly. For at that time, beginning in the 1400s, most of the local people were followers of the Hindu religion. With the influx of Islam, Hindu artists and intellectuals fled en masse to Bali to maintain their faith. So Bali benefited. The migration is said to be the reason Bali is so artistically oriented. The expertise of the people in carving, silverware, painting and the performing arts, especially dancing, was polished through centuries, undisturbed and handed down through families, always linked to the Hindu faith.

But as far as outside world contact was concerned, Bali slept until the 20th century, when Dutch invasions began. Perhaps more important was the later, post-World War II invasion of tourists. First Australians from close by, then people from all over the world, lured by reports of idyllic island life, the superior artistic temperament and unspoiled natural wonders, began to flock to Bali, prompting tourist development that came to exceed that in Java by far.

Java, meanwhile, a financially richer island, nourished its intellectuals and artisans in Yogyakarta and Bandung primarily, although arts and skills similar to those of Bali were discovered by the outside world more slowly. Tourism developed later, too. Java, even while its capital Jakarta was becoming one of the world's largest cities, retained many pockets of unspoiled nature and isolated villages relatively untouched by time. The size alone, not to mention the ruggedness of the interior, hid these treasures.

While Bali's major attractions in the southern half of the island are becoming overwhelmed by tourism, the bigger Java affords a glimpse into the past that Bali once shared, so that the two neighboring islands complement one another, each providing what the other lacks—an ideal situation for visitors. A full panorama of island life reaching back more than a thousand years awaits the traveler, and a full range of experiences—from the ancient and rustic to the most modern, from the smallest village to the largest metropolis, from endless uninhabited wilderness to teeming cities.

Indonesia is today the fifth largest nation in the world, trailing just behind the United States in population with a conservatively estimated 185 million people, the greatest percentage of which lives on Java and Bali. The capital city of Jakarta, with approximately 8 million people, is bigger than New York or London, and Java has four other cities with more than one million in population.

Young people tend to trek from small villages to the cities to seek their fortune—a movement which the government tries to discourage. Yet most of the people (83 percent) are farmers still and poor, the wealth of the islands never having filtered down to the masses.

Farming, the major occupation of the islands, was largely dictated by geology. The volcanic Ring of Fire islands are blessed with fertile lava-rich soil. Meanwhile, the need for irrigation systems promoted cooperation between neighboring peoples, which spurred social interaction and development. Tribes had to learn to get along with one another, and when they did, they learned the advantage of trade.

Indonesia is a young nation, in more ways than one. The constitution dates back only to August 1945, and it was only several years later that the Dutch, under pressure from the United Nations, put down their guns and agreed to let the Indonesians live in peace and freedom. Today 65 percent of the burgeoning population is under 21 years of age, and it is likely that, despite government pleas for small families, there will be a new baby boom.

The vital statistics of the republic (see Appendix) are not just words. The government has adopted a progressive attitude toward public welfare, forest and animal preservation, and global responsibility. One telling example: while other nations turned their back on refugees, the already crowded Indonesia sheltered more than ten thousand Vietnamese boat people on their northern islands in 1990, and their foreign minister stated, "We will always uphold the Geneva Convention [on refugees] and we will be true to it as well. We never have any intention to chase the boat people away. Never."

In religion 87 percent of the Javanese are Muslim, but the Balinese are predominantly Hindu. Both situations reflect the native acquiescence to foreign creeds brought to their shores centuries ago. But whenever a new religion spread in these islands, it always was infused with traditional native beliefs of ancient origin involving animism and reverence for ancestors. Christians and Buddhists practice on the islands with complete freedom despite being minorities, and Islam is practiced with far more latitude than anywhere in Arabia. Women do not wear veils and they enjoy all the freedoms that men do. Regional differences are noteworthy. Tribes in pockets of west and east Java observe the Christianity taught to them by missionaries. In the area of Bandung, Islam is less influenced by Hinduism than in the east.

The dress is Western style; the favorite music comes from America, Europe and Australia, and outsiders are not regarded as infidels, but rather with considerable esteem. After all, to the average person from Java or Bali, all tourists are rich, a desirable trait which has a way of transcending national borders and religious differences.

The per capita income in Indonesia today is estimated at approximately $700, which is roughly the annual earnings of a government worker or teacher. An upper-rank army officer makes more than twice that amount. There are wide gaps between the rich and poor which can be seen in homes ranging from shacks to mansions.

The government of Indonesia—although its bureaucracy is as corrupt and inefficient as that of any modern nation—seems sincere in its efforts to improve the economic well-being of the people through educational programs financed by increased exports. Indonesia has more oil than Kuwait but suffers the fortunes of OPEC's wildly wavering market.

If at all possible, the visitor should avoid getting involved with any level of the government. The local people themselves observe this principle from long, hard-earned knowledge that being buried in red tape amid indecision does not quickly solve a minor problem, but often confounds and magnifies it.

The religiousness of the people should not be underestimated. Although the young are becoming increasingly aware of designer jeans and Western luxuries and crave them, their whole attitude toward life is more spiritual than that of the average visitor. Whether Hindu or Muslim, they cling to an ancient heritage or *adat* which grants respect not only to all living creatures but to the trees and flowers, the mountains and the smallest rock. They even set a day aside for the blessing of all metal objects (including automobiles). Everything is considered a part of a life force.

On Bali especially one sees signs of religion pervading every-day life. When a family sits down to a meal, one of the younger members will often place a small token plate of their food on the shelf of a backyard shrine dedicated to an ancestor, in order that the dearly departed one, unforgotten, may still share in the ritual of family life.

The food staple is rice, which is grown everywhere in centuries old, sculptured paddies on the slopes and flatlands. As a broad generalization, it could be observed that the cuisine of Bali and Java blends the oriental and Arabic worlds.

Oriental dishes are plentiful and diverse. Fried rice, mixed with bits of chicken, meat or fish, forms the basic meal for most families, but *sate* (sah-tay) a stick of barbecued, seasoned meats that resembles shish-kebab, is another widely popular dish. Fish, shrimp—seafood in general—is plentiful and, for the visitor at least, quite inexpensive.

Chinese restaurants are numerous and even small villages will provide Chinese favorites. Larger cities, especially those with a tourist trade, usually have Japanese, Korean, Thai, Mexican, and even American-style fast-food outlets. The hamburger is everywhere. Imported steaks are available at reasonable prices, and visitors lucky enough to sample a buffet feast will be amazed at the variety and excellence of the food spread on the groaning tables, and the cost. The islands have not, however, caught on to providing Western-style desserts, and sweet dishes may be rated more as "interesting" than reminiscent of home.

Native grown fruits and vegetables, including the exotic and tantalizing, are abundant and tasty.

American, British and Australian visitors will find that many of the exotic dishes have been modified to their taste, a result of the long Dutch occupation, during which island cuisine was adapted to European palates. Those who wish to be more adventurous in eating will find that different villages and regions have their own specialties, which usually rely on whichever basic foods are most locally available.

Dishes that are labeled "Sumatra-style" rather than Javanese will likely be hotter, because the Sumatra people run wild with chili peppers. Javanese food is spicy enough for the average visitor, who will find a variety of menu items that intrigue. *Nasi goreng*, which is fried rice with sate, is very popular, as is *gado-gado*, a salad served with peanut sauce. The meat, vegetable, fish and fowl dishes available—all touched with typical local flavorings like coconut, peanut, or whatever spice is most plentiful locally—will appeal to many visitors, while others will face no problem in finding foods prepared the way they are used to. It is part of the politeness of the Indonesians that they will discuss their menu offerings and let visitors sample sauces.

A visitor talking to a Java or Bali resident should try to reciprocate their over-politeness. Discussion of religion should be avoided just as in any mixed company. Atheism is a taboo subject because it is associated with communism, another taboo. Other subjects to be avoided in conversation include Arab-Israeli conflicts (Indonesians opposed Iraqi president Saddam Hussein but lost thousands of jobs due to the 1991 war), the question of rightful rule in East Timor or Irian Jaya, and generally, any controversial politics. If one said to a burly Australian in a boisterous tavern, "I don't like your face," his reaction would be quite predictable; but when talking to Indonesians on sensitive subjects, one must remember that these are people straining to be polite at all costs and that certain topics will place them in an embarrassing position. They do not wish to offend you by disagreeing.

This same attitude often results in misdirections. If you ask a Java or Bali native where something or some place is, he or she will never say, "I don't know." They would rather make something up, or guess. It would be too embarrassing not to be able to help you. So when asking for directions, get a consensus (two votes out of three) and consult your maps anyway before proceeding.

They are a young-old people. They are humble and proud. Did their history make them so? Many historical allusions are cited in this book in reference to particular monuments. A capsule review of significant dates in the Java and Bali record shows the diversity of their background:

500,000 B.C.	Date fixed for Java Man fossils discovered near Solo.
2500	Beginning of Asian migrations to Java.
500	Bronze artworks in evidence on Bali.
50 A.D.	Trade with China, India, bringing Hindu and Buddhist influences.
150	Trade expands. Export caravans reach Greece and Rome.
650	Buddhist Srivigaya Kingdom based on Sumatra rules Melakka Strait and Java.
675	Arab Muslim traders form Sumatra settlements.
760	Borobudur (Buddhist) temple built. Hindu and Buddhist kingdoms coexist.
860	Mataram Kingdom (Hindu) arises in East Java.
1290	Majapahit Kingdom (Hindu) prospers in Java.
1400	Islamic influences spread in Java.
1511–12	Portuguese take control of Melakka Strait and Maluku Islands spice trade.
1596	Dutch land in West Java.
1641	Dutch take control of Melakka Strait.

1640	Batavia (now Jakarta) becomes trade capital of East Indies.
1755	Dutch split weakened Mataram Kingdom into Yogyakarta and Solo districts.
1811–16	British interregnum in Java and Bali.
1825–30	Java war led by Prince Diponegoro against Dutch occupation.
1846–49	Dutch expedition to conquer Bali
1906	New Dutch military conquests, occupation of Bali.
1927	Sukarno Nationalist Party arises out of study group in Bandung.
1930	Sukarno imprisoned by Dutch.
1942	Java, Bali, other islands occupied by Japanese war forces.
1945	Independent Indonesia proclaimed as defeated Japanese depart.
1946–49	War with Dutch.
1949	Dutch abandon Indonesia as colony.
1965	Attempted Communist coup and harsh retaliation.

Peace.

CHAPTER TWO

The Travel Planner

What you see and do in Java and Bali should be molded more to your heart's desires rather than the published activity schedules of travel agents or hotel recreation directors. With a little advance planning, you can tailor your experience of the wide variety of island attractions to your own personal perferences.

Would you prefer a hike in a rain forest, a crawl around metropolitan pubs, a plunge into sea and surf, an endless shopping spree—or just idling in the sun?

Tastes differ. There seems to be a presumption among some travel circles operating in Java and Bali that all visitors have an insatiable appetite for traditional dances, puppet shows, volcano climbing and temple photography. This is not always so, of course, although such pursuits have been very popular.

Nevertheless, some people will feel that island theater is obscure, complex and contrived, and that the drama, originating however long ago, may be of historic or cultural curiosity but that its entertainment value is minimal. If you are such a visitor, the colorful costumes and exotic atmosphere will quickly pall and such presentations will go on your list as "maybe see it once."

People also will say in all honesty that puppet shows really are for children. Sample one or two if you wish, but do not get roped into more unless they genuinely intrigue you. Despite the historic nature of these presentations, they generally fail to educate the westerner in the lore of daily Indonesian life. Don't take them too seriously. A pageant depicting the Boston Tea Party may be of passing interest to an American who is familiar with the story but would likely mean little to a foreigner; likewise Indonesian presentations of ancient themes have distinct value in enriching their lives rather than that of the average visitor.

There is so much to see and do in Java and Bali that one must be selective. Try to see it all and do it all if you can and wish to, but when you have to choose, and you will, go where your heart says to go, do what you feel like doing. This is the place for it. You are in paradise. There are no rules. There are no obligatory schedules.

To facilitate your planning for Java and Bali, we offer a simple calendar of choices called the Travel Planner. It is basically a skeletal framework on which to proceed from day to day—simple memos to yourself with enough flexibility to allow the occasional lapse into poolside idling or beach bummery, urges that tend to overcome the most energetic when in Java and Bali.

Sample charts can be seen on the next few pages, along with a blank chart for you to fill in. Those which are already made out might serve the traditional visitor who wants to see as much as can be seen in two weeks. Note that the designated "two weeks" only covers twelve days. The Balinese would understand such a calendar. This is a deliberate design to provide for relaxation—for relief from the schedule itself, lest it become too slavish—as well as to allow for those unexpected travel incidents and choices which always come up and throw the best laid plans awry.

Forming your own chart is a simple exercise.

As you read the upcoming chapters describing the attractions of Java and Bali, pick out those which especially appeal to you. Write them down like a shopping list. Pare your list down to ten entries.

THE TRAVEL PLANNER

DAY ONE—
Fly to Bali

DAY TWO—
Rest and relax in Bali

Poolside
Seaside

DAY THREE—
Excursion
to Ubud
Mas
Celuk

Sightseeing

Shopping

Late afternoon at pool

Evening, dine out

DAY FOUR—
Poolside a.m.

Late afternoon excursion to Tanah Lot

Dinner at seaside

DAY FIVE—
Morning walk on Kuta beach strip
Shopping

Afternoon poolside

Evening show, Bali dancers or drama

DAY SIX—
Early start, Day trip to Mother Temple
Sightseeing enroute (or monkey forest)

Night pub crawl, Kuta

DAY SEVEN—
Fly to Jakarta

Check in at City Hotel or Beach Hotel

Leisurely lunch, dinner

DAY EIGHT—
City tour

See monuments, Ancol or Mini Indonesia park

Round off day at Surabaya Market

Evening nightlife

DAY NINE—
Fly to Yogyakarta

Check in relax in a.m.

See palace, market in afternoon, night

Dinner at hotel

DAY TEN—
Day tour to Borobudur temple

Poolside afternoon

Dinner show

DAY ELEVEN—
Prambahan Plain, temple at Solo

More shopping!

Dine at hotel

Pack

DAY TWELVE—
Fly home

THE TRAVEL PLANNER

DAY ONE—
Fly to Jakarta

DAY TWO—
City Tour

See monuments, Ancol or Mini Indonesia park

Round off day at Surabaya Market

DAY THREE—
Carita Beach or Thousand Islands

Swimming, surfing, snorkeling or tanning

Quiet evening, hotel dining, pub

DAY FOUR—
Krakatau visit or tour of nearby villages, forests

Boat riding

DAY FIVE—
Side trip to Bogor and/or Bandung

Return to hotel

Quiet evening or show.

DAY SIX—
Train to Yogyakarta

Check into hotel

Visit marketplace

DAY SEVEN—
Visit Borobudur

Dinner show in evening

DAY EIGHT—
Prambahan Plain

Shopping in Solo

Return to hotel

DAY NINE—
Travel to Bali by train, plane or bus

Sunset excursion to Tanah Lot

Seaside dinner

DAY TEN—
Poolside a.m.

Afternoon trip to Ubud, Mas and Celuk

Evening stroll of Kuta streets

DAY ELEVEN—
Denpassar shopping in morning

Afternoon seaside or poolside

Quiet hotel dinner and/or pub crawl

DAY TWELVE—
Fly home

THE TRAVEL PLANNER

DAY ONE—
Fly to Jakarta

DAY TWO—
City tour

Shopping at
Surabaya market

Dining out
beachside

DAY THREE—
Train: northern
route via Cirebon
and Semarang to
Yogyakarta

Check into hotel

DAY FOUR—
Visit Borobudur

Dining
downtown

Shopping
downtown

DAY FIVE—
Prambahan Plain

Train or bus to
Surabaya

Overnight in
Surabaya or
Probolinggo

DAY SIX—
Relax in a.m.

Begin Bromo
tour

DAY SEVEN—
Bromo tour

Return to hotel

DAY EIGHT—
Bus and ferry to
Bali

Check into Bali
hotel

DAY NINE—
Relax in a.m.,
poolside or
seaside

Denpassar
shopping

Explore Kuta
streets

DAY TEN—
Rest at beach or
poolside

Afternoon tour
to Ubud, Mas,
and Celuk

Monkey forest

Dine in Kuta

DAY ELEVEN—
Mother Temple
tour

Lake Bedugul

Evening pub
crawl in Kuta
beach area or
quiet hotel
dining

DAY TWELVE—
Fly home

THE TRAVEL PLANNER
(The Shopper's Delight)

DAY ONE—
Fly to Bali

DAY TWO—
Denpassar shopping

Tour of city

DAY THREE—
Tour Ubud, Mas, Celuk for shopping

Return via Mengwi or Batubulan

Optional stop at Goa Gaja

Dining out

DAY FOUR—
Relax in hotel or seaside

Stroll around Kuta streets, shops

Quiet evening in hotel

DAY FIVE—
Early morning flight to Yogyakarta

Settle in hotel, relax in a.m.

Visit marketplace in late afternoon, evening

DAY SIX—
Borobudur tour

Stop at villages en route

Dinner and show in evening

DAY SEVEN—
City tour in a.m.

Fly to Jakarta

Check into hotel

Relaxing dinner

DAY EIGHT—
Surabaya Market

City shopping tour

DAY NINE—
Side trip to Bogor and/or Bandung for sightseeing and shopping

Dinner out

DAY TEN—
Tour arts, crafts outlets and city landmarks

Night life with early bedtime or substitute evening departure for Carita Beach

DAY ELEVEN—
Side trip to Thousand Islands or Carita Beach

Evening return to hotel

DAY TWELVE—
Fly home

THE TRAVEL PLANNER

Make your own travel plans here.

Your list will differ from most other lists, of course. If you are an outdoor person your list may be totally unlike one made out by a person interested in monuments and museums.

For example, the list of an adventurous, outdoorsy traveler might include a day trip to unforgettable Krakatoa volcano in the Sunda Strait, a camera safari on the Ujung Kulan peninsula of West Java which could take two days, perhaps a frivolous visit for a few hours to a monkey forest, a waterfall hike in the jungle, a drive to the Tankuban Prahu Crater and/or an overnighter at Mount Bromo.

Someone who wants a less exerting exposure to wildlife in Java and Bali, for photography, might opt for the monkey forest, the Rangunan Zoo in Jakarta, the Taman Safari Park near Bogor, and perhaps the Sadengan wildlife preserve in East Java.

Scenic-minded individuals who want to capture sweeping vistas may pencil in a tea plantation, the botanic gardens of Bogor, waterfalls and a rain forest excursion, the lake at Bedugul, Turtle Beach and a volcano or two. Rice fields and temples surely would fit into the schedule.

Those who want above all to shop the exotic bargains of Indonesia will put Jalan Surabaya in Jakarta down among their musts, as well as the Yogyakarta marketplace, Kuta Beach and Denpassar town; and Celuk, Mas and Ubud also belong on such a list.

The attraction of temples, monuments, museums and native villages present a formidible array of choices to those interested in history, culture and ancient beauty, but surely the world famous Borobudur, Merdeka Square in Jakarta, the Jakarta "Elephant" Museum, the Dieng Plateau, Prambahan Plain, Tanah Lot and the Mother Temple belong on the list.

Artistically inclined people may choose to focus their entire trip around Bali and Yogyakarta where there are numerous performances of dance, traditional theater, wayang puppetry and gamelan music as well as many shops, galleries, and outdoor displays of painting, sculpture, woodcarving, batik and weaving, silverwork and pottery.

Make a list of ten "musts" for yourself. Consult the maps provided to get an idea of the distances involved and look over the lists of typical travel excursions in each chapter to get an idea of the time period which each item entails. Then begin to pencil in your day-by-day calendar. Most people will end up with a variety of projected excursions that cross over from one special-interest domain to another. This is good. The richer the mixture the merrier.

Consult intercity airline, bus and train schedules to chart your travel from one point to another (nothing is much more than an hour away by air).

Once you have filled in the blanks on your Travel Planner and purchased your airline tickets, you can ink in the items on a real calendar. Be prepared to do some cross-outs and ink-ins as you travel.

There are of course overland bus tours between Bali and Jakarta, providing a rich sampling of the Indonesian experience, but their schedules are rigid and at times can be wearying, so their main appeal is to those who want to put themselves completely into the hands of a tour operator. The decisions on where to go and what to do are by and large already made for you. If this is to your liking—and there are advantages, such as built-in company—inquire about such packages with Smailing Tour or Setia Tours for example. Such overland excursions are represented through travel agencies in principal cities in America and Europe.

In preparation for your trip to Java and Bali, you will require three things: (1) approximately $2,000; (2) about two weeks time; and (3) a valid passport.

Shots are not required for entry into Indonesia from most countries, including America and Great Britain. Only persons entering from nations where small pox is a problem need inoculations. Generally speaking, it is not necessary to take preventive steps against malaria either, especially if your planned trip sticks to the beaten path, that is, Bali and the principal cities of Java. However, if you intend to trek through jungle or in low-lying areas where mosquitoes can be thick, it might be a good idea to ask your doctor to prescribe the pills, which are taken over a period of weeks—before starting out as well as after arrival.

Your airline ticket will be the most expensive single outlay for the trip and advance planning in this purchase can really pay off in big dollar savings.

Garuda Airlines, the national airline of Indonesia, flies from the west coast of the United States to Bali and Jakarta, offering competitive fares on advance purchases. They also have special programs with a blanket ticket covering broad travel inside the nation for a budget fare.

Garuda flies with refueling stops in Hawaii and in Biak, an island off Irian Jaya (New Guinea) where a side show of native dances and art works is presented at the airport on day or night stop-offs as a bonus for the traveler.

Another plus on the Garuda ticket is that their fares to Bali and Jakarta differ little, so that if you want to take in both places, your travel inside Indonesia already is paid for. The same ticket will take you to both places and back.

Continental Airlines, which flies from the west coast of the United States to Bali via Hawaii and Guam, offers an excellent round trip at a very reasonable price. They are often teetering on the brink of bankruptcy and/or take-over, but if the ticket buyer keeps tabs on them, the odds favor a completed trip without cancellation problems.

Some excellent packages, including airline fare and a week of hotels, all for less than $1,000, have been advertised in West Coast newspapers, and the offer is genuine, although not available at short notice.

In these days of periodic airline fare wars it is a good idea to check into the possibility that someone is offering a spectacularly low rate, and actually a number of different airlines serve Jakarta and/or Bali by their own special routes.

Singapore Airlines, for example, brings you within a half hour's hop of Jakarta. Cathay Pacific, China Airlines, Japan

Airlines, KLM, Luftansa, Malaysian Airlines, Philippines Airlines, Qantas, and Thai International are among those serving Indonesia itself, often with stopovers in Hong Kong, Tokyo, Hamburg, and other out-of-the-way places. It doesn't cost anything to have a travel agent look over all the possibilities for comparison.

Speaking of money, do not bring rupiah to Indonesia. You can bring in or take out up to 50,000 rupiah if you wish, but the dollar will bring a much better rate of exchange inside Indonesia. For example, while banks in California were giving out 1,567 rupiah per dollar, the rate in Jakarta and Bali was 1,830, a considerable difference. Rupiah come in denominations of 100, 500, 1,000, 5,000 and 10,000, with coins (seldom used by travelers except for telephones) available in amounts of 100, 50, 25, 10, 5 and 1. Considering that 1 rupiah would be worth less than one-hundredth of a penny, the coin has limited use.

Dollars, carried in singles, fives, tens and twenties, have good bargaining power in some places, but don't flash wads of money. Common sense tells us not to do this anywhere. And in using dollars inside Indonesia, be careful about major purchases from government-affiliated enterprises such as airlines. You save a considerable amount of money by purchasing domestic airline tickets in rupiah, for example.

It's a good idea to keep a pocket calculator handy and when in doubt, ask the price both in dollars and in rupiah, taking a moment to figure out which is most advantageous. You won't be considered impolite. Almost everyone doing business has a cheap calculator and does the same thing.

The clothing you bring to Java and Bali should generally be light, in consideration of their average temperature of over 90° Fahrenheit. Consider, too, that in some mountain areas a sweater will be desirable, and a collapsible umbrella is a handy accessory even in the dry season because showers do fall.

Dress is informal. The climate is hot and humid so shirts and light dresses are advised, but men are required to wear a jacket and tie for formal occasions or official business calls. Brief attire, such as shorts and halter tops, is not considered proper except in sports facilities and on the beach. In the local villages this is considered in bad taste and flagrant displayers of skin are pointed out as brazen foreigners. Actually, tourists who do go around in brief female attire invite more than the occasional stare: the young men of a rural area will give more attention than probably is desired.

General office hours for businesses run from 8 a.m. to 3 p.m. Monday to Thursday, to 11:30 a.m. on Friday, and to 2 p.m. on Saturday. Some businesses stay open until 4 or 5 p.m., bank closing hours vary from 2 p.m. to about 4 p.m., and stores usually are open evenings.

Tipping has slowly become a part of local expectations as tourism has increased, but most hotels and many restaurants add a service charge of 10 percent and then no further tip is required. Where a service charge is not added to the bill, a tip of 5 to 10 percent is appropriate, depending on the level of service. At airports, tip the porter 1,000 rupiah (about 50 cents) per bag, and cab drivers lately expect a 500 rupiah tip. This is not expensive surely, but adjust your tipping to the occasion.

There is a tradition that one does not take or give things with the left hand. This is taboo, as is touching someone else's head, even a child's. But everywhere handshaking is customary. Smiling is a national characteristic.

Customs allows you to bring cigarettes into Indonesia, but since the same brands cost only half over there, it doesn't seem too good an idea. On top of the usual prohibitions against drugs and arms, there also exists an official ban on bringing in TV sets, radio/casette recorders or anything printed in Chinese. If you bring in video cassettes, their very strict censors will ask to review them before returning them to you.

No matter what Karl Malden says, do not rely entirely on traveler's checks. First of all, they aren't accepted everywhere. In some villages they don't even know what they are. Of course, they are handy in large cities, but if you lose them in an inconvenient place, you may have to go back to Jakarta or Denpassar to have them replaced. And if you don't have the cash to do that, Mr. Malden won't be there to pass the hat for you.

But for now, on to the cities and the scenes that make the magic of Java and Bali. . . .

CHAPTER THREE

Jakarta

Jakarta, the burgeoning island capital of the Indonesian Republic, the world's fifth most populous nation—just behind the United States—can be heard as well as seen. The city creates its own lively music. At least, it's a kind of music mixing two different styles, the minuet of a sleepy colonial past and the exuberant beat of today and tomorrow.

You hear both in Jakarta. You can *see* both worlds. You can listen and watch while they seem, impossibly, to be building a brave new Honolulu smack on top of a Tijuana in this faraway tropical land.

Cock one ear and you'll hear birds sing from lush and colorful foliage that thrives everywhere. Other chants rise too: the native craftsmen and sidewalk cooks hawking their goods from canvas-draped huts stacked side by side for blocks. The smells of cut leather and carved hardwoods blend with fried rice that crackles over fire. Laughter is heard everywhere, and eager conversation. At dawn and dusk the wail of Muslim prayer sends an exotic echo facelessly into the skies, from which fall, almost daily, the briefest of thundering showers, pelting the elephantine leaves of tropical

MAP OF JAKARTA
MAIN STREETS AND PLACES OF INTEREST

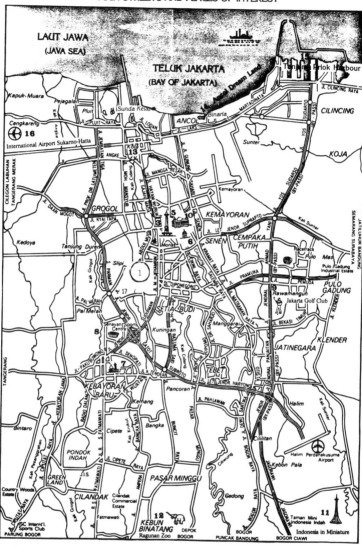

1 . **Welcome Statue**	6. Cathedral	12. Ragunan Zoo
2. National Monument	7. Agung Mosque	13. China Town
3. Merdeka Palace	8. Senayan Sports Complex	14. Fantasy World
4. M u s e u m	9. Jakarta Golf Club	15. Tanjung Priok Harbour
5. Istiqlal Mosque	10. Post Office.	16. International Airport Sukarno - Hatta
	11. Indonesia in Miniature	17. Sarinah Shopping Centre

trees and almost hissing on sun-baked ground, cooling and cleaning the air.

Sometimes in the late evenings and early mornings it becomes so quiet that you can hear palm fronds caressing one another.

Or you can tune an ear to the modern beat, which is kept by pile drivers, it seems. The melody is carried by giant cranes creaking in the air and humming as they hoist steel and concrete aloft in the construction of towering buildings that are muscling out the colonial era. For a chorus, hammers pound. Staccato riveters and jackhammers explode in rapid-fire bursts and the horns of thousands of vehicles join in. All the drums go bang and the cymbals clang.

Everywhere you look new buildings, new shopping centers, new bridges, new roads are under construction: hotels, apartments, offices, stores. Construction experts say it will be ten years before the city really can assume its new identity. The government says five. Businessmen, with a beckoning eye for tourists, say tomorrow. Today, say others: look at the hotels we already have, our monuments, our museums.

Three foreign technicians in hard hats stood shouting to one another in front of a construction site where the noise was so loud they couldn't hear each other. A motorcyclist skidded to a stop in front of them. There was more shouting. Arms were waved. The cyclist couldn't hear either. One of the technicians scribbled furiously on a blueprint, as if the fate of the entire project hung in the balance. The paper was torn off and handed to the cyclist who looked at the writing and sped off. The technicians sat. They had just ordered lunch from the local A&W Root Beer franchise.

Finding the things to love about this island metropolis while it screams with its own birth pains requires reflection on its past and future, the marks of which are everywhere. While the modern towers thrust their skeletal steel frames up above the tree line, neighborhoods of low white buildings, homes, schools and offices crouch behind walls and long green expanses of grass.

Across a busy street a traditional bazaar occupies a long stretch of unpaved sidewalk, offering a wide array of handicrafts for tourists and native vegetables for residents. In the schizophrenic sky a helicopter hovers over century-old schooners in the harbor.

Heroic sculptured monuments rise in every part of town, celebrating the young nation's colorful history—all forty-four years of it.

But despite the nation's youth, Jakarta boasts structures and artifacts as old as anything you'll find in Europe, standing or in ruins. Remember, Java Man, a significant link in the story of human evolution, was discovered on this island. Jakarta itself is one of the oldest capitals in southeast Asia, founded some 1,500 years ago by a Hindu king, even though its present name, which means "Perfect Victory," wasn't bestowed until about 1525 by a Javanese conqueror.

You will arrive in Jakarta, more than likely, via taxi from the pleasant modern Soekarno-Hatta International Airport, which sports its own special Javanese touches, architecturally, in colors, and even in aromas, immediately signaling the exotic nature of the Indonesian experience. Your taxi into the city should be a $10 ride (certainly no more than $15 including tip and road tolls). Tell the driver you want to see the nicest areas en route. The normal way will take you through some beautiful countryside and some forlorn fields, but unless instructed otherwise, taxi drivers tend to enter Jakarta through the least visually attractive parts of the city. The shortest route passes run-down buildings and beleaguered people.

If your first glimpse of Jakarta shows you its most decrepit side, do not be discouraged because this is a huge city and there are many contrasts from area to area. Jakarta's most splendid structures occupy land next door to hovels.

Just when you might begin to get depressed at sights of Third World squalor, a magnificent square or a row of old colonial mansions will uplift your spirits. Just when the sultry atmosphere begins to close in on you, a rain shower will breeze in and sweep away the memory and leave everything momentarily cleaned and refreshed. Everything is in transit here, changing daily, being upgraded and bettered in many ways.

Jakarta sits in the far northwest part of Java but east of the airport. The ever-expanding city sprawls in all directions from the ancient port of Batavia, except northward, of course, into the sea. If you arrive by sea, bus, or train (and train travel is enthusiastically recommended for at least one leg of your journey) you will wind up close to the central city. The heart of the city, where the major hotels cluster amid towers offering every imaginable service for the visitor—banking, businesses, restaurants, shops—forms in the area around Merdeka Square, due south of the old harbor. Monuments, museums and amusements all lie within short, inexpensive cab rides.

Streets (*jalan*, often abbreviated "Jl," means street) can be as confusing as an inside joke to the traveler because of the Indonesian disrespect for straight lines and the local tendency to name the same street after more than one minor hero. Adding to the puzzle are the ubiquitous construction projects which detour traffic like a maze. Jakarta, like New York City, is best left to cabbies, an inexpensive and unexasperating means of conveyance.

Diversity best describes the city. Modern shopping centers gleaming with neon and glass compete with rickety flea-market stalls for the souvenir-hunter's dollar. Tacky, honky-tonk bars ("Girls! Girls! Girls!") vie with posh hotel lounges. Sidewalk vendors heat food on inefficient burners in makeshift wood and canvas enclosures outside lavish restaurants with European and Javanese menus.

There are no really dangerous parts of Jakarta for the visitor with common discretion, but any block or two of splendid modern skyscrapers can suddenly give way to an area of 1940s, low, seedy stores serving the locals, and the next block in turn may be occupied by the former mansions of Dutch colonial bigwigs, charmingly set back behind walls, trees and expansive lawns. Most of these have been converted to commercial and government uses.

Miami architecture, Indonesian flourishes, and colonial nostalgia mix everywhere with squat and squalid concrete block boxes such as are usually relegated to the outskirts of major cities—probably because the outskirts of Jakarta are constantly being swallowed up by the city as it expands year after year. Traffic is a laughable mess and people are everywhere, predictable conditions in a city of eight million built for two. The city really is an incredible hodge-podge.

The sharp contrast of old and new will be apparent everywhere in Jakarta. Near a sparkling, flood-lit Hilton-esque hotel, a thatch-roofed temple with elaborate stone carvings opens into a bird sanctuary. Just two blocks behind a modern office building narrow alleys, pockmarked and puddled with the most recent rain, are cluttered with people and the crude stalls of small entrepreneurs selling herbal tonics.

The People of Jakarta

Buildings, monuments, museums and other attractions do not make up a city. A city is people, and in this Jakarta is rich indeed.

The Javanese are strongly patriotic, fiercely anti-communist and, although their government is officially nonaligned, eagerly pro-West. The people and their government respect and value tourists.

The faces of Jakartans (and other Indonesians who flock here from the countryside if they can) seem to be made by an artist: high cheekbones under golden skin, eyes that are wide and unlined, full lips that break into ready smiles over good white teeth. Their rice-fed bodies are almost uniformly slender.

On the streets young women walk together hand in hand or with an arm around one another. This is not sexual; it is friendship, sisterhood. Men tend to be less demonstrative in public but equally caring about people whom they know, and curious about strangers. When they talk, they stop and look into each other's faces, searching. They ask questions of strangers, sometimes too many, just to practice their English.

Limited English is spoken almost everywhere. It is the second language, recognized as the universal tongue of the future.

A man who dined regularly in his hotel tried graciously to compliment his ever-cheerful waitress, a young woman who seemed a little unsure on the job but tried hard and always seemed to be on duty—dawn, noon or evening. Her English was flawed. She smiled and thanked the man for his compliment, but left hurriedly, bringing back the manager. The manager, almost apologetically, explained to the guest, "She says she can only like you as a father." Embarrassed that his intentions were misconstrued, he forced a laugh and said, "Oh, that's fine, fine, you know, because you are way too young; you are young enough to be my daughter." The manager and waitress exchanged a concerned glance. Then they brought him an attractive, older woman. In her thirties. The chagrined guest resolved to go to his room and make a quick study of the native language, Bhasa Indonesia. The basics—the most useful phrases—really are simple to learn.

Most foreign visitors to these islands—until quite recently— came pointing guns instead of cameras. They were on site-seizing tours.

In recent order were the communists whose failed attempt at a coup in the 1960s incurred the permanent wrath of the entire populace and persuaded them to embrace the West. ("U.S.A. number one," you'll hear often.) Then there was the Japanese occupation of the 1940s. Prior to them, the Dutch, who thought they'd pick up business as usual after the war, only to have their colony reject them decisively. And before that there were the Portuguese and the swords of sultans and other conquerors warring for a thousand years, as long as memory and the written record.

The conquerors always built temples, palaces and other monuments, usually to themselves, and all along the people stayed poor while their natural resources were sapped. These one-time Space Islands had treated the world to flavor. Today it's oil and gas and gold, and still the people are poor.

Except in spirit. Something about the way they walk, swinging their arms freely, heads high. They act like, and quite well may be, the wave of the future, with a birth rate that rivals Mexico City despite the pleas of the government, "Two kids only." The hormones aren't listening. Some estimates of Jakarta's population run to ten million.

Although largely Muslim by inheritance, the people act Westernized, or at least lean in that direction. Women have never adopted veils, which are as rare as Arabian headdresses and ankle-length robes. Indonesians are different.

In a roaring disco at Hotel Bentang II near the downtown area, young women in miniskirts and a variety of modern fashions, a la suburban mall, swing and jerk their bodies to rock music under strobe lights. Their men wear jeans and batik shirts. The place is packed, the music deafening. The girls ask men to dance if they wish or independently do it girl-girl.

Female equality, a rule of the republic, is very much in evidence. You see it in the lower ranks of government and in clerical, shopkeeping and other traditional female positions, but you see it as well in higher political and social careers. There are female entrepreneurs, telecasters and similar highly visible professionals. Divorce is quite common, as is the concommitant single-parent family. Sex appears to be treated quite casually, but traditionally there is emphasis on choice and pride in relationships.

The girls of Jakarta—small, slim and pretty—only want to have fun. They love to dance, to listen to Western music, to laugh, to dine and even to drink a little. Especially to laugh. And, as they will readily admit, they need a man now and then. Scrupulously clean, they love to splash in the shower at nice hotels, probably because the one at home doesn't work any better than a crude mandi.

And if they ask for taxi fare that attains heights suspiciously similar to a hooker's fee, one needn't insult a lady by branding her a professional. After all, as ladies do, they make their choice, and they do not go with someone they do not like. They can't help it if they need money; they consider it quite natural to ask the only person in bed with them who has some. A philosophical comparison of this practice with the Western world would take another book apart from this one.

Most women visiting from Western countries do not find Indonesian men attractive. Perhaps it is partly due to size. Asians tend to be smaller in stature. Also, few Indonesian men have the aggressiveness, money, cars and nice places which, along with size, have become part and parcel of the traditional courtship ritual and image of sexual potency in the West. And, while in groups Indonesian men may voice appreciation of a passing woman's moving parts, they tend to be shy when acting individually.

They are a little in awe of the wealth and lifestyle which they imagine the visitor enjoys. Fear of intrusion upon another's relationships also holds back the Asian man, who respects marriage and other pairings. Who knows if these mysterious visiting women might be married or otherwise involved, in their jet-age way of doing things? The language barrier, too, poses a problem if a man is expected to take the initiative. But again, even though fanny pinching is not a national pastime, as everywhere, there are some bold ones.

Jakarta residents mix easily, readily with visitors.

One striking way to view young Jakartans in massive numbers presents itself weekly. On Sunday mornings thousands of young Indonesians line the streets in pairs, wearing colorful matched shirts, as they engage in a long walk and run which is part of a health program conducted like a parade—and not an overweight youth in ten dozen. It's impressive.

However, to walk at roadside in Jakarta for one's health, considering the general madness of vehicle operators without exception, seems doomed to be a self-defeating enterprise. Something akin to a soldier doing set-up exercises in the trenches edging no-man's land.

Javanese families mix with tourists at a number of local attractions. On the islands beyond the harbor, cottages lure many city-weary Jakartans as well as travelers from distant places, especially on weekends. It is not unusual to see schoolchildren and other locals in the Indonesia in Miniature Park, which exhibits samplings of the diversity of the whole far-flung nation, or in such areas as Old Batavia, the restored Dutch capital, as Javanese acquaint themselves with their own past. In the nearby Fantasy World, Jakarta's junior version of Disneyland, tourists usually are outnumbered by residents.

Getting Around Jakarta

Travel within the Jakarta city limits runs the gamut from helicopter to human-powered rickshaw, but one tourist brochure suggests pricelessly, "The easiest and most convenient method of getting around Jakarta is a chauffeur-driven limousine."

Of course, this attitude works just as well in other cities, as does transmigration of the soul. Meanwhile, you can rent a car quite inexpensively, but don't. This is a city for expert drivers. This is taxiland, or *Taksi*-land, the way they spell it. Besides, cab fare is cheap; you can get almost anywhere in town for two or three dollars. And every ride is a little adventure.

The visitor in suit and tie stepped out of his hotel lobby and, as a blue taxi (Japanese made) drew to a halt in front of him, he pointed out his destination, a building which was prominent on the horizon. It seemed to be about a five- or ten-minute walk. The cab surged forward into traffic. It looked like a blockade. Not only bumper-to-bumper autos but mini-cars like golf carts, bicycles, motorcycles, two-wheel wagons and pedestrians swiveling their hips like bullfighters as they dodged and sidled through. The cab lurched into this standstill mass as if there was an opening. Then the driver made a U-turn. In minutes the visitor was bouncing on the back seat at breakneck speed down alleys almost wide enough for a car. The cab rushed in where Anglos fear to tread, inserting itself into congested traffic in daring maneuvers that always appeared to be dancing with death. Detours abounded. After forty-five minutes of this, the visitor reached his destination trembling, glad to pay and get out.

He needn't have worried. Jakarta taxi drivers must be among the most skilled in the world, able to negotiate their steel within inches of others in a perpetual game of chicken played by thousands of motorists at every intersection, rotary or detour. Accidents are few.

The faint of heart will resort to the mini-bus, which is scheduled, or the human-drawn *becak*, for the illusion of safety. Regular buses are too packed for the taste of most tourists.

And it is actually possible to walk in Jakarta, although usually not all the way from point A to point B. The best approach may be to take an organized tour first for familiarization. Your concierge or any travel bureau can provide information on starting points, pickups and costs, which are quite reasonable. There are many city bus tours, employing small, comfortable buses, and there's even a quite inexpensive helicopter tour for a bird's eye view. While on the tour, make notes on interesting-looking bazaars or other attractions, their names and addresses. Then take a cab there later, get out and walk. That way you'll see not only the tour organizer's "musts": you'll also see what you want to see.

A word of caution about dealing with cab drivers. An English-speaking guide and a taxicab driver are not the same species. In Jakarta, all would-be cab drivers are given a test. They are presented the following questions: (1) Do you speak English? (2) Do you know where this address is?, and (3) Is this cab air conditioned? All these questions must be answered by the word "yes" in order to qualify. Thus the word "yes" has become overused in taxidom.

So be sure of the limits of your guide's language powers, be sure he knows where you want to go, and be sure the air conditioning works on that hot, sultry afternoon. Many taxis have air conditioners that they will charge you an extra 10 percent to use. However, the air conditioner has not been serviced since the vehicle left the factory so you are paying for hot air.

If you are setting out on anything more than a brief trip, these little details can be very important, so it can be worth tipping a bell man or door man to get you a cab and driver that suit your needs. Otherwise you can spend an afternoon failing to communicate with a driver who nods yes to all your queries but doesn't have the foggiest idea what you want or where it is.

If you want to experience the local way, try the *becak* (pedal-powered) rickshaw. But you'll find few on the main streets during heavy traffic hours; mostly they stay to the back streets and alleys—all the better for survival. The two-passenger mini-cars, or *bemos*, also make an interesting ride, but do it for the experience rather than the savings, which can be elusive and often misleading.

In dealing with those types of vehicles, one must bargain and agree in advance on precisely what the fare will be. The rule is exactly the same as in dealing with taxi drivers who say their meter is broken: offer half of what is asked and settle for some mid-point figure, if necessary.

Cabs in Jakarta are regulated by meter, with 500 or 600 rupiah charged for the first kilometer (depending on whether there is air conditioning) and an additional 250 or 300 rupiah for each additional kilometer. In cases where drivers don't turn on their meters, the one-half rule applies, unless some other fee is bargained in advance. The driver is in the wrong if he demands a certain fare and does not have a meter to back him up. It's the law. Don't let them get away with it.

Safety First

We have already pointed out that there are no really dangerous areas for travelers in Jakarta, but common sense dictates that hanging around dark alleys or seedy bars in the late hours is not wise in any city, anywhere. If you mix in crowds or stay in a less than first class hotel, or attach yourself to strangers, a measure of care must be taken to protect your money, papers and other valuables.

A dazed-looking Australian blonde, attractive despite un-combed hair and rumpled clothing, was led into the white-tiled police station, a building that appeared to have been converted from a colonial era hotel. She was ushered to a low counter where five uniformed women were typing theft reports for others, all tourists. She had to wait in line. Next she would have to go to American Express to replace her traveler's checks, and after that to her embassy for a new passport. And then shopping. They even took her clothes. It would be a long, hard day.

Thieves used to be brazenly abundant in Jakarta until the tourism-conscious government started weeding out the worst of them (reforming them in group therapy sessions that involved gunshots, it is said, but that was a decade ago). Nevertheless, some stealing still goes on, as it does in any large city, anywhere. Perhaps here it is less aggressive: mostly sneak-thieves in empty hotel rooms and pick-pockets—non-violent criminals well aware that the authorities deal harshly with any sort of violence.

Don't begrudge a thief or a con man a little; that is, try not to let it spoil your trip. Look at it with perspective. When you pay an ordinary cab fare it's enough money to feed an average Javanese family for about three days—or about half of what most people earn weekly. So if someone gets the best of you in a bargain, or steals a little of your money, it's not the end of the world.

There are ways to prevent losing *a lot*.

Follow the recommended rules and your money will be relatively safe: use the hotel depository for valuables or carry your money zipped and secure, where you can feel its presence after every bump in a crowded city; it's not advisable to carry money in an unbuttoned, back pocket wallet. It might be most convenient to carry two front-pocket packages, one of small, 1,000 rupiah notes for routine transactions and the other with larger denominations, anchored to your pocket lining or zippered up, if possible. It's not wise to flash bundles of 10,000 rupiah bills, and one should remember that there's a big market in stolen traveler's checks, which can be a nuisance to replace.

All About Tipping

From the money you save by being careful, tip wisely.

The intellectual German, tall, young and handsome, winced visibly as a foreign diner at the next table left a 2,000 rupiah tip (slightly more than $2). "They shouldn't do that," he said. "They're going to spoil it. Everybody already thinks all Europeans and Americans are rich."

Even though the tip was not extravagant, he pointed out, most restaurants already add a service charge to cover tips, and for others a 1,000 rupiah note or 10 percent would be generous—a day's wages for many. The German was not rich. He lived in the hills near Semarang, a port in East Java, where his Indonesian wife worked. He visited Jakarta regularly to buy quantities of inexpensive "give-away" items for export as business premiums.

However, the tipper under criticism had a different philosophy. A young, red-haired Scandinavian who lived in Singapore with his European wife, he made regular trips to Jakarta to teach Indonesians basic technical installation and sales. He believed that those who could afford it *should* tip generously. He mentioned a friend who had purchased a house in the Jakarta suburbs for less than $3,000, an astounding bargain, and argued that foreigners who take advantage of Indonesia's bargains shouldn't be stingy with small amounts of money.

The fact is most hotels do routinely add a service charge that covers tips in their restaurants. Where this is not done, a diner is expected to leave approximately 10 percent as a tip, more or less, depending on service and the level of satisfaction. Regarding taxis, tips are not mandatory but drivers have come to expect about 500 rupiah, which is adequate in most circumstances.

Airport and hotel porters expect to be tipped 500 rupiah per bag, and, for room service, the same rule of thumb applies as does in restaurant dining.

Armed with this basic information, you are ready to take a close look at Jakarta. There's plenty to do and see.

Jakarta Attractions

National Monument

The Monas, or National Monument, stands out as a landmark at Merdeka Square in the heart of Jakarta, visible from all directions. It's a 450-foot-high (137 meters) marble obelisk topped with a gold-coated bronze flame symbolizing the Indonesian proclamation of independence in 1945. Atop is an observation deck which gives viewers a sweeping view of the city. Below, the basement houses a museum of national history with dioramas representing the republic's past.

Diponegoro Statue

At the front of the Monas stands a life-size statue of a man on horseback, honoring Pangeran Diponegoro, whose failed attempt to overthrow the Dutch colonial empire more than 150 years ago led to his exile in Sulawesi. The surroundings are park-like, and many Indonesians picnic on the grounds. The monument is within walking distance of several other Jakarta attractions.

Merdeka Palace

This regal structure, built for the Dutch in 1879, now serves as the government seat for important state functions. Behind it another, smaller palace is connected by a courtyard.

National Museum

Dating from 1778, this reputedly is one of the finest in Asia, housing diverse collections of Indonesian cultural, historical and anthropologial relics. Outstanding displays of giant stone statuary, exquisite porcelain, prehistoric bronze, and other curios are capped by the spectacular wealth of the Treasure Room where jewel-studded weapons and ceremonial objects of solid gold may be viewed, everything from trinkets to a throne. The museum itself is a landmark with its dark statue of an elephant on a huge pedestal located at the entrance. Tours are offered in several languages.

Istiqlal Mosque

Although trumpeted as one of the largest mosques in the world and open to (shoeless) visitors, this structure, apart from its unique dome, unfortunately suffers a too-great similarity in architecture to any large hotel, is only about a decade old, and has an interior which, although elegant, is quite simple. The inside can't be photographed. There are older and more splendid mosques and temples elsewhere throughout the countryside.

Roman Catholic Cathedral

Close by the Istiqlal Mosque, one finds the Roman Catholic Cathedral, built about 1900, and near it, the Protestant Immanuel Church, built in 1835. Their main significance lies in demonstrating the Indonesian tolerance for all world religions, most of which are represented to some degree in the islands.

Harbour Area Attractions: *Sunda Kelapa*

In the 1500s, this dock area was the principal Java trading port, occupied by a Hindu Kingdom and frequented by the Portuguese. Today, among other things, it is a busy fish market where native boats unload their daily catchs. At one pier, open to the public, tall-masted sailing schooners (called *pinisi*) hand-built on South Sulawesi island by the Bugi tribe, historic seafarers, dock daily between voyages. This probably is the last active fleet of sail-powered cargo vessels in the world, with sailors and dockmen working shirtless, going ashore by a slender plank, as has been done for centuries. Small boats operating from here also transport passengers to nearby island resorts and some punts will carry tourists around the harbour in a 30-minute oar-powered ride that costs about 2,000 rupiah (a little over a dollar) per person.

Old Batavia

The former Dutch capital, many of its original buildings restored, is also known as Jakarta Kota, interesting for its old watchtower, maritime museum, art museum, and the Jakarta Historical Museum, with an excellent souvenir and arts and crafts shop, all located in original colonial structures. Also part of this complex is the Wayand Museum, which displays art puppets made of wood and leather, and schedules some performances.

Jaya Ancol Park

Built on reclaimed marshland, this is Jakarta's largest recreational park, modeled somewhat after Disneyland but featuring mainly a child's eye look at the world. Different parts of the world are represented by small complexes—a little jungle for Africa, and for America, a Wild West street from frontier days. Rides, including "space cars," bumper cars, rowboats and a ferris wheel delight children and there are games arcades and a fantasy castle. There are also restaurants, adult activities and an especially interesting array of handicrafts. Many artists demonstrate their work as they sell it. Sailboat rides are offered on a sandy beach.

Taman Mini Indonesia

No one can possibly visit all of Indonesia because it includes thousands of different islands, but this park, with a name meaning "Beautiful Indonesia in Miniature," presents compact samples representing each of the 27 provinces in the sprawling archipelago. Life-size replicas show traditional housing, the

cone-shaped homes of wild Irian Jaya and the prow-like structures from Sulawesi—everything distinctive about the islands
from mud huts to temples. Exhibits of handicrafts and performances of traditional dances are scheduled regularly. In an ar-
tificial lake a miniature version of the entire island nation has
been built, and in the Golden Snail, a modernistic cinerama
theater, one can view a spectacular film showing life in the
republic's diverse communities. Orchid gardens, bird sanctuaries
and elaborate woodcarvings are among other features of the park,
which attempts to carry out the national motto, "Unity in Diversity."

Ragunan Zoo

Also south of the central district of Jakarta is the Ragunan
Zoo, one of the few places in the world where one may see the
famous Komodo dragon, the world's largest lizard, growing to a
length of ten feet. The lush tropical setting also features the Java
tiger, apes, cassowaries and the rare bird of paradise. The "dragons," which abound on the island of Komodo near Flores,
hundreds of miles to the east, are not just big lizards but a distinct
species seen nowhere else.

The southern part of Jakarta is its elite district, the most
desirable area for homes, and one can see a marked difference
between the richness of the houses in this section and those in
most other parts of the city, which remains pocked by shanty-
towns in too many "older" parts. Significantly, the southern
section also is marked by the Youth Statue, a monument depicting a man with a platter of plenty. The people of these islands
want their share of the world's plenty. They want the cars, the
TVs. They work hard; why shouldn't they have these things?
Someday, they say.

Any listing of attractions usually covers broad general tastes
and the "beaten track" round the places visitors most often go,
but personal tastes do vary widely. Special interests generally can

be met, whether the preference is for a factory tour or a pub crawl. For these, directions are most easily available from the information desks of prominent hotels or the English language newspapers that are found in hotels and kiosks.

The English language newspapers do carry a regular "Night life" listing which can be invaluable in selecting the right spot for a night on the town. These newspapers, and *Jakarta* tourist magazines piled on bell desks, advertise what is current and hot, and the choices are many.

Not surprisingly, the newspapers and magazines also hawk the wares of many a merchant, from the individual store to the shopping center.

Shopping in Jakarta

Bargaining is expected at most booth-type stalls and smaller shops which are scattered around Jakarta—as are the slicker shopping centers. A good tactic is to offer half of what the seller initially asks. (If he or she accepts too quickly, you've probably been outsmarted.) You'll feel you've really gotten a good deal if the salesperson has to consult the owner before accepting your offer. Knowing comparative values and quality is your best advantage in such bargaining, however. Compare, too, what you would pay back home and you'll find that the prices are small enough to make almost everything a bargain. Try not to insult with too low an offer.

By the way, certain mannerisms or body language that come into play in bargaining should be mentioned here. Aggressive stances, such as placing the hands on the hips or crooking a finger to call someone, are considered grossly impolite, and the Jakartans insist on politeness even in petty larceny and bargaining. The smile is always acceptable, no matter what thoughts it may hide. Remember the strict rule: one does not use the left hand for giving or receiving.

Among the articles of greatest interest to shoppers in Java will be batik, opals, statues, woodcarvings, puppets, *kris* daggers, dance masks, antique pottery, porcelain, silverwork and other jewelry, woven goods, bamboo crafts, glass paintings, oils, tribal art, small wood chests and leather items.

By far the best traditional bazaar-type shopping in Jakarta will be found on Jalan Surabaya, where a mind-boggling array of everything from valuable antiques to trinkets and sheer junk is displayed in jam-packed stalls lining one side of the street for blocks.

In this hodge-podge one will find blowpipes from Borneo, sarongs from Bali, silver bracelets from Yogyakarta, dragon-festooned vases from Kalimantan, spears from Irian Jaya, musical instruments and lanterns, vases six feet tall, puppets and plaques, doorknockers, kettles and tools, an ancient adding machine, swords, telephones, turtles and totes, bows and arrows, paintings by the dozen and immense piles of junk.

That's the trick. If you can tell the junk from the real goods you may find an excellent bargain. One can conjure up the romantic image of binging sailors selling their prized compass, their only source of direction, for money to drink, but the truth is that these instruments, along with almost everything else, probably are sold wholesale to the merchants through secondhand dealers operating like pawnshops.

Firearms, clocks and daggers, pipes and axes, ships wheels, baskets, wind chimes, war drums, old trunks, gramophones, canes, shields, buddhas, furniture and whole shrines, gods included . . . . it is endless.

Apart from this flea market type of shopping, which has smaller competitors elsewhere, Jakarta offers several excellent department stores and art-souvenir shops. In many of these, prices are fixed.

Artshops

Amry Gallery (paintings, batik), Jalan Utan Kayu 66E.

Arjuna Craft Shop (statuary), Jalan Majapahit 16A.

Bali Kerti Souvenir Shop, Borobudur Intercontinental.

Bandung Artshop (paintings, batik, silverwork, coral), Jalan Pasar Baru 15.

Banka Tin-Art Shop (tin art work), Jalan Wahid Hasyim 178

Batik Keris (batik), Jalan Jend. Sudirman 9.

Danar Hadi (batik), Jalan Raden Saleh 1A.

Djelita Art Shop (paintings, statues, carvings, batik, basket work), Jalan Paletehan 37.

Djody Art & Curios (statuary, paintings, garments), Jalan Kebon Sirih Timur 22.

Garuda NV (statues), Jalan Majapahit 12.

KGBI (batik), Jalan Jend. Sudirman 28.

Hadiprana Gallery (paintings), Jalan Paletehan 38.

Irian Art & Gift Shop (statues, batik, silver, leather), Jalan Pasar Baru 16A.

Johan Art Curio (statues, Chinese porcelain), Jalan H.A. Saliom 59A.

King's Gallery (paintings), Jalan KH Hasyim Ashari 36.

Piguara Art & Gift Shop (statues, paintings, carvings, batik, tin, silver, leather, antiques), Jalan Paletehan 1.

Royal Batik Shop (batik, paintings, carvings, ceramics), Jalan Paletehan 1.

Shopping Centers

Alderon Plaza, Jalan Melawi Kebayoran Baru.

Duta Merlin Shopping Center, Jalan Gajah Mada.

Jalan Sabang, Jalan Agus Salim.

Matahari Department Stores (various locations), Ratu Plaza; Pasa Senen; Pasa Baru; Jatinegara.

Ramayana Department Store (four locations), Project Senen Shopping Area; Block M Shopping Area; Jalan Melawai IV/27; Jalan Haji Agus Salim 22A.

Ratu Plaza, Jalan Jend. Sudirman.

Sarinah Department Store, Jalan M. H. Thamrin 11.

Sarinah Jaya, Jalan Iskandarsyah LL/2.

Most of the above are Singapore-style steel and glass shopping centers with a wide variety of merchandise in the main store and at smaller outlets adjoining them. Some shops allow bargaining. You won't have any trouble distinguishing which.

For jewelry, except for the department stores and shopping centers listed, the lobby or arcade of all the major five-star hotels have their own specialty shops, and unless one knows value, this kind of outlet, althrough pricey, may be safest.

Again, many of the outlets mentioned have handicrafts sections, but there are a number of handicraft specialty shops, including Jakarta Handicraft Center, Jalan Pekalongan 12A, and

Pasar Seni in the Taman Impian Jaya Ancol. Shoppers who plan more extensive travel through Java also should keep in mind that some handicrafts may be less expensive in the villages where they are made. On the other hand, saving a few dollars or cents in anticipation of a greater bargain that may or may not come about is not a happy choice if one truly likes a particular article on sale in Jakarta, where some values are outstanding.

When shopping for batik, in which Indonesia is regarded as the leader, every visitor, time permitting, ought to visit a batik factory and/or the Textile Museum where every kind of batik and weaving done in Indonesia can be seen, before rushing to the shops. The colorful materials can be bought at flea markets, department stores and specialty shops. Some batik specialist stores are:

Batik Mira, Jalan MPR Raya 22.
Berdikari, Jalan Mesjid Pal VII.
Hajadi, Jalan Palmerah Utara 46.
Iwan Tirta, Jalan Panarukan 25.
Semar, Jalan Tomang Raya 54.
Sidamukti, Jalan Prof. Dr. Sahardjo 311.
Srikandi, Jalan Melawai VI, 6A.

For antiques, connoisseurs still find bargains in the Jalan Surabaya bazaar, but also worth looking at are the cluttered curio shops along Jalan Majapahit and Jalan Kebon Sirih Timur Dalam. Handicrafts, antique furniture and Chinese porcelain are among the treasures to search out.

About Street Food

On the streets of Jakarta, food stalls issue aromatic signals everywhere, and inside their doors or canvas flaps—or just standing beside a vendor's cart—Indonesians enjoy the fried rice, noodles, meat and vegetable dishes, some hotter and spicier than others, but all tempting. Since the Indonesians eat at the food stalls regularly and they all seem quite healthy, why shouldn't the adventurous visitor try some?

Well, anyone can, of course, and anyone is welcomed. But sanitation at these outlets is not on a par with that at finer restaurants (listed later on in this chapter) which serve similar dishes, and the risks are obvious for visitors whose stomachs are not accustomed to the strange foods offered. Let the diner beware.

Adventure, and the attitude that goes with it, ought to be encouraged, but in gastronomic matters, prudence must prevail lest you ruin your trip with cramps or more serious sickness that require weeks of medication to cure. The food stalls (called *warungs*) release their aromas on every block but the food served on their folding tables under their tent flaps is not quality-controlled, to say the least; it can be dangerous.

There are other options for sampling authentic local cuisine, the spicing of which is enough for the average visitor to deal with. One hygenic alternative, called Puja Sera 4 and located near the Sari Pacific Hotel, collects a veritable smorgasbord of independent warungs in one place. More than twenty different foods from all over the Indonesian archipelago can be tried here safely. And, of course, many fine restaurants offer Indonesian specialties tailored for the visitor.

Restaurant Food

A wide variety of foods—European, American, Chinese, Indonesian, Japanese, Korean and others is available in the restaurants of Jakarta. They are numerous and generally inexpensive.

Depending on taste, one may also rejoice to find such fast food outlets as A&W Root Beer, Pizza Hut, Dairy Queen, and Big Boy.

In restaurants and elsewhere, one should only drink bottled water, or bottled anything. (Don't even use hotel tap water for brushing your teeth.) Bottled water, imported beer and popular spirits are served at most restaurants.

To present a comprehensive list of all the restaurants in Jakarta would take the space of a good-size telephone directory. However, here are some excellent choices:

Western Food

Big Boy, Jalan H. R. Rasuna Said Kav C 11-14. Phone 514900.

Bistro Barbecue, Jl. Wahid Hasyim 75. Phone 364277.

Cafe Expresso, Jl. Kemang Raya 3A. Phone 797754.

Casablanca, Kuningan Plaza. Phone 514800.

Club Noordwijk, Jl. Juanda 5A. Phone 353909.

Club Room, Mandarin Oriental Hotel. Phone 321307.

East-West Barbecue, Jl. Rasuna Said. Phone 587731.

Gandy Steak House, Jl. Gajah Mada 82A. Phone 622127.

Jl. Melawai VIII 2. Phone 774337.

Jl. Cokroaminoto 90. Phone 333292.

Jayakarta Grill, Hotel Sari Pacific. Phone 323707.

Kallista Restaurant, Jl. Panglima Polim Raya 35. Phone 714696.

LaBodega, Jl. Terogong Raya. Phone 767798.

Memories, Jl. Jend. Sudirman. Phone 5781008.
Oasis, Jl. Raden Saleh 47. Phone 326397.
Orleans, Jl. Aditiawarman 67. Phone 715695.
Peacock Cafe, Hilton International Hotel. Phone 583051.
Pete's Club, Jl. Gatot Subroto. Phone 515478.
Ponderosa Steak House, Jl. Medan Merdeka Selatan. Phone
    348045.
        Jl. Jend. Sudirman. Phone 583823.
        Jl. Gatot Subroto. Phone 5780480.
        Arthaloka Bldg. Phone 583280.
Sahid Grill, Sahid Jaya Hotel. Phone 587031.
Steak & Seafood (Black Angus), Jl. Cokroaminoto 86A.
Phone 331551.
Taman Sari, Hilton International Hotel. Phone 588011.
Toba Rotisserie, Borobudur Intercontinental Hotel. Phone
370108.
Topaz Music Lounge, Jl. H. R. Rasuna Said Kav. B-1. Phone
510210.
Town Club, Jl. Jend. Sudirman 31. Phone 5781659.

Additionally, there are several French and Italian restaurants
which properly belong to this category, too:
LaParisien (French), Hyatt Aryaduta Hotel. Phone 376008.
LaRose (French), Jl. Jend. Sudirman. Phone 5780909.
Rugantino (Italian), Jl. Melawai Raya. Phone 714727.
Pinocchio (Italian), Jl. Jend. Sudirman. Phone 514736.
Pizzaria, Hilton International Hotel. Phone 583051.

It should be observed that many Western and European-style
restaurants offer a quite varied menu, often providing a sampling
of the local cuisine and perhaps a Chinese or Japanese-style
meal. On the other hand, Indonesian restaurants generally do
the same, recognizing that their customers come from a variety
of backgrounds.

Indonesian Restaurants

Atithya Loka, Jl. Gatot Subroto. Phone 516102.
Handayani, Jl. Abdul Muis 36E. Phone 373614.
Indonesia, Jl. Jend. Sudirman. Phone 735904.
Ikan Bakar Kebon Sirih, Jl. Kebon Sirih. Phone 351465.
Natrabu, Jl. Agus Salim. Phone 331728.
Prambanan, Hotel Kartika Chandra. Phone 511008.
Salero Bagindo, Jl. Panglima Polim 107. Phone 772713.
        Jl. Wolter Monginsidi 67. Phone 713212.
        Jl. Kebon Sirih 79. Phone 3103047.
Sari Kuring, Jl. Batuceper 55A. Phone 341542.
        Jl. Silang Monas Timur 88. Phone 352972.
        Jl. Matraman Raya 69. Phone 881968.
Satay House Senayan, Jl. Kebon Sirih 31A. Phone 326238.
        Jl. Paku Buwono VI/6. Phone 715821.
        Jl. Tanah Abang II/76. Phone 347270.
        Jl. Cokroaminoto 78. Phone 344248.

Seafood Restaurants

Seafood, that universal favorite, also is the specialty of many Jakarta restaurants, but again, rare is the menu that does not diversify a little in the interests of a diverse clientele:
Aquarium Grill, Horison Hotel. Phone 680008.
Phinisi (A Restaurant Afloat), Pantai Marina. Phone 680947.
Happy Valley, Jl. Asia Africa 6A. Phone 582309.

There are many other seafood restaurants, where the preparation is aimed more for Chinese tastes, for example, and of course, many Japanese restaurants feature sushi and other delicacies in an oriental style. If in doubt, call the restaurant on the telephone before making your reservations.

Oriental restaurants abound: numerous Chinese, Japanese,

Korean, Thai and even Vietnamese specialty houses offer a varied choice for the adventurous food seeker. In most cases, your hotel is the best source of information for sorting out the best of these, and their price scale.

The best hotels of Jakarta all have one or more outstanding restaurants. The Peacock Cafe at the Hilton, with its carved Javanese screens and exotic decor, is famous. At the Hyatt Aryaduta, the serving tables of the Teratai off the lobby fairly groan with an abundance of breakfast-brunch offerings, further sweetened by the music of a sextet playing never-intrusive classics. The Hyatt's Tavern pub, also with live music in a contemporary beat, will bring to your table a two-inch-thick imported steak as it grills on a violently hot stone. You finish the cooking to your taste and they supply potatoes and condiments.

Amid the bamboo and rattan decor of the Horison Hotel's Coffee Shop, overlooking the beach at Ancol, excellent Indonesian and Western dishes are inexpensive. The Ramayana Terrace at the Hotel Indonesia is a bright and cheerful place for small snacks or a full meal. The list is unending.

"A cup of Java" is a phrase that traces its origins to Indonesia and the country's reputation for good coffee is well deserved. Insist on cream rather than milk if you like it at its richest. The hotels take special pride in serving excellent coffee.

Hotels

Five-Star hotels in Jakarta, with prices in the neighborhood of $100 and up, are topped by the Hilton International, which was awarded a special "Diamond Five Star" rating by the Department of Tourism. The Hilton and the Hyatt Aryaduta succeed best, perhaps, in capturing the perfect mixture of the exotic taste of Java and the comforts of first class international travel. At the other end of the scale, hotel rooms are available for the equivalent of approximately $20 or less, and various types of guest houses and hostels, their accommodations at the bare minimum, can be found for $5 and $10 a night.

Five-Star hotels, offering the best in luxury rooms, facilities and services, including shopping arcades, range in price from $100 to $170 for a single, $138 to $179 for a double, and $219 to $675 for suites. They are:

Hilton, Jalan Gatot Subroto, P.O. Box 3315. Phones 587991, 583051, 46698. Telex 46673. Fax 583091.

Borobudur Inter-Continental, Jalan Lapangan Selatan, P.O. Box 329. Phone 370108. Telex 44150. Fax 359741.

Hyatt Aryaduta, Jalan Prapatan 44-46. Phone 376008. Telex 46673. Fax 349836.

Mandarin Oriental, Jalan M. H. Thamrin, P.O. Box 3392. Phone 321307. Telex 61755. Fax 324669.

Sahid Jaya, Jalan Jendral Sudirman 86, P.O. Box 41. Phones 587031, 581376. Telex 46331. Fax 583168.

Four-Star hotels, also with a full range of services and facilities, with prices from $50 to $100 for a single, $60 to $120 for a double, and suites from $120 to $450, including the following:

Horison Hotel, Jalan Pantai Indah, Jaya Ancol, P.O. Box 3340. Phone 680008. Telex 42834. Fax 684004.

Hotel Indonesia, Jalan M. H. Thamrin. Phones 320008, 323942, 322008. Telex 44233. Fax 321508.

Jayakarta Tower, Jalan Hayam Wuruk 126, P.O. Box 803, Phones 6294408, 6496760. Telex 46470. Fax 6295000.

Kartika Chandra, Jalan Gatot Subroto, P.O. Box 85. Phones 510808, 511008. Telex 46470. Fax 5204238.

President Hotel, Jalan M. H. Thamrin 59. Phone 320508. Telex 61401. Fax 333631.

Sari Pacific Hotel, Jalan M. H. Thamrin 6, P.O. Box 3138. Phone 323707. Telex 44514. Fax 323650.

All **Three-Star hotels** in Jakarta have air conditioned rooms, attached bath with hot and cold running water, telephones in the rooms, restaurant, bar, room service and laundry. Most have swimming pools, nightclubs and some shopping arcade areas. Three Star prices range from $30 to $90 for a single, $40 to $100 for a double, and $45 to $350 for suites. Three-Star hotels are:

Garden Hotel, Jalan Kemang Raya 21. Phones 715808, 7995808. Telex 47166.

Grand Menteng, Jalan Matraman Raya 21. Phones 8581524, 8581537, 8580752.

Kartika Plaza, Jalan M. H., Thamrin 10, P.O. Box 2081. Phone 311008. Telex 4579.

Hotel Kemang, Jalan Kemang Raya, P.O. Box 763. Phone 7093208. Telex 47243.

New City Hotel, Jalan Medan Glodok, P.O. Box 1575. Phones 62997008, 6490931.

Orchid Palace, Jalan S. Parman Slipi. Phones 593115, 596911. Telex 46631.

Patra Jasa Hotel, Jalan A. Jani 2. Phone 410608.

Sabang Metropolitan, Jalan Agus Salim 11. Phones 345031, 357621. Telex 44555.

Wisata International, Jalan M. H. Thamrin, P.O. Box 2457. Phones 320308, 320408.

Two-Star hotels also are supposed to have air conditioning, attached bath with hot water, telephones and food service, but quality and maintenance often suffer. Although most are quite clean, they tend to be older hotels and some of them are past their better days. Rates supposedly are from $10 to $30 for a single, $15 to $40 for a double, but in practice it is difficult to get a room for less than $20 to $25, the maximum prices applying during high season. Two-Star hotels are:

Asri, Jalan Pintu 1, P.O. Box 3076. Phone 581949.
Chitra, Jalan Toko Tiga Seberang 23. Phone 6291125.
Cikini Sofyan, Jalan Cikini Raya 79. Phone 320695.
Dias Hotel, Jalan Kran 20. Phone 416237.
Djakarta Hotel, Jalan Hayam Wuruk 35. Phone 377709.
Febiola, Jalan Gajah Mada 27. Phone 6394008.
Hasta Hotel, Jalan Asia Africa Senayan. Phone 581559.
Interhouse, Jalan Melawai Raya 18. Phone 716408.
Kebayoran Inn, Jalan Senayan 87. Phone 775968.
Marcopolo, Jalan Teuku Cik. Phone 3107131.
Menteng, Jalan Gondangdia Lama 28. Phone 325208.
Metropole, Jalan Pintu Besar Selatan 39. Phone 676921.
Paripurna, Jalan Hayam Wuruk 25. Phone 376311.
Sabang Palace, Jalan Setia Budi Raya 24. Phone 514640.
Surya Baru Hotel, Jalan Batu Ceper 11. Phone 368108.
Surya Hotel, Jalan Batu Ceper 44. Phone 378108.
Transaera, Jalan Merdeka Timur 16. Phone 357059.

One-Star hotels have the lowest rating granted by the Jakarta government, and rooms in this category should rent between $7 and $30 a night, with a $10 to $15 average, single or double. In this grade, as with Two-Star hotels, one should inspect the place before signing in, to separate the seedy from the sanitary. Again, the level of cleanliness and hospitability vary considerably with the ownership and management. Good, clean, adequate One-Star and Two-Star hotels exist but there is a great deal of latitude in quality and the would-be guest should choose carefully:

Dirgantara Hotel, Jalan Iskandarsyah 1. Phone 71210999.
Gama Gundaling, Jalan Pal Putih 197. Phone 354251.
Karya Hotel, Jalan Jaksa 322. Phone 322597.
Melati Hotel, Jalan Hayam Wuruk 1. Phone 377208.
Nirwana, Jalan Otto Iskandardinata 14. Phone 8191708.
Pardede, Jalan Raden Saleh 9. Phone 323868.

Petamburan, K. S. Tuban 15. Phone 593393.
Prapanca, Jalan Prapanca Raya 30. Phone 712656.
Rensa Sofyan, Jalan Duren Sawit Raya 108. Phone 8197354.
Royal Hotel, Jalan Ir. H. Juanda 14. Phone 348894.
Salemba Indah, Jalan Paseban 20. Phone 882909.
Sriwijaya, Jalan Veteran 1. Phone 370409.
Senen City Hotel, Jalan Bungur Besar 157. Phone 412826.
Tebet Sofyan, Jalan Prof. Drs. Soepomo 23. Phone 829311.
Wisata Jaya, Jalan Hayam Wuruk 123. Phone 632208.
Wisma Indra, Jalan KHA Salim 63. Phone 337556.

Jakarta also has a variety of hostel-type rooms and domitories in accommodations called *losemans*. Since these must be inspected and bargained for, the best practice is to ask your cab driver enroute from the airport for the loseman area. Some streets are lined with these budget accommodations.

Hotel reservations not only in Jakarta but all over Indonesia can be made through most travel agencies and there are well over one hundred tour operators and travel agents in Jakarta. They can find rooms when no one else can and they often can save you money because they have their own special rate arrangements.

Tour Operators

Most top-rated hotels have an in-house travel agent specializing in city and area tours. Seeing Jakarta on one of these tours can save time and trouble for visitors unfamiliar with the city. City tours can cost from $6 to $60 in minibus groups of ten or more.

Tour and travel agents also book more extensive tours, some running from Jakarta to Bali and beyond; or by ship and plane to the other islands of Indonesia.

A few agents, chosen for broad qualifications, are:

Apexindo Express, Hotel Borobudur, Third Floor. Phone 376598.

Anta Express, Jalan Hayam Wuruk 88. Phone 6395908.

Astrindo, Jalan Ir. H. Juanda 21C. Phone 3806661.

Colors of Asia Travel, Jalan Wahid Hasyim 86. Phone 333640.

Data Tours, Jalan Ir. H. Juanda 30. Phone 375909.

Deha Tour, Jalan Metro Pondok Indah 31 (Plaza). Phone 7500250.

ESA Tour, Jalan Lautze 17K. Phone 356254.

Ista Indonesia, Interhouse Hotel. Phone 714878.

Kostour, Jalan Otto Iskandardinata. Phone 8190052.

Media Tour, Jalan Melawai. Phone 7202680.

Midas Tour, Jalan Cideng Timur 68B. Phone 346254.

Natrabu, Jalan H.A. Salim 29A. Phone 331728.

Nitour, Duta Merlin Shopping Center. Phone 346462.

Pacto, Jalan Surabaya 8. Phone 332634.

Panorama Tours, Jalan Balik Papan 22B. Phone 350438.

Priaventure Tours & Travel, Jalan Bungur Besar 39. Phone 417070.

Protours, Sari Pan Pacific Hotel. Phone 323707.

Satriavi, Jalan Prapatan. Phone 3803944.

Setia, Glodok Plaza. Phone 639008.

Smailling Tour, Jalan Hayam Wuruk 2B. Phone 3800022.

Tedjo Express, Jalan Sultan Hasanuddin 60. Phone 731003.

Universal, Jalan Pintu Besar Selatan 82C. Phone 6907981.
Vayatour, Jalan Batutulis 38. Phone 354457.
Vista Tour, Jalan Cikini Raya 58A. Phone 321917.

These travel agents, among others, also offer day trips and overnighters to Bogor and Bandung, subjects of the next chapter, which are within easy reach of Jakarta.

CHAPTER FOUR

Bogor & Bandung

Departing from Jakarta to the south by expressway, the first city encountered is Bogor, now almost a suburb of the capital, which is extending itself year by year over hill and countryside. And going east from Bogor, the first major city will be Bandung, with a population of approximately two million.

Both of the cities are interesting of themselves, but day trips there, using Jakarta as a base, should highlight the hill areas enroute and around the two cities, not only for the scenic beauty but also for specific attractions including tea plantations, an active volcano you can drive right up to, a wild animal farm, and hot spring areas.

Bogor

In Bogor the chief attraction is the botanical gardens which can transport you into the 1800s. There's a distinct feeling of walking into a 19th-century impressionist painting as you stroll amid lines of towering, majestic trees of every variety and color.

Everywhere rampant root systems sprawl above ground, radiating from these century-old giants, some tangled like the tentacles of monstrous squid and others as tidy as ribbon candy. There are fifteen thousand species of plants and trees in the park, which opened in 1817, inspired by the grand-scale character Sir Thomas Stamford Raffles, founder of Singapore and one-time (briefly) governor and benefactor of Java.

Vines droop luxuriantly as if in a tended jungle and children play in the loops. Colorful blooms abound in season and every imaginable species grows, some as rare as the Rafflesia, the world's largest flower, with blossoms literally a yard wide, weighing ten to fifteen pounds.

This is the ultimate park, an exaggeration of every perfect hometown park that has ever been strolled. Lovers walk hand in hand or cuddle in secluded bushes. The sound of running streams is never far. Young people with guitars congregate and sing. Family picnics are held. Games are played.

On Saturdays and Sundays, locals and visitors throng to the gardens. Admission is reduced to 600 rupiah (almost half the weekday fee) and tourists will be outnumbered by Javanese.

Teenagers—especially the boys showing off for their peers—can be boisterous and fresh. They'll ask to take pictures of you. The girls only smile brightly, flashing their eyes and a word of greeting. Everyone says hello. Some will try to practice their English on visitors, who are pointed out—not treated as intruders but definitely noticed. Foreigners who dislike crowds ought to plan to visit the gardens on weekdays when peacefulness is assured.

At one corner of the park stands a seldom-used presidential palace with deer on the lawn and, reputedly, an impressive Sukarno art collection, paintings and sculptures favoring the female form. Special permission is required for entry and reportedly such arrangements can be made at the aging Hotel Salek across the street, with a colonial facade which looks as if it belonged on a beach in New England.

The city of Bogor is another thing. It has little to recommend it. A market of stalls adjoins the park and enters the town itself but on weekends it's devoted mostly to produce and refreshments for the crowd. The market area in the town itself, more touristy, offers nothing special. Tourism and economics pretty much have done the place in. Traffic from the entrance to town piles up. Businesses and their signs jar the peace—a collection of insurance agents, electric appliance shops, hardware stores and other commercial specialties no different from any mid-American town.

The central part of the city seems to counteract the whole concept of peacefulness that the park presents, but the contrast of the city beside these ageless gardens accents their beauty all the more, because while the city grew and changed, the park remained the same, like a jewel from the past.

Just beyond Bogor, on the road towards Bandung, the road rises through the picture perfect Puncak Pass area, its stunning views sometimes misted out in the afternoons. Small mountain resorts and tea plantations fill the foreground when long-range views are obscured. Also in these hills is the Taman Safari Indonesia, a park in which anoa, rhino, giraffe, white tiger and Asian bears—as well as animals from all over the world—roam freely and can be seen at roadside from the windows of your vehicle. And you can ride an elephant, too, if you wish.

Overnight facilities are available, but the whole trip can be made on an eight-hour tour from any Jakarta hotel for about $30. If you travel on your own, there are recreational areas for picnics, freshwater springs, waterfalls and, at Telaga Warna, a lake which appears to change color several times a day.

They call Bogor "Rain City" because it catches so much precipitation. Situated just below the basin area of Jakarta, with mountains at its back, Bogor is the precise foothill spot where rain clouds build up enough to break. Visitors should keep this in mind when traveling the area.

One interesting Bogor site usually overlooked by mainstream tour operators—for good reason—is the proclamation cut in stone in the middle of the fifth century A.D. by King Purnawarman, who designated himself conqueror of the world. He also left his footprint (à la the Hollywood Chinese Theater) but it's a washout of sorts. The huge boulder on which he left his marks in Sanskrit some 1,500 years ago is clear enough, but it sits in a creek more than a mile off the road. Not a high traffic location.

Some Bogor visitors keep going south to Pelabuhanratu Bay (two hours drive beyond Bogor), a popular weekend resort for Java residents. A beautiful, dramatic, cliff-lined beach, but treacherous. Lives have been lost in the surf and people blame the Queen of the South Seas, an angry green goddess. One resort hotel at the beach, the Samudra, keeps a vacant room full of fresh flowers in an effort to stay on the goddess's good side, if she has one.

Also south of Bogor, in the Sukabumi village area, are several natural recreation sites, the Lido Water Park and Pangrango with water sports, hotel and restaurant facilities, and Situ Gunung, another lake area suitable for camping.

Heading eastward, the road to Bandung seems engineered for sightseeing, its mountain forks branching to Lembang, Maribaya, Jatiluhur Dam, Cibodas and Tangkuban Prahu, the only Java volcano crater where you can drive right up to the rim and look down into benign hell on earth, still reeking with sulphur fumes.

Cibodas Botanic Gardens, called "Paradise on Earth," is a later (1890) version of the Bogor park featuring trees and plants that prosper in the higher altitudes. All of these highland and mountain areas south of Bogor, due to their elevation, can be cooler than Jakarta, especially after the sun goes down, so a sweater or light jacket is useful.

Lembang, site of a natural lake that the government has been developing to attract visitors, provides magnificent mountain views and also is the location of the Bosscha Observatory, a planetarium operated by the Bandung Institute of Technology. Visits require advance permission.

The nearby Maribaya, with invigorating mineral springs and the Ciomas waterfalls, has become popular with nature walkers, as have the sixty-foot Cimahi waterfalls on the road below, approached by a steep, rather demanding walkway.

The Tanghuban Perahu crater 10 miles beyond Lembang got its name, meaning the upturned boat, after a succession of ash and lava cave-ins made it resemble a capsized vessel. The road to the crater was started in 1906 when Java was still dominated by the Dutch and its construction experiencd delays due to wars and eruptions, one in 1910 and the last in 1926.

Inside the giant canyon blown out by the earth's upheavals is a panorama of about ten baby volcanoes poking up from the floor of the colossal crater, some significant enough to have earned their own names: Jurig, Omas, Ratu and Upas.

At an entrance gate about fifteen minutes drive from the Queen's Crater carpark, visitors are charged a small fee (about $1 for car and driver or 250 rupiah per person). Those who wish can descend part way into the crater by foot but a knowledgeable guide is advised because fumes still spout from the earth at many spots.

The first European to scale Mount Tangkuban Perahu, back in 1713 when the contours might have been quite different, was the same man credited with bringing coffee to Java, Abraham van Riebeck. The climb was so strenuous, they say, that he died on the return trip. Today the view that he gave his life for can be achieved by car and road, without exertion.

On the other side, just below the crater is a popular holiday resort, Ciater Hot Springs, where visitors can bathe in man-made pools or the springs that feed them. The view of tea plantations which occupy the rolling hills on the downslope is beautiful.

Near Purwakarta in the same mountains one can visit the Jatiluhur Dam and its reservoir, the latter developed with facilities for swimming, boating, water skiing, tennis and camping.

Closer to Bandung on the north are Cimahi, where the famous craftsmen of Cibeureum display their bamboo art, and the Juanda Forest Preserve. The forest, nicely improved with walking paths, formerly was known as Dago Pakar and is the site of many man-made caves left over from the Japanese war occupation. The Dago Tea House, only eight miles north, offers a spectacular overview of the city of Bandung and is a popular sightseeing location.

Bogor Hotels

Rates in Bogor hotels, which might be used as an escape from Jakarta or a base for mountain excursions, range between $8 and $40:

Bumi Parahyangen Hotel, Jalan Raya Ciawi Puncak 10. Phone 87147.

Cibogo Hotel, Jalan Raya Puncak 133.

Evergreen Village, Jalan Raya Puncak. Phone 4075.

Lembah Nyiur Hotel, Jalan Raya Puncak 79. Phone 4891.

Mars Hotel, Jalan Raya Cipayung 133. Phone 4488.

Parama Hotel, Jalan Raya Puncak 32. Phone 4728.

Pondok Genggong Hotel, Jalan Raya Jakarta-Bogor. Phone 870875.

Salak Hotel, Jalan Ir. H. Juanda 8. Phone 22091.

Safari Garden, Jalan Raya Puncak 601. Phone 28225.

Ussu International, Jalan Raya Cisarua. Phone 4499.

Bandung

Bandung itself, the metropolitan capital of West Java, stands on a plateau at an elevation that keeps it cool year-around, a refreshing alternative to the sultry air of the coasts and lowlands. And the pace of Bandung is slower, calmer, despite its big-city size.

It gives you an idea of Java's burgeoning population problem when one realizes that Bandung in pre-war days, about 1940, had about 150,000 residents; in a period of fifty years the city has multiplied more than ten times. Bandung has been called "The Paris of Java" and "The City of Flowers." Once it was known for elegant colonial homes set back on wide streets lined with shade trees, and, despite a ravaging fire decades ago, these elements are still there, if somewhat overpowered by commercial and industrial growth.

The people are Sundanese (an ethnic distinction of the area, less influenced by Hindu inheritance than the Javanese of central and eastern Java) and, according to at least one official government publication, the women of Bandung are reputedly the most beautiful in all Indonesia.

The city also is noted as an educational center. It has an interesting geological museum with replicas of the famous Java Man among other rocks and fossils. An institute in Bandung monitors the volcanoes of Indonesia, which is important because the whole nation sits on the most active, unstable part of the Pacific Ring of Fire.

But once a visitor looks over the local campuses, perhaps strolls through the Bandung Zoo and shops in the touristy section called Babakan Siliwangi, there is nothing much more to do. All of the attractions are in the outlying areas around the city.

Even culturally, although the city is known for Wayang Golek wooden puppet shows and for Anklung (bamboo pipe) music, a performance accompanied by drums and horn, the best bambo music instruments are said to be made and demonstrated at the

Mang Udjo Anklung Workshop in the village of Padasuka, a short distance east of Bandung.

In the volcanic area south of Bandung the village of Garut is recommended as typically Sundanese. There are lakes and hot water springs nearby. The view from Papandayan crater is outstanding and, depending on conditions, the curious might also look into Mount Galunggung, which erupted as recently as 1982.

Off the beaten track, to the southwest of Bandung lies the village of Ciwedey where craftsmen fashion exotic knives and daggers. The *kris* blade holds a special spiritual meaning for Java natives who believe the instruments—a favorite collector's item among tourists—carry magical powers if properly made.

Tasikmalaya, southeast of Bandung, largely gets its reputation from bamboo and rattan crafts. Hats, umbrellas, baskets, mats, and many other products, including batik, are for sale everywhere.

At the farthest point southeast in the province of West Java one encounters Pangandaran Beach, a holiday resort popular with Jakartan elites as well as tourists. This sandy beach peninsula, shaded by coconut palms and surrounded by a forest preserve full of wildlife like monkeys, deer and hornbills, offers very inexpensive seaside cottages.

The area is marked with spectacular rock formations, exposed coral reefs (at low tide) and underground caves that can be explored. Or just watch the local fishermen casting their nets. It's really a seaside wonderland.

On the opposite coast of Java, almost 100 miles directly north, the clean, bright port city of Cirebon (pronounced Cheeri-bon) attracts a few visitors who are interested in another approach to touring. No mere sideshow to Java travel, Cirebon is completely different and presents the look of the island relatively untrammeled by the consequences of late 1900s, such as independence, an oil economy and organized tourism.

Cirebon is only three or four hours train or bus ride east of Jakarta, but tours seldom operate that way. Thus Cirebon is best seen as a side trip from Bandung where the road shortcuts across the island northeast through more impressive scenery than the rather dull train tracks afford.

If one single sight could embody the spirit of the city, it is the sultan's coach at the 15th-century palace called Kraton Kesepuhan. This creation combines Chinese, Hindu, Javanese, Islamic and other influences in a vehicle shaped like a winged elephant. The same slightly mad touches can be seen in another attraction on the outskirts of town, the ruins of Taman Arum Sunyaragi, a one-time fortress converted into a pleasure palace that looks like something designed by a tripping Californian in the 1960s but actually dates from 1702, with a fanciful remodeling in 1852.

The name *Cirebon*, one plausible theory holds, derived from a Japanese word meaning mixture. Once among the richest ports in Java, it boasts two palaces with museums, both somewhat neglected, and a grand mosque, dating from 1500, signifying the city's role as one of the original seats from which Islam spread through Java.

But the relics of its history are mere curiosities compared to the atmosphere of the past which clings to the city and its harbor, its warehouses that once bulged with the wealth of these islands which foreign nations were so willing to fight for.

Today it's a matter of a few interesting points, excellent seafood, an intriguing market area and, in the neighboring village of Trusmi, bargains in outstanding batik.

For the seafood try the Calibri Restaurant in the Grand Hotel Cirebon, Cirebon Plaza Restaurant or Mazim's, all of which serve European, Indonesian and Chinese-style menus.

Some people might like to stay in the Bandung area and use it as a base for touring the mountain resorts, volcanoes and Sundanese villages of the area instead of launching their tours out of Jakarta. Either can easily be done with travel package deals.

Bandung hotels, and others in the extended area, are listed with rate ranges for singles and doubles. Suites and bungalows often vary more by season.

Bandung Hotels

Anggrek Golden Hotel, Jalan Martadinata 15. Phone 52537. $8 to $65.

Arjuna Plaza, Jalan Ciumbuleuit 128. Phone 81328. $6 to $40.

Braga Hotel, Jalan Braga 8. Phone 51685. $6 to $40.

Bumi Asih Hotel, Jalan Cilamaya 1. Phone 50419. $8 to $65.

Capital Plaza Hotel, Jalan Jendral A. Yani 75. $8 to $65.

Grand Hotel Lembang, Jalan Raya Lembang 228. Phone 870875. $8 to $65.

Guntur Hotel, Jalan Otto Iskandardinata 20. Phone 50763. $8 to $65.

Harapan Hotel, Jalan Kepatihan 14. Phone 51212. $6 to $40.

Horison Hotel, Jalan Maskumambang 8. Phone 411462. $8 to $65.

Istana Hotel, Jalan Lembang 21. Phone 433025. $15 to $80.

Kumala Panghegar Hotel, Jalan Asia Afrika 140. Phone 52141. $15 to $80.

Melati Hotel, Jalan Kebonjati 24. Phone 56409. $6 to $40.

Mutiari Hotel, Jalan Kebun Kawang 60. Phone 56356. $6 to $40.

Naripan Hotel, Jalan Dipati Ukur 20. Phone 83536. $6 to $40.

New Naripan Hotel, Jalan Naripan 31. Phone 51167. $8 to $65.

Panghegar Hotel, Jalan Merdeka 2. Phone 432295. $15 to $80.

Patra Jasa Hotel, Jalan Ir. H. Juanda 132. Phone 82590. $8 to $65.

Pondok Sonyrosa Hotel, Jalan Hhegarmanah 4. Phone 84100. $8 to $65.

Savoy Hoffman Hotel, Jalan Asia Afrika 112. Phone 432244. $8 to $65.

Trio Hotel, Jalan Gardujati 56. Phone 615055. $8 to $65.

Arrangements for rooms at mountain and beach hotels and resorts, of which there are many, are best made through travel agents (at no extra cost). Cirebon also has a number of good hotels and motels, including:

Cirbeon Plaza, Jalan Kartini 46. Phone 2061. $8 to $40.
Grand Hotel, Jalan Siliwangi 98. Phone 2014. $15 to $40.
Kharisma Hotel, Jalan Kartini 48. Phone 2295. $15 to $40.
Omega Hotel, Jalan Tuparev 20. Phone 3072. $15 to $40.
Patrajasa Motel, Jalan Tuparev 11. Phone 3792. $18 to $60.

Bandung Agents

Some travel agents are listed here for the Bandung area because they can book local area tours, hotels, trains, planes, etc.; but the same business in the Bandung area and other sections south of Jakarta can be handled as well by Jakarta tour and travel agents.

Anta Express, Jalan Cibadak 172. Phone 611774.
Central Raya Mulya, Jalan Lengkong Besar 24. Phone 52616.
Interlink, Jalan Wastukencana 5. Phone 50614.
Java Bali Indah, Jalan Moch. Mesri 34. Phone 52248.
Kaliman Ultra, Jalan Merdeka 56. Phone 52245.
Natrabu, Jalan Sumireja Timur 14. Phone 521141.
Nitour, Jalan Tamblong 2. Phone 50576.
Pacto, Homann Hotel. Phone 58091.
Pacific Megah, Jalan Dewi Sartika 53. Phone 57852.
Satriavi, Panghegar Hotel. Phone 57584.
Union Express, Homann Hotel. Phone 58091.
Vayatour, Jalan Merdeka 2. Phone 58823.
Vista Express, Jalan Asia Afrika 112. Phone 58091.

CHAPTER FIVE

Java's West Coast

The Bogor and Bandung areas, although popular, hold no monopoly on points of interest which visitors can sample using Jakarta as a base. The whole wild west coast of Java awaits those who want a glimpse off the beaten path and into the tropical island's untouched past.

Within a few hours of Jakarta, travelers can find the sandy white beaches of the relatively undeveloped, quiet and uncrowded west coast. They are less than three hours by car from the international airport. Some people like to start their island visit at this point, hastening here immediately from Jakarta to unwind from the rigors of the flight and, at the same time, begin to sample the richness, diversity and dramatic history of the scenic land. Others go west for a brief rest from the hubub and whirl of big city life in Jakarta. Others still will overnight in Jakarta before proceeding west. Whatever one's approach, it's a good place to brace oneself before setting out on a full-length tour of Java.

But the west coast presents two faces to the visitor: You can laze on the beach under palms, sipping tropical drinks and gazing at the dramatic scenery, or you can plunge into an arduous schedule of hiking, climbing, sea-going and even jungle treks and photo safaris.

One real bargain in overland travel is offered through the Carita Krakatau Beach Hotel, located on the Sunda Strait, which separates Java and Sumatra (a ferry ride away) and links the Indian Ocean to the Java Sea. The hotel operates a mini-bus or van daily at 3 p.m. from its offices in a hotel lobby in Jakarta to the beach hotel for only $10, provided a minimum of three people sign up for the trip.

Their accommodations vary widely: luxury cottages, rustic beach cabins and even an inexpensive hostel, Hostel Rakata, are among the options for which you can pay from $5 to $60. To the north at Anyer, the Marina Village offers more luxurious housing in "executive cottages" with a $75 per person special that includes meals and sightseeing.

Probably the biggest attraction on the west coast, visible from Carita Beach, is the baby volcano Anak Krakatau. *Anak* means child, and this active volcano rose from the sea about sixty years ago in the same spot where its father, Krakatau (called Krakatoa in the west), exploded and disappeared in an 1883 disaster that shook the whole world.

That explosion, the loudest ever recorded, was heard by the human ear more than 3,500 miles away. Waves from it were felt as far as the English Channel, halfway around the globe. Skies changed color all over the earth and climate was altered everywhere.

In the immediate area, tidal waves killed 36,000, many of them still buried several yards beneath the sands of Java and Sumatra, up to ten miles inland. For many years after the disaster no natives would go near the Sunda Strait and settlements on the coast still are few and far between.

Anak Krakatau has grown steadily in height since it emerged from the sea and now stands over six hundred feet in elevation. It has erupted several times itself, the last time in 1981, but although it still emits smoke and ashes regularly, it is not considered dangerous—yet. The adventurous tourist can pay a visit to Anak Krakatau.

From Carita Beach (the name translates into "the beach of stories") small fishing boats and larger sailing vessels make the trip according to the demand. It's a ten-hour journey in all, four hours one way. This side trip is advisable only between May and October. After that, the monsoon season moves in and the waters become very rough.

Faster speedboats operate out of Anyer to the north from the luxury resort Marina Village, where almost any kind of fishing or sailing vessel can be chartered. The fishing is excellent, by the way.

But the regular tour from Carita Beach is one for the hardy. An early morning start is required. After the four hours at sea, crossing the spot where the great volcano Kratatau vanished so violently, you land on a black sand beach and commence a two-hour hike climbing up the slopes of Anak Krakatau. Under the punishing sun and humidity of a usual Sunda Strait day, even the most physically fit will wilt a little.

It's more than an opportunity to stand at the spot that shook the world. How many chances do you get to witness the very origins of life itself? Much of life on earth came about through the same process that created Anak Krakatau and, in fact, scientists from all over the world come to study the baby volcano as a "laboratory of life." The clash of fire and water, the emergence of new land from the sea, and the small miracle of how plants and animals colonize this virgin earth can all be seen here.

"This is the bay of stories—that's what Carita Bay means," said Dr. Axel Ridder, a tall, bearded Berlin ex-patriate who has been watching Krakatau for more than twenty years. He added, "And the natives still do tell stories. They can point out high water marks where the tidal waves swept away their ancestors."

Recalling the Dutch warship Berouw which was hurled two miles inland by a surge of high water from the eruption, Dr.

Ridder said, "The wreck remained there, high and dry, for a hundred years. It was only in the early 1980s that a native chief sold it for scrap without anyone finding out until too late. Too bad. It should have been preserved."

If Krakatau were to strike again, the burgeoning population of Java—ten times what it was only a century ago—would certainly swell the casualty figures, experts agree. But most of the scientists attracted to Anak Krakatau come not in fear of death but rather in appreciation of life.

"This is one of the most fascinating spots in the world," exclaimed Dr. Ian Thornton, an Australian zoologist who inspects the volcano regularly. "It's a unique attraction."

The explosive geological history of Krakatau is not being overlooked. The Indonesian Volcanological Institute has placed monitoring equipment around the fussing baby which, Dr. Thorton pointed out, has an ancestry more terrible than its well-known father.

Three islands encircle Anak Krakatau, only one of which is a remnant of the 1883 explosion. All three of the outer islands are thought to be the ruins of one earlier, huge volcanic island called Ancient Krakatau.

According to the Javanese *Book of Kings*, that was a ten-mile-wide monster two miles high which exploded and disappeared in prehistory. Krakatau senior arose in the middle after that, like Anak Krakatau, history repeating itself.

Could it happen again? The science of predicting volcanic eruptions has not advanced a great deal in the past hundred years. Said one scientist, "They're like earthquakes. By the time you hear the rumblings, it's too late."

And as with major earthquakes, it could happen tomorrow, or in a hundred years, or ten thousand. Meanwhile, scientists and satellites are watching Anak Krakatau. Fingers are crossed and the clock is ticking.

No one is too worried. Monitoring equipment is in place and any suspicious rumblings from the earth's interior would be sufficient warning to begin evacuations, it is generally agreed. Before Krakatau the elder exploded, it gave off smoke, ashes and roars, and yet visitors still went there for adventurous picnics, just as they now do to Anak Krakatau.

If you make the trip you win a membership certificate in the Krakatau Foundation that documents your excursion. It's a quite exclusive club.

Travelers might consider the trek bleak and unrewarding if they have no special interest in geology and related earth sciences or in the history of natural disasters. Anak Krakatau certainly is not the prettiest island in Java environs, endowed with only a small, "instant" rain forest that has sprouted up on one side. It's largely a matter of the historic significance of the site and the insight into the way new earth and life springs from the sea.

A good deal of perspective about Krakatau and its offspring can be gained without even leaving the Carita Beach Hotel. There owner Axel Ridder maintains a Krakatau Museum and will show you a documentary film that provides abundant information, historical and current. Besides, you can see Anak Krakatoa from the beach and you can ask about high water marks where the tidal waves—some of them more than a hundred feet high—crashed ashore with such devastating fury. This is the Beach of Stories, remember, and the natives have passed down tales of the disaster.

Krakatau actually has become part of the Indonesian National Parks system, which includes a number of offshore islands and another major west coast attraction, on the southernmost peninsula, a wildlife preserve called Ujung Kulon.

In the dense forest which makes up this reserve, wild animals roam freely, including the last fifty remaining one-horned rhinoceroces, an endangered species. Other animals populating the area include tigers, panthers, monkeys, buffalo, wild ox, deer, wild boar and crocodiles.

Obviously, the visitor cannot roam as freely as the animals. This is not a zoo and there are no bars. Specially supervised tours offer the opportunity to view these wild creatures living in their natural habitat. Your guides, the Indonesian equivalent of forest rangers, will lead you to protected towers that provide excellent vantage points for observation and photography.

Again, this is an adventure, more like a safari than a side trip. The park is accessible only by boat at this time, although there are plans for a road. A permit is required and the usual starting point is the small village of Labuan, just south of Carita Beach. Charters out of Marina Village also make the trip, which takes a minimum of one full day. Visitors must arrange for their own lunch and beverages. This is not like a crowded Yosemite or Yellowstone National Park. You will be in a very real jungle.

Three Californians decided to charter a fifty-foot motor yacht to take them and some friends on a tour of the Ujung Kulon Preserve as well as Krakatau and the westernmost Java island, Panaitan. The boat, a converted fishing vessel which looked more seaworthy than it was, experienced motor failure on the third day, stranding the passengers on Panaitan. No radio, no flares.

Two of the men set out on surfboards to cross to the jungle preserve in search of help. Barefoot, making their own path as they went, they encountered two panthers and a cobra and had to sleep in the brush overnight.

They reached a ranger station the next day, trek-scarred, hungry and thirsty. And not a little scared. Two days later they were taken to Jakarta from which an air and sea search was launched for their comrades who had disappeared from the island in their crippled boat. It was presumed that they had restarted the engine and tried to run for home but didn't make it. They were adrift somewhere in the Indian Ocean.

After ten days the boat drifted into a remote fishing village on Sumatra and all aboard were saved.

But they'll never rent a boat again without being sure of its capabilities, no matter what the captain boasts.

Much of the sightseeing in this undeveloped coastal area is more difficult than you'll find it elsewhere. There's a great waterfall at nearby Curug Gendang, inland, but if you want to see it, you are faced with a three-hour hike through hills and jungle. If hiking is your sport and you love the challenge of a jungle trek, this can be a spectacular sight. On the other hand, if the journey sounds too strenuous for you, don't feel cheated because there are many outstanding waterfalls further east which are more accessible, sometimes by car.

In the hills at Cibea, inland from Carita Beach, there's a Badui village where that mystic tribe has isolated itself from civilization for over four hundred years. They turn their backs on progress. They have no use for money, nor for much government, either. This can be an interesting excursion, but they only allow visitors into the outer villages, not inside the most sequestered inner village.

Even if you spoke Indonesian, it's unlikely you could converse with the natives of the outer Badui village because their dialect, an archaic Sundanese preserved for centuries, prevents communication with outsiders. But your guide will be able to explain the lifestyle of these "wild" natives and you'll gain insight into a tribe that still lives back in the 16th century. It can be a little like stepping into a time machine.

Other mystics also reside in this area. The Bantenese *Debus* are said to be holy men who are able to endure the pain of fire or even torture unharmed. Sometimes visitors, by special arrangement, are allowed to witness their ceremonies, but this is not an event which happens every day. Inquiries must be made well in advance.

In a brief stay of two or even three days on the west coast, it would be impossible to see and do everything: Anak Krakatau, the wild animal reserve, the waterfall, and the village of the Badui. Choices must be made, but there is a variety of appeal in these little adventures.

Some visitors may elect to sit out *all* of the more demanding side trips. There'll still be plenty of other opportunities to explore the many faces of Java at your own pace as you continue the journey eastward.

For those who prefer more leisurely sightseeing, the west coast has a few other interesting places to fill the gaps between extensive beach play and relaxation.

At Anyer to the north there's a historic and impressive lighthouse built by Queen Wilhelmena in 1883 just after the Krakatau disaster, reflecting part of the Javanese Dutch heritage.

Nearby at Merak, where there is a ferry link to Sumatra, the scenery is outstanding and there's a comfortable beach resort called Salira Indah.

There's an 18-hole golf course at Cilegon, usually uncrowded.

In the Bay of Banten, close to Cilegon, an exceptional bird sanctuary and wildlife reserve occupies the island of Dua. Visitors are welcome and the trip is relatively easy.

The city of Banten generally is considered the birthplace of Islam in Indonesia and there you'll find a renovated ancient mosque which boasts the oldest minaret in the islands as well as the Grand Mosque, built in 1566 by Sultan Maulana Jusuf.

Also in Banten you can see the remains of two elaborate palaces which were destroyed by conquerors early in the 19th century, the Speelwijk Fortress where the Dutch first landed in 1596, and an old Chinese temple. Together they give you a general sense of the diverse background of Java concentrated in a single town.

Banten and the other small towns dotting the west coast area all have small marketplaces, sometimes just on certain days of the week, and not totally tourist-oriented. But shoppers can bargain hunt among the limited offerings and it may be a good place to sharpen your negotiating skills. Or you can just look: travel through the remainder of the island will bring you in contact with a much wider array of the art and handicrafts that make Java famous.

At most of the resorts, traditional dance performances can be seen either on a regularly scheduled basis or upon request. If a number of people ask in advance for a certain day, the management usually will be able to arrange, for instance, for a showing of the Tari Topeng or Masked Dance.

At the right time of year—harvest days for example—there are communal folk dances in the local villages and everybody can join in.

Excursions by boat to Sanghiang Island are available at Carita and Anyer. The island boasts excellent sea gardens for skin diving, and relics of World War II such as sunken boats and aircraft can be explored.

For hikers there are nearby ricefields, villages, rubber plantations, tea plantations and even a couple of remote gem shops. For the railroad buff, the town of Labuan operates the oldest steam trains still in service anywhere in the world, they say, with locomotives dating back to 1899.

Meanwhile, back at the hook-shaped Carita Beach bay, there's sailing, surfing, fishing, scuba diving, snorkeling, windsurfing and even tennis. Not exactly exotic or adventurous, but fun nevertheless.

West Coast Hotels

A foursome of first-time Australian visitors was carousing in a fashionable Jakarta hotel bar one day, as is not uncommon, when they decided that they should adjourn their party to the sand and sun of a nearby seashore. They decided on Carita Beach.

At Carita Beach, they reasoned, just a couple of hours drive away, there awaited pleasant, thatch-roofed bungalows, beachside bars. . . . Images of a laid-back atmosphere, the rolling surf, clean air were alluring. But try as they might, they could not raise a west coast hotel on the telephone. Telexes went unanswered. Attributing the lack of instant communication to some unknown technical flaw, and having read that the west coast resorts are so uncrowded during weekdays that they lower their prices and make other concessions to lure travelers, the foursome decided to plunge ahead unannounced, certain of their welcome.

They hired a car at a cost of approximately 50,000 rupiah (about $30 U.S.) one way, checked out of their four-star hotel and soon were swaying to the lilt of a two-lane highway westbound.

Upon arrival, they found the hotel of their choice jammed.

Inexplicably, the place was so overcrowded in fact that not another human of any size or appetite could be accommodated.

Thus began a wearying round of alternative hotels and resorts. All full. No one knew why. A few special parties, an unusual number of tour groups taking advantage of mid-week rates, and the remaining spaces filled by other, earlier spur-of-the-moment guests.

By nightfall, the foursome had to abandon their quest for the beach life and return to Jakarta. Cost, another 50,000 rupiah.

But, once back in the big city, the hour late, their nerves ajangle, unfed and weary, the group found that the rooms they had vacated were no longer available. So another round of hotel hunting was begun without enthusiasm. Time and again the tourists were turned away, except at the restaurants and bars.

Finally, in the wee hours of the morning, with daylight cracking on the horizon and the Muslim calls to prayer ringing in their ears like moans for the dead, they had no choice but to accept seedy rooms in a hotel whose unsavory appearance was probably the principal reason for its availability, if not the smell.

A day was lost, a whim squashed. The sun did not rise on cheerful faces.

Certainly one ought to encourage such spur-of-the moment decisions, for they can make life interesting. However, if the urge strikes you, put yourself immediately in the hands of a capable travel agent; authorize him or her to telephone, telex or FAX (or bribe) as necessary to confirm your reservations in advance. Then have another drink and wait. Don't go near the checkout desk until you have confirmed reservations in hand.

No matter what you hear, no matter what you read, no matter what common sense tells you, do not make the assumption that a certain area will have plenty of rooms available. Don't go anywhere without confirmed reservations. Leave your traveler's checks at home, or even lose them if you will, but don't go without reservations.

The best places to stay on the relatively undeveloped Java west coast are listed below, with their Jakarta telephone numbers for advance reservations:

Abadi Hotel, Serang area, $5 to $50. Phone 81641.

Anyer Beach Hotel, $11 to $80. Phone 367594.

Carita Krakatau Beach Hotel, $5 (hostel) to $65. Phone 325208, Ext. 5.

Desiana Cottages, $25 to $55. Phone 593316.

Mambruk Beach Resort, $25 to $85. Phone Anyer Lor 421.

Marina Village, $30 to $100. Phone 363948.

Merak Beach Hotel, $5 to $100. Phone 367838.

Pulorida Hotel, Merak, $5 to $40. Phone 367508.

Travel agents in Jakarta maintain their own system for contact with other hotels in the west beach area. Among these are the Selat Sunda Wisata Cottages in Labuan, with accommodations from $39; the Serang Hotel, $5 to $65; and the Wisma Wira Carita, $20 to $30.

Jakarta travel bureaus also are the contact point for a place that can't really be called the west coast because it's north of the capital, but nevertheless serves as a close-by escape from the metropolis: the Thousand Islands resort, also called the Seribu Islands.

There are really not one thousand (but more than a hundred) islands and some dissent was raised about giving these recreational outposts a non-Indonesian name, but the resort primarily occupies a half dozen different islands stretching from the Jakarta harbor northward for 60 miles or more.

The islands have a speckled history as the bases for forts, lighthouses, shipyards. One of them, whose name intriguingly translates to Heavenly Nymph Island, was once a leper colony.

Crowded during the weekends when Jakartans and expatriates flee the city to occupy the beach bungalows and cottages available, the Thousand Islands offer a Bali-like holiday close to the

city. Sandy beaches, clear water and an abundance of colorful
fish and coral formations attract snorkelers and other divers.

Accommodations vary from basic to luxury, and costs vary
from $80 to $190 per person for a two-night stay. Arrangements
must be made through travel agencies and most openings are
during the work week.

Day trips are available to the closest developed islands, departing at 7 a.m. by motorboat and returning at 4 p.m., but travel
time, depending on the type of boats available, can take between
one and four hours from the Jaya Ancol Pier. Light aircraft also
make the trip, which is not recommended in the rainy season.

Tourist development is progressing in these offshore islands—
as it is along the more advanced west coast beaches—but is still
light years away from rivaling Bali. Only because of Java's general
lack of beach development does the Thousand Islands get much
attention. Those with the time and money will consider Bali
their best escape from Jakarta.

But one of the greatest attractions in these islands lies about
midway between Jakarta and Bali: the alluring vicinity of
Yogyakarta.

CHAPTER 6

Yogyakarta

In one compact area, the Yogyakarta vicinity has everything that is outstanding and intriguing about Java: the Borobudur temple, a world-class monument that makes the pyramids seem unambitious by comparison, ancient palaces and ruins of kingdoms, smoking volcanoes, beaches and caves, sprawling, colorful markets, comfortable hotels, big cities and small ones, lots of good food and millions of friendly people. And yes, palm trees too, palm trees everywhere.

If a visitor could stop at only one city in the whole eight-hundred-mile span of Java, Yogyakarta should be that one.

It can be reached by plane, train or bus conveniently from all major points of Java or Bali, with multiple daily flights from Jakarta and Denpasar. The airport at Yogyakarta (commonly abbreviated to Yogya in local conversation) compared to Jakarta or even Denpasar is relaxed, relatively uncrowded and fairly close to any hotel.

It's a big city—three million people, they say—but it doesn't act like one, doesn't look like one and doesn't feel like one. The pace is noticeably slower than Jakarta or Denpasar. The lack of tall buildings, the open street scene, the unhurried and courteous behavior of everyone except motorists, all contribute to a comfortable atmosphere.

Yogyakarta is not perfect, far from it, because it *is* a city, but it has an ideal location.

It is early morning, just about daybreak, and everybody is headed somewhere. A man in a suit pedals along beside the highway, his bicycle mounted with twin baskets balanced astride the rear wheel, each carrying a precious cargo of one child as he edges along toward a baby-sitting relative. In the parking lot in front of a hotel, a small tourist bus begins loading for a trip to the temples of the Prambanan Plain. Motorscooters buzz in fury past sleepy, horse-drawn wagons. Fruit vendors begin unpacking crates and displaying their produce in stands. Above them all looms the cone-shaped Mount Merapi, the unfriendly local volcano, which appears for less than an hour shortly after sunrise, almost as if to remind everyone that it is there, then disappears in mists for another day.

The greatest attraction by far in the Yogyakarta area, about twenty-five miles out of town to the northwest, is the Borobudur temple, a Buddhist monument so massive and intricate that it makes Egypt's pyramids seem unimaginative. It dominates the Kedu plains with a work of art that is truly a wonder of the world and can be seen for miles around. The drive to Borobudur, pleasantly rural once one clears the disorder of Yogyakarta traffic, passes through tidy mountain villages and high over river bridges.

The stone monument, so gigantic that the hundreds of life-size Buddhas lining the various levels are virtually lost to the eye from a distance, dwarfed by the overall stateliness of the structure, stands starkly alone, a cathedral without a city. Walking the terrace, climbing to the top, one realizes that almost every exposed vertical stone is carved with reliefs and designs.

The Borobudur temple, by the best scientific guesses, was constructed more than a thousand years ago, between 778 and

856 A.D., and mysteriously abandoned soon after completion, probably because of some unrecorded natural disaster rather than an unchronicled war. How long the ediface stood intact also is unknown although there are clues in etchings from the 1600s, before the settling of America, that it was then relatively un-damaged by time.

But by the turn of this century, around 1900, Borobudur was mostly in ruins, partially buried in volcanic ash and overgrown with rampant wild foliage. Raffles, when lieutenant governor in 1814, had sent an engineer to partially clear the area and confirm reports of what was hidden there. His men barely scratched the surface. History records that when the king of Siam (whose predecessor is better remembered than he from memoirs and the outstanding Broadway musical) visited in 1896 he was made a present of eight cartloads of Buddhas and carved relief panels from the site. Scavengers and art collectors looted even more.

But gradually there began a movement to restore this un-believable creation. Attempts were repeatedly frustrated by wars and economic barricades. As recently as the 1960s the United Nations officially recognized the structure as a world treasure and unanimously ordered a rescue mission. It took ten years of devoted work which was completed in the 1980s at a cost of approximately 25 million dollars.

Standing at the top of the Borobudur one is compelled to imagine the empty, peaceful green fields all around filled with Javanese workers and worshipers, as they must once have been. One wonders if a metropolis that housed them is buried some-where, too, or if Borobudur was a place of pilgrimage from afar in its brief period of use.

The place abounds with mysteries: could such a monument have been constructed with slave labor or was this a work of devout, sacrificial labor by the faithful? Why was this great shrine abandoned so abruptly? Who designed it so that more than a million heavy stone blocks were assembled in a configuration with every dimension, every elevation replete with religious significance? All of this was built before the Tower of London, before the dome of St. Peter's in Rome, before Notre Dame cathedral in Paris.

Visitors of all religions from all over the globe come to see this remarkable monument, which is open daily and, being a tourist attraction, has become surrounded (at a respectable distance) by the sheds of souvenir hawks and soft drink stands. A clear, level park separates the commercialism from the Borobudur itself. Nothing of much value is sold in these places or by the individual entrepreneurs who flock to the environs but are banned from the temple itself. Mostly they try to sell books and booklets about Borobudur, which are a good buy at half the price they ask, but are also obtainable in any bookstore or newsstand in Java.

Mount Merapi, usually hidden from Yogyakarta during most of the day, is clearly visible from Borobudur. Somehow a feeling of great tragedy pervades the atmosphere of the empty fields around. A weed that grows in the park surrounding Borobudur (called *putri malu*), seems ominous. If you reach down and touch it, it shrinks and withers at the point of contact.

Little is known of the short-lived dynasty that constructed this enormous temple. How the people rose, and why they fled, perhaps will always remain a mystery.

Two smaller temples on a line within a couple of miles of Borobudur are believed to have been part of the original complex, serving as acolyte shrines. They are called Candi Mendut and Candi Pawon.

The pyramid-shaped Mendut temple houses an outstanding, ten-foot-tall Buddha sculpture with the deity seated western style, hands in the teaching mode. Some historians consider this the finest Buddha in existence. It is flanked by a pair of statues almost as big. Huge relief panels also adorn the temple, which, were it not in the shadow of Borobudur, probably would have become the focus of visits by pilgrims and tourists. The other temple, Pawon, restored in 1903, is believed to serve as the tomb of a king.

Resident island visitors to Borobudur, who are many and come from considerable distances, are every bit as awed by the structure as are foreign tourists. For some reason visitors from America are still so rare that the locals will ask to take your picture with them. It may be a bit disconcerting to be at one of the wonders of the world and have someone want to photograph *you*. Be sure to turn your own cameras on them in turn.

Then picture this: the Borobudur, the world's largest Buddhist temple, sits in an empty field atop a hill twenty-five miles west of Yogyakarta. Go about eleven miles eastward to encounter an equally startling monument, this one to Hinduism: the Prambanan temples, once a conglomerate of hundreds of individual temples located in an equally stark plains area and also built about a thousand years. The Prambanan temples, dozens of which survive in various states of restoration, also include Candi Larad Longgrang, or the Temple of the Slender Virgin. The Prambanan temples are taller than Borobudur but spire-shaped rather than pyramidal and, like Borobudur, contain countless exquisite carvings.

The Buddhist and the Hindu temple sites experienced a similar history, too, both abandoned soon after construction, their ruins only rediscovered in recent centuries, overgrown and covered with volcanic ash.

Because of the two different religions that inspired these temples, some historians were tempted to theorize that a devastating war broke out among rival kingdoms, but the common symptom of destruction, volcanic ash, and the fact that some temples in the area display both Hindu and Buddhist carvings, indicating a common peaceful use, point more to a natural catacylsm—earthquake, volcanic eruption or both—as the blow which depopulated the entire region . . . or if not the only blow, then the final one.

The slender virgin referred to in one of the temple's names is believed to have been a legendary princess turned to stone after trying to trick an ugly but powerful giant out of marrying her. Her transformed image forms part of a gallery of sculptures credited among the most beautiful Hindu art in the world. There is Siva, the destroyer, with four arms, standing ten feet tall in a special niche facing the east, while the other points of the compass are filled by statues honoring Ganesha, the elephant-headed god of wisdom, Bhatara Guru depicted as the pot-bellied high priest, and the Slender Virgin, who some say is merely the consort of Siva. Ornate reliefs show many of the Hindu religious legends, and entire tales from the Ramayana are carved in a series of elaborate panels.

The principal shrine has been completely restored quite recently, and two other life-size images stand close, representing the other figures of the Hindu trinity, Vishnu and Brahma, but they are marred by scaffolding erected for the as-yet incomplete reconstruction. Piles of stone are all that remain of some outer temples, but perhaps in time—a decade or two, or more—the entire, majestic complex will be restored to its original beauty on the Prambanan Plains.

The Prambanan group of temples is open for visitors daily for a token admission fee and, during full moon nights monthly, May to September, ballet performances of the Ramayana are given at the site.

Within a few miles of the Prambanan, several other significant temples are located, including Candi Kalasan, with its cross-shaped monument marking the late-8th-century marriage of a Hindu king and Buddhist princess; and the Buddhist sanctuary at Plaosan which existed amid hundreds of Hindu holy places. Around these plains are strewn the remains of crumbled temples and shrines uncountable, some partially restored. It's almost as if the whole outdoors for miles around had been consecrated as one boundless religious meeting place.

At the main temple, some visitors study the sculptures and relief details for hours. Others barely give them glance, as if perhaps trying to absorb an over-all sense of this overwhelming repository of the faith of a million people—which was about the total population of Java at the time these magnificent temples were erected and adorned.

One vantage point for an overview of the temples of Prambanan Plains is the site of King Boko's palace, also called Kraton

Ratubaka, atop a plateau about two miles south. Although there is little left of the once-great palace, some excavations of the ruins are underway. The brief climb is worth it just for the view.

Archeologists and volcanologists must consider this region a sort of professional heaven on earth.

If the stunning temples of Prambanan and Borobudur so overload the senses, how could any other similar attractions from antiquity compete for the attention of visitors? Well, at least two major sites do. Both of them a little further afield, they nevertheless lure a stream of tourists regularly, one as the oldest Hindu temple site on Java and the other for its rare architectural derivation and erotic imagery.

The temples of the Dieng Plateau, in cooler mountains more than fifty miles northwest of Yogyakarta, once numbered in the hundreds and are said to predate Borobudur. Often mist-shrouded and adorned with strange and highly individual sculptures, they were carved with bas-reliefs which unfortunately have eroded considerably through the years. These temples too, like Borobudur and Prambanan, experienced a history of abandonment and relatively recent rediscovery.

The visitor who has already seen Borobudur and Prambanan from a Yogyakarta hotel base probably will consider the Dieng Plateau temples themselves nowhere near comparable to those other great monuments, but the trip up through the scenic mountains can redeem the whole excursion for those who can relax and enjoy it.

More people make the trip northeast instead to Candi Sukuh, the "Erotic Temple" on the slopes of Mount Lawa east of Solo, also named Surakarta. Aside from carvings depicting the male symbol *(lingga)* and the female *(yoni)*, which by the way are not obscene but rather, perhaps, a trifle garish in their preoccupation with fertility (some viewers find them worthy of a giggle), the Erotic Temple is striking for its resemblance to the ancient Mayan pyramids deep in Mexico.

This is perhaps the sole architectural kinship shown in Java but scientists have found linguistic, anthropological and cultural parallels between Central America and Indonesia and Malaysia, believed to be the common point of origin for peoples of these widely distant areas. One can also hear in Yogyakarta the music of Sumatrans whose instruments and songs clearly and amazingly evoke Old Mexico.

At the entrance to Candi Sukah there stands a fertility stone. The stone, carved with a lingga and yoni, was apparently used as a test of the fidelity of young women. A woman wearing the traditional sarong had to leap across the stone. If her sarong tore or fell off, this was clear evidence that she was no virgin, or, in the case of a married woman, not true. Considering the leg-stretching leap required to clear the stone, many a sarong must have torn or fallen, exposing limbs and perhaps secrets that must have been grist for much speculation among observers.

The same tours that take Yogyakarta guests to the Sukuh temple, which is beyond Surakarta, usually stop also at the Surakarta Kraton, or palace, center of an ancient Mataram kingdom which rivaled Yogyakarta. Guided tours of the palace, built in the mid-1700s, and its subsidiary museum, are available daily in the morning. Visitors are ushered, shoeless, to view the grand throne room, main hall and exhibits. Music and dance pavilions adjoining the palace offer glimpses of students engaged in gamelan music and dance rehearsals.

A second palace, with a museum in its ceremonial hall, houses the collection of another branch of the royal family, including art objects and curiosities which whet the visitor's appetite for shopping. Tour operators also provide for this, in Solo's extensive antique market.

Yogyakarta, of course, has its own rival royal palace, a white-walled complex in the heart of downtown. Its marbled throne room features an indoor moat, crystal chandeliers and other touches of regal splendor. Among articles in the sultan's private collection are ancient gamelan instruments and exquisite statuary.

Open to the public daily, with shorter hours on Fridays and Saturdays, the palace does not look too impressive from the outside, since all the visitor can see is the thick wall running for more than a mile, and the entrance is a dusty courtyard with a faded piazza. But the palace is practically a city within a city, its luxurious buildings and shaded courtyards betokening a life of splendor within.

The sultan, who occupies a private portion of the palace, enjoys special status with almost total autonomy in some aspects of the government of the city-state of Yogyakarta, a privilege granted because of his support for the anti-colonial forces at the time when Indonesia was trying to forcibly eject the Dutch. Prince Mangkubumi, forty-three years old and the eldest of seventeen sons of Sultan Hamengkubuwono, assumed the title of sultan in 1989, as tradition decrees that the oldest son take the throne upon the death of his father. The claim to the throne was contested by another son but their father never had declared any of his five wives formally his queen so the eldest son officially succeeded.

Curiously, a two-hundred-year-old banyan tree in the palace courtyard, noted as a place of meditation, collapsed upon the arrival of the new sultan.

Another interesting palace, almost adjoining, is the Taman Sari or "Water Castle," an enclosed complex of bathing pools and rooms where the sultan could watch the women of his harem bathing. The Water Castle, which originally had a moat, has subterranean passageways which are said to run under the walls of the main palace. Some restoration work is underway on the neglected stonework.

In the downtown area near the palace—within walking distance, or, more comfortably by pedicab—a number of small museums and a variety of other attractions await: for example, a bird market where hundreds of singing and/or squawking budgies, turtle doves, cockatoos, macaws, parrots and other exotic winged creatures and cages are sold. A colony of young batik artists nearby also are trying their wings, so be careful what you buy; and then there is the great indoor-outdoor, day and night market that Malioboro Street has been turned into. Across the way from the first-class Hotel Garuda and stretching for blocks, this is more a sidewalk bazaar than a shopping center. You can purchase batik, gold and silver jewelry, puppets, carvings, leather goods, paintings, novelties, produce, books and even shaving cream. If you don't see it, ask. It's there somewhere.

It's a crowded place with lots of young people. Be sure your rupiah or dollars are secure because it is an ideal operating ground for pickpockets. Some incidents have been reported but they are becoming less common.

As a center of Javanese culture, Yogyakarta also features a number of good art galleries and home-studios where paintings are displayed and sold. Indonesia's most internationally known artist, Affandi, who died in 1990 at the age of 80, owned an unusual house-gallery complex on Jalan Solo near the Ambarrukmo Palace Hotel, and his daughter is expected to keep operating the establishment, a favorite stop for the art-loving visitor.

The Ambarrukmo Palace Hotel, by the way, may be the only one in the world built on the grounds of an occupied palace. Dance, drama, puppetry and crafts shows often are staged at a large pavilion adjoining the hotel and palace property. Guests and visitors at the hotel can see classical Javanese dance and gamelan performances in the theater restaurant as part of a dinner show.

The schedule of dances, drama, gamelan music and other performances in Yogyakarta varies from week to week but there are always numerous events. Hotel desks, tour agents and the government tourist office (on Jalan Malioboro) will be happy to supply current lists of the extensive showings. Academies where students train in dance, music and other arts also are open to visitors, as is the government's batik research center in Yogyakarta.

Kota Gede, once the capital of a Mataram kingdom in Java, today is better known as the silver center suburb of Yogyakarta. Visitors can watch craftsmen creating jewelry and ornaments and can bargain in the display stores. Those shops which do not bargain, by the way, will at least grant a 10 percent discount for the asking.

If the city area itself fails to keep a visitor amused, there are various alternatives to sightseeing tours of palaces, temples and museums. The mountains around the city contain cool resort retreats such as Tawangmangu on the slopes of the inactive volcano Mount Lawu, Kopeng on Mount Merbabu, the holiday resort Bandungan near Semarang on Mount Ungaran, and, when it's safe, Kaliurang on Mount Merapi's foothills.

And there is the seashore, too, popular with many locals. Parangtritis Beach, about sixteen miles directly south of Yogyakarta, offers rolling dunes and rugged cliffs leading to sandy beaches on the Indian Ocean. On the western edge of this beach the sultan of Yogyakarta annually makes flowery offerings to the goddess of the South Seas.

White and black beaches are found on this coast. At Baron, a few miles to the east, the beaches are white and sheltered and the waters are safer than elsewhere in this area. Visitors unaccustomed to the undertow at south-facing beaches on the Indian Ocean should exercise extreme caution.

One of the most interesting coastal areas in all Java—if remote—is near Gombang, a solid eighty-mile drive west of Yogyakarta. The Jatijaja Cave is located in this region; it is an auditorium-size cavern in limestone, well-lit and lined with life-size statues representing the entire cast of an ancient legend. The entrance has been prepared for visitors and there is a floored area inside with benches.

Directly south of this natural phenomenon are the cliffs of Karangbolong, riddled with smaller caves on the slopes facing the sea. Natives risk their lives here on a workaday basis, scaling the steep cliffs at low tide to gather swallows' nests, which are sold to Chinese restaurants around the world.

The cave and cliffs are actually more accessible from the Cilicap area than from Yogyakarta. Cilicap, the only commercial-class harbor on the south coast, at the border between west and central Java, is a five-hour train ride west from Yogyakarta with an hour's bus ride tacked on at the end.

Another possible side trip from Yogyakarta would be a visit to the north coast and Semarang, a deep-water port which is the administrative center of Central Java and a docking place for passenger liners. Air-conditioned, reserved-seat buses or comfortable inter-city Colts make the two-hour (75 miles) trip, but trains only go a far as Surakarta.

Those who are interested can, of course, overnight in Surakarta, taking in its city and area attractions including the Erotic Temple and, nine miles north, the village of Sangiran where significant archeological explorations are underway on the banks of the Solo River. This was the site of the discovery in 1891 of the Java Man (Pithecanthropus erectus), an important milestone in anthropology.

Semarang has been described as one of the most pleasant cities in Java, and the setting certainly is alluring, rising from the waters of the harbor up the inland mountain slopes to the south. The newer residential area of this city of one million occupies the hillsides which offer a breath-taking view out to sea.

This is a commercial rather than a tourist center, however, and most of its colonial charm and waterfront color has been sacrificed to progress. The few surviving concessions to the past include Semarang's old Chinatown of narrow streets and temples, an 18th-century copper-domed Dutch church, and some European mansions.

Apart from the view from the city, visitors probably will find the outlying areas around Semarang more appealing. Jepara is famous for its teak wood carvings, especially reproductions of antique furniture and screens evoking scenes from the Ramayana and other legends. Ambarawa, to the south of Semarang, features a collection of old steam locomotives and carriages. They operate what they say is the last existing cog railway on Java and arrangements can be made in Semarang (through the Central Java Exploitation Office) for tourist groups to ride.

Significantly demonstrating the racial mixture of Java are two predominantly Chinese villages east of Semarang, Lassem and Rembang, but these are rather far afield. Closer is Demak, site of the Grand Mosque, marking that village as the first center of Islamic conversion in Java, in the 1500s.

So the opportunities for sightseeing and enjoyment from Yogyakarta are many and diverse. It might be said that the only thing Yogyakarta really lacks is a Bali-class beach, but even in Bali people use the swimming pools as often as the surf.

Yogyakarta Tours

Most of the public tours out of Yogyakarta follow a pattern in both destinations and prices. For a Borobudur visit, there is a minibus arranged by the Yogyakarta Tourist Information Service which stops two hours at Borobudur before proceeding to the Dieng Plateau, all for a price of approximately five dollars. It's a value that's hard to beat except by catching the regular public bus for fifty cents, transferring, and spending twice the time riding and more time waiting.

Even with the tourist bus a visitor is at the mercy of other people's schedules, which can be costly in terms of time, free choice and comfort. The public bus to Solo, with a good, frequent schedule, will drop you at the Prambanan temples for the equivalent of twenty-five cents if you just want to roam around.

Many travel agents in Yogyakarta offer similar tours with similar prices covering most of the popular destinations in similar packages. The common choices, and prices, are these:

City Tour: Visit Sultan's Palace, SonoBudoyo Museum, batik home industry outlet and silvercrafts outlet. A three-hour tour. In groups of four to nine persons it's $9 a person. Single person, $23; two people, $12.50 each; three people, $10 each.

Countryside Tour: Visit a dance center, painting gallery, pottery village, leather puppet makers, and mask handicrafts. A four-hour tour, focusing on craft-making and shopping. Four to nine people, $10 each; one person, $26; two, $12.50 each; three $12 each.

Borobudur Tour: Visit the Borobudur temple and its two adjoining temples at Mendut and Pawon. Four hours. Group of four to nine, $11 each; one person, $28; two, $16 each; three, $13 each.

Prambanan Tour: Visit Prambanan, Kalasan, Sewu and Plaosan temples. Three hours. Group of four to nine, $9; one person, $23; two people, $14 each; three people $10 each.

Solo Tour: Visit Prambanan temples, the palace in Solo, the museum and the market area. Six hours. $17 in group of four to nine; $42 a single person; $24 each per couple; $20 each for three. Two variations of the Solo tour usually are available, adding two hours. One tour makes a side trip from Solo to the Erotic Temple and the other makes a side trip to Sangiran, where Java Man was discovered. For this $9 is added for groups, $20 for singles, $14 each for couples, and $10 each for three.

Dieng Plateau Tour. Visit the temples of the Dieng Plateau, active volcanoes, lakes and hot springs. Ten hours. For one person, $90 to $120; for two, $50 to $70 each; for three $35 to $50 each, and the same each in larger groups.

Of course, if you start with a foursome, the tour organizers will put together any tour you want to design for yourself, at comparable rates.

Consider, too, the fact that the best hotel in town will take two people anywhere they want to go, in an air conditioned car with an English-speaking driver, for 30,000 rupiah for a four-hour trip. This amounts to less than $10 per person and could cover either Borobudur or Prambanan. An extra hour, if you decide to stop for lunch, will cost less than $5 for the taxi—not per person.

There is of course an advantage in traveling in small groups by tour bus. You meet people, for one thing, and the tour operators know where to go, or at least where most people seem to want to go. Make sure they are going where *you* want to go.

Six tour operators have offices in the arcade at the Ambar-
rukmo Palace Hotel, Jalan Adi Sucipto, Yogyakarta. They are:
Pacto Tours, phone 86050; Paradise Indah Tours, phone 86552;
Pt. Milangkori, phone 88488; Vista Tour, phone 86353; Rama
Tours, phone 87658; and Satriavi, phone 88488, ext. 742.

Among other tour operators are Chandra Universal, Mataram
Plaza, phone 5483; Ida's Tour & Travel, Sahid Garden Hotel,
phone 3697; Musi Holiday Tour & Travel, Hotel Garuda, phone
86353; Setia Tours & Travel, Yogya International Hotel, phone
86171.

Yogyakarta Area Hotels and Restaurants

The best hotels in Yogyakarta, with rates ranging between $40
and $80 single, $50 and $80 double, depending on the season,
are the Ambarrukmo Palace (phone 88488) on Jalan Solo, a short
hop from the airport; and the Garuda, (phone 86457) handily
downtown on Jalan Malioboro.

At the Mutiari Hotel (phone 4531), also on Malioboro; the
Puri Artha (phone 59345), Jalan Cendrawasih 9; Sahid Garden
(phone 3697), Jalan Babasari; Sriwedari (phone 88288), Jalan
Adisucipto 5; and Yogya International (phone 5318), also on
Jalan Adisucipto, all with air conditioning, bath and telephone,
rates start at $30 single, $35 double, with a maximum of $70.

The Batik Palace Hotel (phone 2149), Arjuna Plaza (phone
86862), and Sri Manganti (phone 2881) all have rooms between
$25 and $35, single or double, and there are many clean
guesthouses centrally located and surprisingly inexpensive, including Peti Mas, phone 2896; Wisma Gajah, phone 2479;
Airlangga, phone 3344; Sumaryo, phone 2852; Indraloka Home-
stay, phone 3614 and Koba Cottages, phone 3697.

In the high season, hotel rooms and airline bookings for
Yogyakarta can be hard to get, so advance planning is required.
The number of flights, like the number of hotel rooms, hasn't
kept up with the demand.

Yogyakarta's best dining is found in the major hotels: the Bale Kambang floating restaurant on the palace grounds adjoining the Ambarrukmo Palace Hotel, and its Borobudur Theater Restaurant both lay out an excellent buffet feast for approximately $10 a person. The Garuda Bar and Restaurant, at the hotel on Malioboro, serves good Indonesian, Chinese, Japanese and European menus, and the Dragon Restaurant at the Yogya International Hotel serves authentic Chinese dishes and a good choice of seafood.

Other restaurants worth a visit are the Mirah Coffee Shop in the Mutiara Hotel downtown, and the Mirasa Coffee Shop off the lobby in the Ambarrukmo. The food is always good and the prices really are surprisingly low.

Or try the Andrawina Loka, Jalan Adisucipto 9; the Ayam Goreng on the same street at No. 7; the Appalosa Pub and Restaurant at Jalan Kyai Mojo 57; the Gita Bujana Snack and Steak House on Jalan Diponegoro; the Legian on Jalan Perwakilan; Natour's Restaurant on Jalan Babarsari; the Sintawang on Jalan Magelang; or the Sparta Steak House Jalan Adisucipto. There's also a Kentucky Fried Chicken franchise on Adisucipto.

The same general rule about trying the hotel food first can be followed in Semarang and Surakarta (Solo).

In Semarang try Bin Lok on Gang Besan; Eva Coffee Shop on Jalan Raya Bedono; Gombel Indah on Jalan Setiabudi; Instana on Jalan Haryono; Kit Wan Kie on Gang Pinggir; New Garden Hill on Jalan Setiabudi; New Mandarin on Jalan Karangyar; Sari on Jalan Y. Jani; and Tan Goei on Jalan Tanjung. Semarang also has Kentucky Fried Chicken.

In Surakarta, European, Chinese and Indonesian dishes are served at Centres on Jalan Kratonan; Diamond on Jalan Slamet Riyadi; Gita Bujana on Jalan Gatot Subroto; New Holland on Jalan Slamet Riyadi; and the Orient, also on the same street.

For those making a side trip who might want to overnight either in Semarang or Surakarta, the best Semarang hotels are:

Patrajasa, phone 27371; Metro Grand Park, phone 314441; and Sky Garden, phone 312733. Rates at the Patrajasa start at $28 and run to $60; at the others the range is from $15 to $40, but doubles usually start at $20.

Less expensive Semarang hotels which have air conditioning, bath, and telephone, with prices from $10 to $30, are: The Bali, phone 211974; Candi Baru, phone 315272; Dibya Puri, phone 27821; Queen Hotel, phone 27603; Santika, phone 214491; Siranda, phone 313272, and Telomoyo, phone 20926.

In Surakarta the best are the Kusuma Sahid Prince Hotel, phone 6356; the Mangkunegaran Palace, phone 5683, the Cakra Hotel, phone 5847, and the Solo Inn, phone 6077. At the Kusuma, where they boast that the king stayed during the inconvenience of a palace fire in the 1980s, rates really begin about $40, with deluxe rooms starting at $60. Still, if you're willing to share a bath, they have economy rooms starting at $25. The Cakra and Solo accommodations start at about $15 single, $20 double and go up to about $35. The Mangkunegaran is slightly cheaper.

Surakarta budget hotels, in the $10 to $25 range, include: Dana Hotel, phone 3890; Gedung Wanita, phone 7508; Sahid Hotel, phone 3889; Sanashtri Hotel, on Jalan Penumpangan Barat 78.

CHAPTER 7

East Java

Many conventional tourists give East Java and its sonorously named capital, Surabaya, a complete bypass, probably because it is wild, unfocused and demanding.

Yet for the same reasons, other visitors hasten to this area, which the maps call Jawa Timur, including the island of Madura, the outstanding volcano Mount Bromo, thick forests, a sea of sand, and dense jungle preserves that protect the few last surviving tigers running free. Even the temples of East Java are more frequently found in ruins than anywhere else in Java or Bali, in keeping with the province's rough image.

When you look out into the harbor of Surabaya today and see sparkling yachts mixing with rust-streaked freighters, it is hard to imagine that Kublai Khan once sent his fleet here from China, armed for war; that square-rigged sailing vessels from all over the world anchored here; and that it was the most prosperous port in all Southeast Asia. Joseph Conrad, the Polish/English novelist, sailed here and wrote about the rugged men who caroused, brawled and schemed in dockside bars amid the intrigue of warring potentates.

But the past of Surabaya sadly is gone, most of it wiped away, like the square-riggers, by the rush of progress. A bustling, hard-working city of three million, a city of factories and warehouses, industry and commerce, it sits dusty and baking in tropical heat and has lost its romance, except in memory.

All that's left is an old Arab quarter, a Chinese district, a few isolated Dutch colonial relics, mostly commercial buildings, and, for the deeper past, little monuments like the park statue memorializing King Kertanegara who incurred the wrath of the great Mongol conqueror Kublai Khan in the 13th century.

Surabaya has become a sort of lesser Jakarta, second in size, second in importance, and second in all the ills that befall large cities if only because of size.

But like Jakarta, where splendid new buildings are thrown up in nests of poverty with seeming disregard for the past, there is an energy here, a vitality similar to that which one feels walking the downtown streets of New York City. The struggle to survive, to make the best of the nation's new-found independence, seems to pervade every mundane activity from crossing the crowded street to haggling over little transactions.

Some excellent hotels serve the city but more of their guests are commercial travelers than vacationers. Most of the tourists here are bristling with eagerness to get on into the countryside, to the little villages and mountains that they really came to see.

Those who linger in the city will hear boasts that Surabaya has the largest zoo and largest shopping center in Southeast Asia. Both claims are exaggerations but the zoo does contain a variety of animals: lions, zebras, elephants, camels, monkeys, Komodo dragons and, in a collection of nocturnal creatures, flying squir-rels and bats. The shopping center, the Delta Plaza, is worth strolling, but there are other mall-type retail conglomerations as well: Tunjungan Plaza, Apollo Plaza and Indo Plaza, none of them in any way exclusively Indonesian.

Delta Plaza is just around the corner from the People's Amuse-ment Park, a concentration of rides and attractions, indigenous theater, modern music presentations and crafts outlets. Despite the bright, banner-decked entry, the interior dims with the functional look common to all government projects.

Monuments are few. There are a couple of temples in the narrow streets of the Chinese quarter with hand-puppet side shows outside, a mosque surrounded by textile craft stalls, the aforementioned statue of a king, and a modern obelisk saluting heroes of the Indonesian independence struggle which followed World War II.

One old dock area on the Kalinas River outlet into the harbor still loads and unloads the colorful *pinisi* sailing vessels of the Bugis from Sulawesi. These and some century-old warehouses in the neighborhood give a brief glimpse into the city's past.

Some visitors catch the ferry to the island of Madura, which is really a bargain water voyage costing less than 250 rupiah (less than 25 cents) for the half-hour trip. The ferries sail at ten- and fifteen-minute intervals all day and evening.

But unless the bull races are scheduled on the cattle-growing island, there's nothing much to see on Madura: rustic scenery and a couple of sandy beaches at Camplong and Slopeng. The bull races, the island's claim to fame which breeders say originated in competitions between cattlemen at harvest time, are an annual elimination series culminating in August and September to the accompaniment of folk dancing and other festivities. The racing bulls, specially bred for the event, reach speeds phenomenal for their size and bulk. Sometimes a race will be staged out of season for a large tourist group.

Of all the attractions in East Java, it's safe to say that visitors come for the volcanoes, especially Mount Bromo, which the natives regard with fear.

It was an ordinary East Java day, February 10, 1990, at the Hindu temples of Panatran, where surviving stone portions date back to the 13th century and carvings recall legendary battles, attracting tourists from nearby Blitar. Ten miles north stood a small volcano, Mount Kelud.

Shortly before noon that day Mount Kelud erupted without warning. Thousands of sulphuric rocks were hurled into the air. Gaseous dust sputtered up and fell on the surrounding villages. Sixteen people were killed, fifty seriously injured. Panic set in as thousands began to flee their homes. Rice fields were destroyed. Trees burned by the hundreds.

How many times in the history of Java has that scene been repeated? The geological scars, left through eons in which the lifespan of man is no longer than the blink of an eye, tell of terrible cataclysms in which the destruction can only be imagined. On that scale, Kelud's outburst was just a minor event.

West of Mount Bromo stand two volcanoes, side by side, twelve miles apart. They are Mount Kelud, which up until 1990 had gained favor with mountain-climbing clubs, and Mount Kawi, where thousands of pilgrims, mostly Chinese and Indonesian, flock every year in the belief, based on legend, that a visit and offering here will bring good fortune. Alongside the stairway to the top, an assortment of sacred springs, Chinese houses of worship, flower and souvenir stalls are open. There are frequent gamelan and wayang performances.

Mounts Kelud and Kawi are only two of 21 "Class A" volcanoes in Java, as rated by the Indonesian Volcanological Service which monitors active volcanoes. Altogether there are about 400 volcanoes in Indonesia, 128 active.

Technicians had monitors installed on Mount Kelud at the time of the eruption, but apparently the signals were not received early enough to evacuate residents or warn them of the latest eruption. Until the science of predicting volcanic behavior advances, all volcanoes have to be treated as potentially very dangerous.

Mount Bromo, although merely one of hundreds of volcanoes in Indonesia, and far from the tallest, nevertheless is a standout, because it rises to its full height straight out of a flat bed of sand, flanked by the perfectly conical extinct volcano, Batok. In this setting, with mist swirling around, the smell of sulphur, and smoke curling up from the live caldera, Bromo achieves a mystic appearance that is other-worldly.

It has terrified natives for centuries. The Tenggerese people in the villages around the volcano, whose forefathers fled the Muslim wave of conversion to retain their own Hindu religion combined with even older Javanese beliefs, revere the god of Bromo and every January make offerings to placate him in a colorful mountainside ceremony.

The sea of sand that surrounds Mount Bromo is actually the caldera of another ancient volcano called Tengger. It died in prehistory, but by size alone one would have to believe that it could knock the earth off its axis in a single detonation.

Most visits to Bromo are scheduled for an early morning arrival, when the rising sun makes the scene especially eerie. It's a three-hour drive from Surabaya south to Probolinggo, the jumping-off point. After an overnight stay at Ngadisari or Cemoro Lawang, a village at the edge of the sea of sand, the routine calls for setting off at 3 or 4 a.m. by horseback across the cold sand flats, where the route is marked with reflective paint on stones. When the sand ends, you climb up steps to the rim of the crater and peer down into the fumes, the sun rising on the other side to light your view. It is a magnificent sight.

There are other more circuitous ways to get there which avoid the tourist-organized atmosphere of the trip through Probolinggo, but when you take these other approaches, you are all alone in the dark. Still, some stalwart souls, trekking with flashlight and backpack, do it the hard way.

In any event, it is advisable to make the trip between May and November, if only to avoid the cold at the high elevations. And rain could wash out the whole expedition.

For those who believe that volcanoes belong on the horizon rather than under one's feet, there are other attractions in East Java worthy of attention. Unfortunately, it is impossible to completely avoid volcanoes in East Java. Spotted around the province are, in addition to those already mentioned, Arjuno, Argopuro, Liman, Raung, Lamongan, Welirang, Wilis, Semeru and another Merapi, almost as tall as the one near Yogyakarta. In this area, anything over five hundred feet tall that comes to a point is likely to be volcanic.

Proceeding south of Surabaya one finds some interesting foothill and mountain villages. Pandaan village holds a ballet festival in the summer months with performances every other Saturday at Candia Wilwatika theater, staging tales from the Ramayana and other legends.

Malang, everyone seems to agree, is the prettiest town for miles around. The streets are clean and winding, the buildings, some quaint, are well kept, and there are parks and squares and little market areas. Dutch colonial civil servants and planters used to live here, and now Indonesians favor it as a retirement center. A youthful element is evident in Malang too, because it is an educational center which attracts many students.

Candi Singosari, nearby to the west, offers temple ruins which have been restored, but these show the ravages of time and looting. The same is true of Candi Dago at Tumpang. The Kidal Temple, east of Malang, is in better condition.

Other hillside resorts in the area with excellent views, hot springs, waterfalls and some ruins, include Batu, famous for flowers and apples, Selecta, Sumber Brantas, Songgoriti, and Wendit.

Trowulan, now little more than a village southwest of Surabaya, six hundred years ago was the capital of a vast Majapahit empire covering most of Indonesia and part of Malaysia. There are ruins to be seen at several sites around town, and the local museum has collected interesting statuary from the empire. The museum is open mostly morning hours, except Mondays. The town of Mojokerto, close by to the north, also is an attractive old town with an informative little museum. Those interested in history will learn intriguing tales of treachery in high places among rival princes of those days—enough to fill a book of Shakespearean plays.

Tretes, on a mountainside near Pandaan, has a reputation as

an excellent mountain resort in a beautiful setting within walking distance to the Karek Bodo waterfall. Horseback riding and camping facilities are available. Tretes is also said to feature a special little red light district, although it is not made clear why tourists would want to buy red lights.

Further west, near Nganjuk, is the Sedudo waterfall, which legend holds will bestow eternal youth on bathers in its cool waters. In the village they make brass gamelan orchestra musical instruments. Ngetos temple also is located here.

Some beaches, on both the north and south coasts of East Java, are open for swimming, boating, snorkeling and skin-diving, but these strips are not as well developed as resort areas in neighboring Bali, of course.

On the north coast, near Situbondo, lies the Pasirputih, a name which means white sands. The waters are calm, hotels and restaurants service the area, and the sands, if not all white, are plentiful. The area is crowded with local residents from Surabaya on weekends. In the other direction from Surabaya, a resort area at the Cape of Kodok, between Surabaya and Tuban, also attracts weekend crowds.

To the south, several beaches draw visitors to the more remote resorts of Pacitan and Prigi, both sheltered by bays which keep the surf down. Prigi beach is rockier but both have dramatic cliffs. On the road to the latter from Trenggalek is a gigantic limestone cave that has become a popular stop for visitors. Along the same coast of the Indian Ocean are Ngliyep Beach and Watu Ulo, and the better-known Sukamade Beach where giant turtles come to lay their eggs.

On the road east on the Jember-Bondowoso-Panarukan route one can detour to Ijen crater lake, a green-water pond lined with sheer cliffs and dammed to keep its sulphuric contents from contaminating the local crops. The quiet little town of Bondowoso stages bullfights, not in the Spanish tradition but rather bull-against-bull, and is also interesting for its megalithic ruins, statues, sarcophagi and stone chairs.

Three large nature reserves occupy wild areas of East Java: Baluran National Park on the north coast, Meru Betiri and Blambangan of the southeastern peninsula.

Baluran is a dry, open area of forests and shrubs, with marshlands along the coast itself. Wild oxen, buffalo, deer, peacocks and other animals roam the preserve, which can be entered with permits from the PHPA (forestry agency) in Banyuwangi. A guesthouse and lookout tower with views of grazing areas are available, and a two-day photo safari to Baluran is one of the popular package tours offered by agents in Surabaya.

Meru Betiri, where the last four or five tigers in Java literally have been cornered, is less accessible. The road deadends after twenty miles of potholes south of Jember, and dense jungle lies all around. The chances of seeing a tiger are almost nonexistent. In fact, environmentalists are discussing a plan to move people out of this area to protect the animal in the preserve. There are leopards, monkeys and wild pigs. You can also reach the protected Turtle Beach on the coast of Meru Betiri.

Blambangan, officially named Banyuwangi Selatan Reserve, also has monkeys, deer, leopards and wild pigs, but the most visible animals here are the herd of hundreds of wild buffalos which can be watched from towers as they graze. Surfers have discovered the coast of this peninsula and crude bamboo shacks have been thrown up as shelters at some points. Permission is required to enter the preserve.

At Kaliklatak, a privately owned plantation offers tours of their operation on the slopes of Mount Merapi where coffee, rubber, cocoa, cloves and cinnamon are grown.

On the Bali Strait five miles north of Banyuwangi is Ketapang, the ferry dock for the crossing to Gilimanuk on the island of Bali. This fifteen-minute voyage costs a small fraction of a dollar per person; you can take an automobile with you for a few dollars. Usually the ferry is included in a bus ticket from Surabaya or Yogyakarta to Bali.

East Java Tours

The most popular East Java tours, offered out of Surabaya, vary in time and price from a few hours at about $10 per person, to ten hours at $150 a person, depending on the size of the group. These tours, available through any agent and posted at most hotels, include the following:

Surabaya City Tour: three to four hours, includes the Heroes Monument, the harbor area, Joko Dolok Park and a quick dash across the strait to Madura. Cost $8 to $15 each in groups of four to nine people; $15 each in groups of three; $20 each for couples, and $35 for a single person wishing to make the tour alone.

Mount Bromo Tour, ten to twelve hours, goes from Surabaya to Ngadisari, crossing the Tengger sand sea on horseback and up to the lip of Mount Bromo crater; and back, of course. Costs $40 to $50 in groups of ten or more; $60 to $75 each in a group of three; $70 to $80 each for a couple, and $120 to $140 for singles who wish to go unaccompanied except by guide.

Singosari-Malang Tour, six to eight hours, goes to Singosari Temple, Selecta mountain resort, a botanical garden, scenic viewpoints and the town of Malang. Costs $38 to $40 in groups of ten or more; $40 to $70 each for a trio, $55 to $80 each for a couple, $100 to $110 for an individual.

Tretes Tour, six hours, goes to the Tretes area and includes a visit to a mountain resort with swimming, hiking, climbing and horseback riding, and to scenic viewpoints and a waterfall. Costs $25 to $30 in groups of ten or more; $35 each for a trio, $40 each for a couple, and $70 for one person only.

Trowulan Tour, six hours, includes Javanese ballet and puppet performances, the palace of the ancient Majapahit kingdom and the Trowulan museum, as well as scenic views. Costs $22 to $24 in groups of ten or more; $30 to $40 each for a trio; $45 each as a couple, and $85 single.

Madura Tour, five to six hours, during bull racing season only, goes from Surabaya to Bangkalan and Pamekasan or Madura island, and returns. Costs $40 in groups of ten or more; $45 to $50 each for three or two persons, and about $100 to go alone.

Baluran Tour, two days, goes to Pasuruan, Baluran Preserve for photo hunting of wild animals, and returns. Costs $55 in groups of up to nine; $70 each for three people, $93 each for two, and $170 for a single person.

Among Surabaya agents organizing these tours are: Intan Baiduri Abadi, phone 20163; Kapasan Oriental Express, phone 314178; Karya Express, phone 26586; Olympic Abadi, phone 25662; Intan Abadi, phone 20163; Natrabu, phone 68513; Pacto, phone 43351; Turi Express, phone 23414; Venus Tours, phone 60110;

If you have your own group of two, three or four people, be sure to check your hotel taxi desk to see whether it would not be cheaper to hire your own cab for a self-designed tour, if that appeals to you.

East Java Hotels and Restaurants

By far the best hotel in Surabaya is the new Hyatt Bumi Surabaya, with hundreds of rooms priced in the $100 and up range, specialty restaurants, a fitness center, tennis court, swimming pool, a shopping complex and other facilities. Naturally it is the most expensive.

Other excellent hotels with high standards and all the facilities expected, at prices of $35 to $80, single or double, follow:

Elmi Hotel, Jalan Panglima Sudirman 42. Phone 471570.
Garden Hotel, Jalan Pemuda 71. Phone 470000.
Garden Palace, Jalan Y. Sudarso 11. Phone 479250.
Majapahit Hotel, Jalan Tunjungan 65. Phone 43351.
Mirama Hotel, Jalan Raya Darmo 72. Phone 69501.
New Garden Park, Jalan Samodra 3. Phone 270004.
Patrajasa Motel, Gunungsari. Phone 68681.
Simpang Hotel, Jalan Pemuda 1. Phone 42150.
Less expensive hotels which still offer all the basic services,

including air conditioning, with prices running in a wide range between $20 and $70, single or double, are:

Cendana Indah, Jalan Duryat 16. Phone 42251.
Lesmana Hotel, Jalan Bintoro 16. Phone 67152.
Pregolan Hotel, Jalan Bunder 11. Phone 41251.
Ramayana Hotel, Jalan J. Basuki Rachmat 67. Phone 46321.
Sarkies Hotel, Jalan Embong Malang 7. Phone 44514.
Semut, Jalan Samodra 9. Phone 24578.
Tanjung Hotel, Jalan Sudirman 43. Phone 44031.

In the Probolinggo area close to Mount Bromo, some new hotels have opened to capitalize on the increased tourism headed that way, but those who make the trip usually have their hotel prearranged by the tour operators. In the Mount Bromo area itself are the Bromo Permai, Grand Bromo Hotel and Tampiar-toplaza Hotel, all three offering rooms in the range from $20 to $70; and there's a camper's special at $2 in the Bromo Permai, which leaves a lot of room for negotiating. The Mount Bromo area hotels naturally are more rustic lodgings than one would expect in the city.

Those seeking options to the Surabaya bustle might try the clean neat hotels in Malang, where rates run from $30 to $75. The best of these is the Purnama Hotel, phone 24066. Others include: Asida, phone 259; Palem, phone 177; Pelangi, phone 27456; Palem Sari, phone 219; and the Splendid Inn, phone 23860.

In Tretes there are the Tanjung Plaza, phone 81102, and the Natour Bath Hotel, phone 81161, but in the case of these outlying hotels, travel agents probably can get you the best rate and take care of reservations.

Mountain lodges and resorts and seaside accommodations throughout East Java also are available, but again, at no cost and sometimes big savings, these are best made through travel agents from a major city.

Food in Surabaya is generally more expensive than in other

parts of Java and Bali, and the night life, aimed at the commercial traveler as well as the tourist, also is more extensive. Seafood and Chinese food are the favorites in Java's second city, and most restaurants offer European plates as well as Indonesian and Chinese.

Popular Surabaya restaurants include the Aloha, Asli, Bima Garden, Bon Cafe Steak House, Dynasty Steak and Satay House, Finna, Fran's Steak House, Gandy's Steak House, Handayani, Mahkota, New Fajar, Oriental Restaurant, Ria, Regent Sea Food, Satellite Garden, Taman Sari Indah, Tiara, Venecia Steak House, and Wisma Sier.

*Javanese dancer in traditional
Ramayana ballet*
(Photo by author)

*Natives dressed for comedy wayang performance,
East Java*
(Courtesy Indonesia Tourist Bureau)

Homes of poor visible across drainage canal from luxury hotel
(Photo by author)

Hotel Putri Bali, one of the islands' largest, most luxurious resorts
(Courtesy Indonesia Tourist Bureau)

Convention Hall, Jakarta, scene of international conferences
(Courtesy Indonesia Tourist Bureau)

Welcome Statue in front of Hotel Indonesia, Jarkarta
(Courtesy Indonesia Tourist Bureau)

Street market, downtown Yogyakarta
(Photo by author)

Market on Marlioboro Street, Yogyakarta
(Photo by author)

Monas national monument, Jakarta
(Photo by author)

Modern and ancient transportation in market area,
Yogyakarta
(Photo by author)

Entrance to Water Castle, Yogyakarta
(Photo by author)

Temple at entrance to Taman mini Indonesia
(Photo by author)

Prambahan Plain, scene of restoration of 1000-year-old temples
(Photo by author)

Turrets housing Buddha statues, Borobudur temple
(Photo by author)

A small corner of the gigantic Borobudur monument, Central Java
(Photo by author)

Prambahan temple, Central Java
(Courtesy Indonesia Tourist Bureau)

Exotic carvings adorning temples
(Photo by author)

Shiva Mahadewa in Candi Prambahan, Central Java
(Courtesy Indonesia Tourist Bureau)

Massive Borobudur monument, Central Java
(Courtesy Indonesia Tourist Bureau)

Tea plantation, West Java
(Courtesy Indonesia Tourist Bureau)

*Woodcarver and popular
fisherman piece, near Denpasar*
(Photo by author)

Tourist searched for peanuts, Monkey Forest, Bali (Photo by author)

Footbridge in Botanical Gardens, Bogor
(Photo by author)

Beach scene, Bali
(Photo by author)

Ancol Beach, Jakarta Harbor
(Photo by author)

The pinisi, a hand-made boat still seen on Indonesian waters
(Photo by author)

Volcano crater, East Java
(Photo by author)

Garuda, Indonesian airlines named for the god of flight

CHAPTER 8

Bali

*You are breakfasting at a table sheltered by flowering vines,
overlooking a white sandy beach through palms abundant with
coconuts. Small boats parade out on the blue-grey sea. Surf
pounds and birds call.*

*A dawn rainfall has just ended, wiping away the sultry burden
of moisture that hung in the atmosphere overnight. A small breeze
stirs, feeling delicious on your skin. Your eyes hold a full feast of
lush greens and blues, vegetation and water, while around you
volcanic mountains soar. People talk cheerfully and laugh, beginning another day hopefully. It will be a glorious day, because you
are in Bali.*

Bali. It has been given many names: The Island of the Gods,
The Last Paradise, The Island of Temples. . . .

What is it that draws hundreds of thousands of visitors to this
60-by-90 mile island, making it the most popular destination in
all Indonesia? What are the Balinese like? Who are these people
with golden skin who inherited so beautiful a land that foreigners
come from all over the globe to see their home?

There are more than two and a half million Balinese. Although extraordinarily endowed with artistic talent and at one with a religious but free lifestyle, basically they are just people. They all have belly buttons, a standard set of limbs, and features consistent with the bilateral symmetry common in the human species.

People with white skins, the Balinese know, are the result of under-done experiments when the gods were trying to bake up the perfect color for humans, achieved only in Bali, of course. But they like westerners anyway.

Really, if the Balinese differ from other people it must be in the way they live, with a temple in every backyard and religion a real part of their everyday life. They do this completely without fanaticism or proselytizing, taking their sacred laws more as a family or community code—a tradition adapted to real life to sweeten its meaning.

Balinese smile a lot. If it's because they know a secret, that secret was brought to them centuries ago and divulged in so artistic a manner that they not only yielded immediately to its beauty, but developed and preserved a whole range of arts in perpetuating it.

The softest of breezes barely nudges in from the ocean in the dark of the night, and Simon, a handsome young Torajan man from a jungle village in inland Sulawesi, bends over a book in the dim light of the open bar at the Bali Mandira Cottages, where he works. The last customer left hours ago.

Simon, who speaks seven languages, is studying the restaurant business from the ground up. He prefers this, wearing the costume of a hotel barman, to what he would be doing at home in Sulawesi, perhaps: entertaining tourists in native costume. Simon is one of the hundreds of smiling, seemingly happy people who serve visitors to the island he calls home.

Simon's co-worker, Ming, a Buddhist from Singaraja, a village in north Bali famous for its hot springs, is the only member of his family to move to the big city, where he is studying hotel management in a government school and working his way. Tonight he dons earphones and props his feet up on a rattan chair in the empty bar. Ming loves American music, especially love songs.

It is four o'clock in the morning when a tourist enters. The two young men leap to their feet and greet the guest with a smile. They say, "How may we help you?"

Aside from the populace, the island itself offers the visitor a seemingly endless panorama of great beauty: majestic volcanoes, strikingly cultivated rice fields called "The Steps of the Gods," glorious white and black beaches, forests and rivers and streams and palm trees everywhere. Comparisons with the Hawaii of a half-century ago, or more, are inevitable.

Until the tourists came, the Balinese never much favored beach property. They preferred to live in the foothills of the mountains where their gods dwelled. Who would want to live next to the ocean? Everybody knows that terrible demons hide out and all the storms come from there. Of course, poor fishermen have to. . . .

Visitors to Bali tend to congregate in the beachy southern part of the island, in the Kuta Beach, Legian Beach, Sanur Beach and Nusa Dua Beach areas, using these locations as a base for short or extended tours to points of interest to the north, east and west. This seems to be the best plan, if only because those who serve the tourist industry have designed it that way, with most facilities in the south and a network of transportation putting all attractions within reach of day tours or two-day excursions.

Kuta Beach is the most popular, especially with younger visitors. For one thing, it offers a broad range of accommodations, including some of the least expensive on the whole island.

Kuta Beach

Kuta Beach itself, a mecca for surfers, offers white sand with vigorous wave action and a strong undertow that chases many bathers back to the safety of swimming pools, of which there is no shortage. On the beach sands the tourists will be swarmed by hawkers selling small items like fans, mats and carved boxes, but they will go away quietly if you tell them you have no money with you. On the other hand, you can strike some excellent bargains in such unavoidable encounters. The sellers are desperately eager and, compared to downtown shops, they operate with little overhead.

Speaking of overhead, there are trees on the beach, cultivated into a wide umbrella sprawl for shade. For sunning you can buy mats for a dollar or two.

The sight of local women naked to the waist is rare these days on Bali. It is usually relegated to their paintings and to inland villages where people still cling to the old ways. The custom began to fade in the early 1900s when the iron-fisted Dutch solidified their grip on Bali. Dutch commanders, in the bloody aftermath of conquest, gave cover-up orders to protect their soldiers from the immoral influences that they feared in this great natural display. (And can it be conjectured, by this act alone, whether it is added to the list of Dutch cruelties or kindnesses, perhaps set back tourism for half a century.)

You still will see bare breasted young women at the beaches and swimming pools, more so than in the villages, but these are not the natives Margaret Mead photographed; they are proud young tourists from Australia, New Zealand, Europe and other more cosmopolitan areas.

A few protests have been voiced by more religious residents, but naked chests do not seem to bother the inhabitants so much as does total nudity. This should only be practiced on the most isolated beaches where there is little chance that the impromptu nudist will emerge from the surf to be greeted by offended locals.

The beach streets at Kota and Legian, adjoining communities, recall Coney Island, Atlantic City and Santa Monica in the 1950s, or honky-tonk beach strips everywhere: narrow streets jammed with pedestrians edging along in front of white-washed stores that somehow lack the look of permanence. Ramshackle is a word that comes to mind, but it's more the clutter than a lack of sturdiness that creates the feeling; leather shops, T-shirt shops, fashions, souvenir shops, money changers, cafes, bars, little hotels vie for attention in an endless commercial chain and the atmosphere is upbeat, holiday. Every day is Sunday at the beach—and every night. Buy a balloon or an ice cream cone, stop for a beer or a coke.

Kuta and Legian beaches are located on the west coast of Bali. Only a dozen miles away, on the east coast, lies Sanur Beach, the next most popular, slightly more upscale.

Sanur Beach

Sanur offers a seaside peace and quiet which Kuta cannot, but the price of peace can be distinctly higher, since this is the location of such comprehensive accommodations as the Hyatt, among other hotel giants. It is quite true that at certain times of the year you can stay in Sanur for as little as twenty dollars a night, but the dominating hotels of Sanur are First Class.

The beach really is a little whiter and, due to an effective reef, less ruffled with waves. The landscaping, the architecture, a variety of in-house restaurants, health clubs, doorstep access to boats, a full array of activities and services, all are yours at this level of luxury.

However, the higher you climb in hotel rates and standards, the greater you will find the distance from the life of the island. In the luxury category, the hotel becomes almost an island in itself, isolating and insulating its guests from contact with real Bali and its people, so that your excursions away from the hotel are journeys into a different world. It's not a bad idea. There's something very nice about being able to harbor in such an environment after a long day's venture into a world to which one is not accustomed.

And you are never far from the world of Bali. It's almost like the old steamship lines, before the passenger ship companies discovered gold in the middle class and abandoned the deck system which segregated First Class from Second Class, etc. When you stay at Sanur or Nusa Dua, you're on a First Class ticket; but the most knowledgeable passengers would abandon their First Class deck at night after dinner and go below. The Tourist Class was always having more fun.

Nusa Dua

Nusa Dua, a name meaning "two islands," actually is a little peninsula at the very foot of Bali and is just a tall wave away from being an island unto itself. The hotels here are resort complexes, isolated even from one another, but you can watch an ocean sunrise and sunset from the same spot if you like, and the beauty of the place is unchallenged.

Quite new, Nusa Dua represents a largely government sponsored effort to create a super-Bali without a pebble out of place, and they appear to be accomplishing this seemingly impossible feat of beautifying the superlative.

Half of the area, which is ringed by three miles of sand, consists of parks: a profusion of palms sheltering gardens so rich in plantings and statuary that it all seems unreal, as if it was just painted there to improve on the shortcomings of the gods. Ornate bridges, fountains and pools—even the puffy clouds seem to pose, as if only there by exclusive invitation.

And yet, every hotel built here—and all of them are so-called World-Class—conforms in its own individual way to local architectural concepts, to the extent that no visitor to this rich playground will lose sight of the very special qualities of the island. Bali, by the way, almost from its inception as a tourist attraction, declared that no hotel would be built taller than the highest coconut tree, a ruling that has held fast amid fears that skyscrapers would alter wind and sun patterns even if they did not offend the eye. So Bali was among the first to fight high-rise development, long before such environmentally conscious campaigns became fashionable elsewhere in the world.

The facilities of Nusa Dua are truly lavish. Elaborate swimming pools, tennis and squash courts, jogging tracks and complete health centers with suanas and massage parlors; windsurfing and snorkeling, horseback riding, boating, cycling. There's little missing, and on the drawing board there are plans for a full-size golf course and a marina. Condominiums can't be far away in time.

One incident perhaps typifies Nusa Dua. One day, high atop a glorious fan palm, seemingly trimmed by an artist, one wilted, slightly discolored frond was spotted. Almost immediately, as if on an emergency run, a service truck braked to a halt at its foot and threw up a ladder. A man raced to the top and the offending piece was quietly removed. Banished probably to the unkempt wastelands of the north.

If you are going there, try to be beautiful. Or quite well off. One out of two is not bad.

Denpasar

A tarnished frond would not be noticed in Denpasar. It's not really a big city despite its population of over two hundred thousand, but as the capital and administrative center of Bali it shows signs of hasty, unplanned growth. Indeed, traffic lights and one-way streets had to be set up to regulate the motorists. It's not a place to stay.

One of the most positive things that can be said about Denpasar is that it appears to have been necessary.

It would have been a perfectly acceptable little city somewhere else, perhaps South America or Montana with an excuse like an extended gold rush, but it doesn't really belong on Bali. It somehow doesn't fit.

But all the services are here, and they have to be put someplace: airline offices, tourist information, governmental branches and banking, not to mention stores and restaurants.

An interesting market—a disorderly line-up of stalls offering everything from fish to fine jewelry—occupies a site just off the center of town, on Pasar Badung. And there are some well-stocked art stores on the narrow streets, some of them non-bargaining, non-discounting, but good places to size up what's available around Bali and the price range—before you set out on the village rounds.

Some interesting monuments as well as other concessions to beauty will be found within the city limits, and the keen-eyed visitor will espy the underlying framework of a once-sleepy colonial town not without a fading charm.

There are tours of Denpasar, and the visit can be worthwhile for a look at the museum and art centre, among other cultural repositories.

The Museum Bali, behind ornate walls in the center of Denpasar, consists of four major buildings dating back to 1910, three of which represent styles from different provinces of Bali.

The largest building reflects traditional architecture in the eastern province of Karangasem and houses displays from pre-history to the early 20th century, including ceremonial and practical objects. Other exhibits feature examples of woodcarving and the many arts and crafts which belong to the religious history of Bali.

In a darkened room with strangely flickering lights, a dozen visitors cluster in front of a screen. It seems identical to that used for slide projections or home movies, but what they are watching has been a presentation in these islands for hundreds of years.

The island of Bali had motion pictures for centuries before Hollywood dreamed of them.

In Bali, however, it is a puppet show that holds the attention. Wood or leather puppets crafted by local artisans perform behind the screen onto which a lamp casts their shadows, so that the whole show is seen in precision-planned silhouette. This is wayang kulit, *one of the types of puppetry that was brought from India more than a thousand years ago by missionaries. Telling Hindu tales, history or myth, they converted the natives to the religion as well as the art form.*

In wayang golek *the same stories are told without the screen. The wooden puppets, expertly carved and colorfully painted, controlled by strings, bamboo rods and the hands of highly skilled puppeteers, appear directly before the audience.*

The Art Centre is another attraction worthy of attention. Occupying a coconut grove in the middle of Denpasar, the relatively new complex brings together exhibition galleries of top painters as well as facilities for the performing arts, including dance and drama. Visitors on day-time tours can watch young Bali students rehearsing dances and music. Since they wear blue jeans instead of the fanciful antique costumes and make-up, observers get a real back-stage insight.

Literature on dance, drama, painting and other arts also are available for those who want to learn the meaning behind the sometimes obscure imagery and pageantry.

Special Interests on the Water

Many surfers and skin divers are drawn to Bali by its reputation for their sports. Surfers, from beginners to highly experienced, find that the waters around Bali suit all tastes. Kuta Beach, facing west, gets most attention from surfers in the months between April and September, but during the rainy season, October to March, most surfers prefer the east coast, at Sanur and Nusa Dua. Uluwati waters, off the southwestern tip of the island, also have a great reputation among surfers but are for veteran practitioners only. The high curling waves and sharp coral bottom pose a constant danger.

People say that Bali is a good place to learn skin diving because of its many protected beaches and shallow inlets with alluring marine life.

Good skin diving areas include the reefs off the coast of West Bali Reserve and the island Palau Menjangan, as well as the islands off the southeast coast, Nusa Penida and Nusa Lembongan, where there are underwater grottoes. Off the beach at Tulamben, near Kubu, the World War II sunken freighter, the S.S. *Liberty*, is popular with divers. The fish who make the wreck their home are said to be so tame that they swim over to greet divers. The north coast, around Singaraja and Lovina Beach, also has popular diving areas.

A number of dive shops specialize in island diving tours, introductory and advanced certificate training sessions, equipment sales and rentals. The best known are: P. T. Bali Adventures, phone 71767; Oceana Dive Center, phone 88652; Bali Marine Sports, phone 87872; Baruna Water Sports, phone 51223; and, primarily for equipment, Raja Sports, phone 35020.

The same sports shops also set up parasailing, waterskiing, water scooter, jet ski, windsurfing and fishing expeditions, and so do most of the major hotels. For ten dollars, some taxi services will take you on parasailing or windsurfing outings of limited duration, or, for slightly more, water skiing or water scootering.

Batubulan

On the northeast outskirts of Denpasar, hardly distinguishable from the city itself, the village of Batubulan churns out thousands of stone carvings of every possible description. It is safe to guess that 90 percent of the gate-guarding demons, gods and decorations that are seen all over Bali come from here, hewn and polished by young men under tutelage of the old.

The carvings, small, medium and large, and some heroic in scale, are cut from a lightweight indigenous stone that easily lends itself to such work. They represent traditional warrior figures and princesses, gods and demons, scary half-animal half-human beings, and other less complex designs. Visitors can watch the men and boys work in their open sheds.

Lined up outside ornately carved ballustrades one can view a wide assortment of this almost mass-produced art: amid the traditional carved images you will see a touch of the more commercial: next to a demon's head stands a Bambi, and beside her, a life-size GI Joe. There are no Elvis statues. The export possibilities are tempting since some of the specimens are no heavier than the average suitcase.

Arts and Crafts

When you decide to set out on excursions into the interior villages of the island, or its more distant coastal areas, you'll find that the attractions—aside from natural wonders like beaches, volcanoes and hot springs—usually consist of artistic products which are created locally and available for sale; or historic, exotic temples; or dances and theater which evoke the spirit and inheritance of the Balinese.

All these are interrelated, in that the works of art created by the Balinese are the product of a tradition of enhancing the religious ceremonies which take place at the temples, of which dance and theater are an integral part.

The art works available chiefly consist of batik and similar fabrics and designs, woodcarvings, gold and silver jewelry and adornments, paintings and puppets—all informally on a manufacturer-to-you basis and incredibly inexpensive.

Has the influx of tourists cheapened and distorted the traditional Balinese arts? These days much of the art—whether dance or design—is prepared for sale to tourists rather than as offerings to the gods, the ancestors or the community, but some say that the presence of numerous visitors has in fact stimulated and enhanced the arts by creating a competitive atmosphere in which the best flourish and infuse the economy with sustaining dollars.

Among the communities most popular with visitors, Mas is noted for woodcarvings. The streets of Mas are lined by artists' complexes including training school areas, carving shelters and, of course, showrooms. In most of these studio factories you can watch the masters and their students work individual pieces of wood into finely polished creations.

Celuk is a center for silverwork and gold. Celuk inhabitants produce sophisticated, modern-looking jewelry, tableware and decorations with a special Balinese touch. Flowers, dragons and other creatures of myth as well as representations of animal life adorn rings, bracelets, necklaces, earrings, hairpins and other pieces. This traditional family art, handed down to sons and daughters with little intervening modernization, is an elite branch of the Balinese arts. Bellows still serve instead of blow-torch heat, but the products show great skill and talent, and hardly look home made.

Almost wherever you buy on the island, however, a little more refinement will be needed in the design of bracelet and necklace clasps and earring studs. This very minor touch should be watched for, mindful that jewelers at home can set right any catch as needed.

Ubud's chief attraction is paintings. Through the years, these have been influenced by an influx of European and American artists who, although they did not turn this peaceful village into a Balinese version of Taos, did focus the local efforts on popular native themes. Village and marketplace views, bathing maidens, Balinese dancers, rice farmers and temples predictably dominate the range of subjects always colorful and characteristic of the island. Local artists will invite visitors into their homes and studios, and will urge that even the largest framed painting can be safely rolled into a tube for transport by suitcase or mail.

Batuan is a village near Celuk where Margaret Mead, the noted anthropologist, filmed her Bali classic. Its people are noted for their dancing skills, as well as painting, batik and some woodcarving. Batuan perhaps is less on the beaten track of tour operator's schedules. The village temple, across the highway from its market showplace, is its foremost architectural attraction.

Of the dozen villages clustered north of Denpasar and all competing for the tourist dollar, Ubud is perhaps the most interesting. It offers the visitor a mile of narrow streets cluttered with shops displaying every imaginable souvenir of Bali. And it is walkable, with the usual admonition to pedestrians to beware of two- and four-wheel vehicles encroaching on your space. Ubud then forms a gigantic, linear outdoor market, a strip which is varied and ideal for browsing and bargaining. Mas and Celuk, for example, where visitors are invited to view craftsmen and artists at work in secluded courtyard areas, do not for the most part offer such accessibility.

The artistic centers at Mas and Celuk, spaced apart and set back from the one-and-a-half-lane road in separated complexes of several buildings, require the visitor to turn off the road and park. An escort will greet you and take you around, eager to bargain with you for any object in which you show the slightest interest. This omnipresent pressure—if not a hard-sell approach—makes browsing difficult. If you ask the significance of an excellent and aromatic sandalwood carving in Mas, for example, you are likely to receive more salesmanship than information.

The woodcarvings, mostly in teak, ebony, mahogany and sandalwood, come in a plethora of sizes, designs and images. Behind intricately carved nets in fragile wood, life-size natives cast for fish; Balinese bathing girls stand boldly nude; Buddhas, gods and demons, jewel boxes, animals, mothers with children, pairs of lovers and even some erotic statuary à la Kama Sutra—in a single piece you can find enough beauty to make the entire trip worthwhile, and one regrets that one cannot linger long.

Many of the villages along the way on a tour inland are superficially nondescript: too many tin roofs, too much construction underway, too many crumbling or impervious walls, but there is beauty to be found, if one looks. Most of it is off-road, beyond the pavement and walls.

One reason for so many walls, apart from the normal separation of property is too many times, at private homes where some invitation-only ceremonies or festivities were underway, tourists would wander in; or worse, a tour van would pull up, unleashing a horde of the uninvited led by a brazen and inconsiderate guide. Many small gatherings, however colorful or quaint, are private affairs and tourists should make sure of their welcome before intruding with clicking cameras.

Many perfectly kept houses and businesses—and sometimes

it's difficult to distinguish one from the other—stand behind walls in ornate splendor, and even the poorest dwelling displays its own backyard shrine where the family makes offerings to the gods of wind, fire and water—little things like rice, incense or flowers—in the name of unforgotten grandfathers or others.

The ubiquitous carvings of gods and demons will never let you forget that religion pervades the daily life of the Balinese.

You may rightly guess that the specific art factories and stores to which you are taken by taxi or tour bus are chosen more for the reasons of the driver or his employers than yours, whether that be friendship, convenience or a favorable percentage of whatever sales result.

Quality, of course, varies widely from place to place and what appears to be the same figure, of the same material, at one artistic compound may sell for less at another place, but look carefully. Much care and painstaking effort go into a finished work—a single statuette offered for approximately thirty dollars may have taken three weeks to complete—not to mention talent on top of that. Variations in the gracefulness of lines, the perfection of small details, and the purity and grain of the wood itself may be the real difference in what seems at first to be a bargain.

There is prolific duplication in statuettes, frames, screens and jewelry boxes, as if someone had decided that certain images and designs are particularly favored by tourists. Or perhaps it is a matter of art students paying for their lessons by copying an old favorite. But the items are beautiful, and varied enough for all tastes. Except of course, no Elvis statues.

Hundreds of outlets for exquisite art work bombard the senses until one feels that they are everywhere, in quantity inexhaustible; but most people will leave remembering one or two pieces of art that they wish they had looked at longer, or even taken.

Since the cluster of villages already mentioned are among the foremost shopping attractions of Bali—though by no means an exclusive franchise—a word or two about bargains and bargaining might be useful.

First of all, Indonesians know that all Americans, without exception, are rich. Australians, Japanese and Europeans, too. It will do you no good to protest. How else could you be walking around with such a thick wad of rupiah in your pocket like loose change, often more than a year's pay to the native Indonesian?

The rule of thumb in bargaining, whether streetside or in a shop (unless it's clearly marked "Fixed Price," and even then it's worth asking for a discount) is that the asking price is at least twice what will be accepted. But they know that you know that, which complicates the picture, because sometimes they will quadruple the asking price to allow for this.

If the artist or merchant accepts too quickly the sum you offer, chances are that you have blundered. You've probably gotten a bargain anyway, but could have done better. If the seller walks away or turns to others, you might have hurt his feelings with too low an offer. But that's a risk you must take. It may be just a tactic, and if so, the seller will come back with a compromise offer.

It can sometimes be effective to act like you might possibly be interested in a piece which you adore, but which the asking price puts out of the question forever, even for bargaining. If the seller hasn't had much traffic that particular day, he may feel that he must sell something; he may need the money more than he needs the merchandise.

Much artwork that you see is being sold on a sort of consignment basis and the starving artist who created it will accept almost anything above the negligible cost price. But these sellers have more experience in the tourist trade than most tourists do. If you are able to deal directly with the owner of a shop or the artist himself, there may be more leeway for bargaining. Sales clerks generally must operate within a certain range, below which they cannot go without consultation.

A few examples of bargains struck: A batik sarong of good material, nicely colored, artistically designed, the asking price, 25,000 rupiah (about $14 U.S.), the selling price, $5. Large gold and silver earrings, asking price, 100,000 rupiah (about $55

U.S.) selling price, $18. A carved box, asking price, 15,000 rupiah (about $8 U.S.), selling price, $4. A silver necklace trimmed with gold, asking price, 180,000 rupiah (about $100 U.S.), selling price, $50.

If you travel with American dollars in small amounts (lots of $1, $5 and $10 bills), your bargaining edge may be considerably improved in some quarters. But count carefully. Most merchants in stores carry pocket calculators to figure the rate of exchange, and it's not a bad idea for customers to do the same, unless you're a whiz at doing figures in your head. Merchants are supposed to make their sales in rupiahs, not in dollars, and sometimes that works in the buyer's favor, so a comparison is always worth trying.

It is quite easy and not too expensive, even being quite selective, to stuff a large tote bag with souvenirs and gifts to take home, if only because the prices are so good.

But what is so grand about a bargain batik sarong if you don't really like batik and never wear sarongs? Ah, a nice gift for a friend or relative maybe; or is it because you're afraid you'll regret not buying when you had the chance? This is a quite common reaction that hits when it's too late. After all, we regret more the things we don't do than the things we do.

And besides, Bali is special. The rules of common sense do not entirely apply, or why is this a holiday?

Temples and Holy Places

There are approximately five thousand major temples on the island of Bali. Don't expect to visit them all in two weeks.

Everywhere you look you will see temples: little ones posted in rice fields, the aforementioned backyard shrines; your taxi driver may have converted his dashboard into a mini-shrine. These, of course, are minor temples and do not count toward the five thousand.

An earlier census put the number of temples at ten thousand but the Balinese inclination for building them on or near active volcanoes has caused a severe reduction through the years. Many of the sightseeing locations on Bali are tied in with temples and the religious tradition of the islanders, such as the monkey forest at Sangeh as well as many scheduled dances and drama performances.

To understand the importance of their temples to the Balinese, without naming and classifying the hundred or so traditional gods and demons, heroes and villains who figure in the religious myths and histories, only a few facts are really necessary:

Isolation is part of it. While most of Indonesia is Muslim, due to the activities of Arab traders about five hundred years ago, Bali not only retained its older Hindu religion, but accepted from Java the migration of Hindu artists and intellectuals who would not convert to Islam. And Bali's blend of Hinduism, preserved for centuries, was infused with prehistoric native beliefs in ancestor worship and the omnipresence of god in nature.

The religion of the Balinese came initially from a region in eastern India called Orissa, which, in the pre-Christian era, fostered the kingdom of Kalinga, southwest of Calcutta on the Bay of Bengal.

The Kalingans, besides becoming accomplished seafarers and traders, developed a society enriched by architecture, arts and crafts, dance and drama, and they originated a form of puppet theater which in those days was as enthralling an invention as television is to this age.

When the Kalingans landed in Bali to spread their religion along with their commercial interests, they used this puppet theater to captivate the imagination of the natives and explain to them the workings of Hinduism. The effect was as striking as if the Crusaders had brought motion pictures, in full color, and projection equipment with them, instead of swords. The Balinese, to coin a phrase, took it as gospel, and not only accepted the teachings, but also the techniques. This was theater—show biz—to which the natives must have had an instinctive proclivity.

Bali already had its own set of gods at the time and its own animist religious codes, but the people were willing and able to assimilate them into the new system without conflict. They began creating their own puppets, their own puppet theater and later, live shows illustrating the same themes. They also developed artistic accoutrements as part of this live theater: dances, paintings, woodcarvings, silver and gold decorations.

So it is a very ancient art that sparks the modern-day lives of the Balinese.

TRADITIONAL DANCES

No island in the world has cultivated the art of dance to the extent that has Bali, where highly stylized performances in ornate costumes, sometimes with masks, can be viewed daily. Literally thousands of dancers, trained from childhood in villages throughout the island, participate.

Strongly influenced by the Hindu heritage of Bali, the dances are sometimes human representations of the the same traditional tales as the puppet shows have related for hundreds of years, exploring common themes of good and evil, love and hate, war and peace. Graceful, colorful, beautiful, the steps are ritually choreographed, except in the wild "trance" dances.

More than fifty dance types are performed, but the best known are the *kecak*, or monkey dance, with scores of chanting males;

the *barong* dance featuring a mythical animal protector of mankind; and the *legong* dance, the most classical of forms, also called the dance of the heavenly nymphs, and presented by a bevy of richly clad young women chosen for their beauty as well as their talent. Once it was a dance of virgins.

The noted British writer Aldous Huxley once likened Balinese dance to "a poem or a piece of music."

Dance schedules are posted in villages all over the island.

Every village of any size has at least one performing group associated with it, and children begin to learn the dances and drama as soon as they can walk because it is part of their religious life. Every modern ceremony, and there is at least one major ceremony somewhere on the island each and every week, includes these colorful set pieces.

It is perhaps unnecessary for those who are not historians or serious students of art to understand the themes that are played out here by an astounding number of Balinese people of all ages. The themes are simplistic, the plots sometimes childishly complicated and outlandish but universal in the triumph of good over evil, love over all. These are tales of princes and princesses, and the villains embody evil so clearly as to be hissable. Don't look for philosophical subtlety. These are ancient parables, their beauty evident in the presentation rather than hidden in the depths.

It's an elementary Bible class come to life. To the Balinese all of life is connected to ritual: birth, death, adolescence, marriage, old age, rain, harvests, volcanic eruptions—whatever happens. Today, when a Bali family cooks up a pot of rice for dinner, they'll often put out a taste of it at their home shrine as an offering for Uncle Edgar or Aunt Myrtle, recently deceased.

The marriage ceremony, too, is a bit of a stage play. The wife-to-be carries a market basket depicting her role as homemaker, and the groom bears the food that he will be charged with bringing from the fields. Instead of "tying the knot," as Westerners say, they cut it. It's a ribbon-cutting ceremony, a grand opening of a new life.

Babies are almost sacred to the Balinese family. Because the newborn child is believed to be fresh from heaven and thereby closer to the gods than others, an infant is not allowed to touch the ground for the first 105 days. They still belong to the gods until then.

They have a coming-of-age tooth-filing ceremony to reduce the sharpness of the canine teeth, which signify animal ferocity. The filing thus favors the non-violent aspect of humanity.

And the Balinese believe in trance, inviting the spirits to occupy them, such as can be witnessed in the performances of the *barong* dance.

These dances and rituals take place all the time, not just in special shows for tourists. Yes, while the tourist showers or dives into his ceramic pool, children still bathe in little streams hidden by mountain foliage, and village life goes on despite 20th-century intrusions.

(P.S. It is forbidden to photograph naked maidens bathing out of doors. One is not likely to be jailed for such an offense, but an appropriate fine, usually exacted on the spot, might be one direct punch in the nose.)

The Balinese can be sensitive about interlopers at their private rituals, and tourists should observe some restraint. Never walk in front of praying people, always wear a sash and/or sarong as required for entering temples, and make sure that permission has been obtained for an outsider to attend a ceremony. Common sense should prevail. A woman who would not enter a church at home in a bathing suit, should not expect to be welcome in Bali thus clad. No one would climb church walls, monuments or statuary at home, and the same would be frowned upon in Bali.

On the other hand, it is joked that the tour organizers can arrange anything, short of a human sacrifice, at twenty-four hours' notice, and will be stymied only if a virgin is required.

To some degree the tourist trade may actually reinforce, rather than trample upon, the native traditions and ways of life. Some hotels support the dancing and other manifestations of this heritage because the tourists expect it, and the expectation reminds the Balinese of their special origin and makes it all the more important.

Tour agents cover the island well, organizing itineraries that can be undertaken in varying periods of time, from a few hours to a matter of days, and their schedule of rates is modest enough to fit the budget of almost any visitor. They can arrange visits to ceremonies and processions and they maintain a regular list of upcoming dances and other costumed performances that are intended to be public.

Really, when one computes the time and money that can be lost by a stranger searching out his or her own routes, locations and schedules, twice as much can be taken in at less cost by resorting to the tour organizers. And even if one does not wish to travel in a group, there are compromise plans available.

Certain temples are high on the list of the tour operators:

The holiest of all temples on Bali, Pura Besakih (*pura* means temple), located about thirty-five miles north of Denpasar (as the crow flies; allow an hour plus for driving), really is an aggregation of thirty temples in all. The principal area enshrines the holy trinity of Brahma, Vishnu and Siva. It is an elaborate complex linked by terraces and steps, built on the slopes of the formidible Mount Agung, which last erupted violently in the 1960s, causing widespread death and destruction.

For the great ceremonies, worshipers converge at Besikah from all over the island, bearing their offerings. Ceremonies follow an annual religious calendar, but the most impressive gathering of all only occurs once a century. Not to wait, the last such ritual was performed in the 1970s.

At some temples it will be the ceremony that impresses. At some the dances. Often the temples themselves, by their sheer beauty, age, or other physical attribute, draw the visitor.

Probably the most photographed of all temples on Bali is Tanah Lot, which occupies a small promontory swept by tides on the west coast. The water ebbs far enough to permit access by foot at certain times of the day, but this is not when ceremonies or dances are scheduled. They say that the giant rock which supports the temple is riddled with caves, and in these caves dwell guardian snakes.

Although Tanah Lot photographs best in the morning hours, tours almost invariably arrive there in late afternoon when the picturesque scene turns almost to silhouette, but they do this for a good reason: the sunset is truly spectacular.

At Tampaksiring, the Tirtu Empul temple is noted for its supposed holy springs which bubble up in an inner courtyard. Special bathing pools, with water spouts gushing from mossy walls, attract thousands to the site, where the water is believed to have magical powers.

This is a thousand-year-old temple but today it is surrounded by souvenir stands especially promoting the local arts of bone and ivory carving. The temple's close neighbor is the 1954 palace built for Sukarno.

On the southernmost cliffs of Bali, high atop a sheer precipice dropping straight to the sea, stands the Pura Luhur Uluwatu, linked by legend with the goddess of the waters, Dewi Danu. Monkeys scamper all over the site, protected by the designation "holy" and said to be guardians of the temple. From vantage points the visitor can see surfers far below, negotiating waters that are exciting but made dangerous by sharp coral formations. A Hindu saint once took up occupancy here for ideal communication with the gods.

Pura Kehen at Bangli is considered the second most sacred temple in all Bali but it was damaged by volcanic upheavals and has not been restored to the condition of the island's other great attractions. The town itself is interesting as the former center of a powerful kingdom. Pura Kehen, a mountainous site with panoramic views, is reached by a high fight of stairs lined with stone gods. A monster head and a giant banyan tree mark the entrance.

Nearby, a temple of the dead called Pura Dalem Penunggekan is carved with reliefs representing demons punishing evil-doers in the hereafter with such violence as rape, castration and burning, the Balinese equivalent of fire and brimstone.

At the village of Mengwi, also once the center of a kingdom, which ruled until a century ago, the Pura Taman Ayun, spacious and open to the skies, is surrounded by a moat.

In a serene setting, adjoined by a collection of shops and handicraft displays that are part of a government project, the temple is overlooked by a terraced restaurant called the Royal Gardens. (Try the tunapi or chicken sati, excellent and inexpensive, as in most of Bali).

Out of the thousands of temples in Bali, it is difficult to point to a half-dozen and say that these are the most interesting, when the fact is that they are just the most often visited for a number of reasons.

There is Pejeng, noted for ancient archeological findings amid a profusion of thirty functioning temples, and for Penataran Sasih, the "Pejeng moon," a gigantic copper drum that dates from three hundred years before Christ. Close also are the Yeh Pilu temple with brass reliefs from the fourteenth century, and Blahbatu with its Paseh temple dedicated to the giant Kbo Iwa, whose head stands out in a relief carved more than five hundred years ago. At the nearby river banks, relics from the eleventh century are now being unearthed.

There is Penelokan near Batur Lake with the Ulun Danu Temple and its 285 altars, but most people come for the spectacular views of the volcanic region. At Penulisan, it takes 344 steps to reach the highest temple location in Bali, dating back nine hundred years.

In the north there are temples to the rice goddess Sri, and temples honoring mysterious sea gods. In the southwest there are Pura Sadat Kapal, a restoration of an ancient temple, and Pura Bukit Sari in the holy monkey forest at Sangeh.

Enroute to the temples one is distracted by a variety of interests: the lively local market at Sukawati, known for its leather puppets and wind chimes; Kapal's prodigious production of stone

ballustrades and wall decorations; the royal tombs of Gunung
Kawi; or Jagaraga, where the temple carvings are contemporary
renditions of steamships and automobiles. The diversity is head-
spinning and endless, as is the beauty of stepped rice fields,
plains, forests, mountains and the sea.

If temples abound, so does the designation "holy," which is
applied almost without discretion, more on historic or legendary
criteria rather than sanctification. There is at least one holy
monkey forest, a holy bat cave, and even the volcanoes are tagged
with reverence.

At Sangeh's popular monkey forest there is a "lost" temple in
the interior crawling with the creatures, who have really learned
the tourist game and play it to their best advantage, begging,
borrowing and stealing with the aim of procuring give-away
bananas and peanuts.

Here one must believe that it is the forest and not the monkeys
who have earned the designation as holy. There is a legend that
the monkeys were dropped here along with a loose mountain
from the hands of a fumbling god, distracted by other pursuits.

The best approach to the monkey forest is to take along one of
the young guides who congregate outside the entrance where the
visitor must pay a tiny contribution for admission. The young
guides know how to treat the monkeys and will not let them take
too much advantage of you, and this service alone is well worth
the thousand or two (or more) rupiah that you'll pay the guide.

If a monkey climbs on your shoulder, as they will unless
stopped, the guide will get it down when *you* want it down, not
when the monkey does. It's simple, really; you stoop down, the
monkey leaves; they know the routine. This can be important
because sometimes an uninitiated tourist will become frightened
or panicky. It's not everyday that we have wild monkeys jumping
on our person and a hasty reaction such as swatting at the aggressive creatures could make the monkey panic, too.

Bags of peanuts and bunches of midget bananas are sold to
tourists on the way in, and the monkeys know this. They crowd
around visitors, encircling, knowing that even if you do not

immediately proffer goodies, you are hiding them somewhere on your person. If you hold your treats out too obviously, they'll swipe the lot—just grab them and run. The more experienced monkeys will steal your sunglasses, a hairpin, or even your camera, and run off, waiting at a safe distance for you to pay a ransom in bananas for their return.

Remember, it's a jungle out there. It's a good idea to carry a stick. Just tapping it between yourself and the monkeys will keep them at a distance. They respect a stick even if you don't intend to use it on them.

They can be a lot of fun. The monkeys are clean, rabies free and, thanks largely to their intelligence, seldom bite or scratch humans, although there have been instances, usually involving unnecessary panic.

The monkey forests are not a good place to visit when it has just rained. Picture a muddy-pawed monkey climbing on you and grabbing your clothes, or hugging you with a sopping wet belly. Also watch out for monkeys at Sangeh who have been cooling off in the handy roadside sewer stream. If you have a guide with you, he'll keep the wet ones away, which alone makes it a good investment.

Another popular monkey forest lies near Peliatan and Ubud. The monkeys are a little less aggressive, but all the creatures fight among themselves for dominance and squabbles can break out over any gift banana. The Ubud monkey forest also hides an old temple of the dead, and, off the beaten track, in a hollow between two slopes can be found a pacific natural pool that seems little visited.

The forest at Sangeh, however, is more beautiful, with its towering nutmeg trees and slightly mysterious, disused interior temple. At both monkey forests the tourist department collects a few hundred rupiah as admission (about 25¢), but even if they had to charge a little more, it would be nice if they could provide a flier with basic information about the monkey preservation project. One sees foresters with clipboards inspecting the creatures as if they knew each one personally, and they do provide feed, which is a mixture of rice and corn grains, for the feebler monkeys who are bullied out of their share of tourist handouts by the dominant ones.

Monkeys seem to play a rather large role in the legend of Bali and the creatures are given free rein at many sites. Even at the much visited Tanah Lot temple on the west coast, the dance most performed is a mass imitation of chanting monkeys, the *kekak* dance.

Other spots of variable holiness are also linked with live creatures, most prominently the Bat Cave near Kusamba and the Elephant Cave near Bedulu and Ubud.

Bali has no elephants but its Elephant Cave is among the most popular tourist attractions. Some say that it was so named because the huge carvings at the entry resemble an elephant from a distance; others say the name comes from a Ganesa statue inside.

You enter this roadside attraction through an open-air market that is more Tijuana than Bali, just parallel rows of canvas flap stalls thrown up to capitalize on the tourist parade, where leather goods, T-shirts and drinks are offered for sale. Nothing very special, unless you need a cool drink.

Down a long incline with steps leading into a serene valley, one comes upon an ancient cave carved into a solid rock formation sometime in the eleventh century. Over the entrance, images of demons and other frightening creatures swarm, as if meant to scare away the uninvited from what apparently began as a monastery.

In recent years, equally ancient carvings and an elaborate, once splendid bathing pool area were discovered adjacent to the cave, and have now been excavated and restored with fountains running and mosses growing. This whole area of the hidden valley must have been dedicated to secluded worship on a massive scale.

At roadside above there is an excellent restaurant called Puri (meaning palace) Suling, which offers a good buffet lunch, quite inexpensive, with tables overlooking a spectacular green valley with tiered rice fields climbing the opposite hillside. Somewhere down below you can hear water running. The peace alone is worth the price.

The Bat Cave (Goa Lawah), a dozen miles to the east on the coast, will not appeal to everyone, but if you happen to catch one of the rare ceremonials there, in which offerings are carried on the heads of women to appease the spirit of a Hindu god believed to dwell in the cave, it's well worth the trip.

Inside there is a ruined temple which must have been a showpiece at one time, but the odor of bat dung does something to the stomach that inspires less than awe. The creatures themselves, screaming by the countless thousands, flapping and soaring, clash with the serenity that one expects of Bali.

Someone will explain to you that bats are really cute, harmless little creatures who keep their cave and environs free of mosquitoes, and none of the locals show any overt vampirish tendencies, but if your instincts tell you otherwise, then even the violins of an accompanying waltz from *Die Fledermaus* will fail to make the Goa Lawah inhabitants more presentable.

If you don't love bats or monkeys, how about turtles or birds? Or bulls?

In the tiny village of Petulu Gunung, population three hundred, thousands of white birds called kokokans take up lodgings every night. Some fifteen thousand of them fill the trees and all available roosting areas each evening at sunset, leaving the next morning. Despite being vastly outnumbered by the winged creatures, the villagers regard their feathered guests as holy.

At Negara, in the west district of Jembrana, bull races are staged, a tradition picked up from the island of Madura off the northeast coast of Java. Dressed in silks and bells, the specially bred cattle put on a thundering display of speed in imitation of thoroughbred horses, which they outweigh considerably.

On Serangan, also called Turtle Island, south of Sanur, giant sea turtles lay their eggs by night. This is a popular off-shore trek for tourists, perhaps overcommercialized, but so close to all the hotel centers that it never lacks for visitors.

Volcanoes and Hidden Villages

There are hundreds of things to see, scores of places to go. The variety, like the beauty of Bali, seems endless.

The volcanic regions alone can occupy days of sightseeing. The village of Kintamani, gateway to a much-visited volcano, Mount Batur, is itself fascinating for its market days—every third day, actually—when men and women travel long distances from all over the countryside to bring a variety of wares and turn the sleepy town into a bustling bazaar. Oranges and passion fruit are the chief local crops, which thrive in the volcanic soil and high altitude cool, but tourists' interests certainly are not neglected in the marketing.

The view from Penelokan, a village on the rim of the ten-mile-wide Batur caldera, is awe-inspiring. A geological wonder that's almost beyond description, the Gunung Batur mists and smoke obscure it photographically much of the time. Different aspects of the crater can be viewed from the villages of Batur, Kedisan, and Penulisan, among other vantage points, because this is one of the few volcanoes with a road running along its rim. Picture the largest modern outdoor sports arena that you have ever seen. About a hundred structures of such size could sit inside this colossal dent in the earth. The violent upheaval which created such a gigantic natural bowl must have rivaled Krakatau.

A relatively new, smoking volcano with a crescent lake beside it sits inside the caldera; the lake alone is some five miles long.

Visitors can cross the lake by boat and stop at the mysterious village of Trunyan where natives, secluding themselves from the rest of the island, surviving untold volcanic assaults, still cling to ancient tribal ways that even predate the Hindu influence on Bali.

Near the east coast of Bali the palace of Klungkung, the court of justice and the floating pavilion are the focus of tourist attention where centuries ago a powerful kingdom centered.

Klungkung's most noted attraction is the court of justice or Kerta Gosa, a structure whose ceiling murals depict the bloody retribution due to those who violate the laws of earth and the rewards that await the virtuous in heaven.

At the crossroads town of Gianyar there is an interesting royal palace, but the town generally is visited more because it is a center for the weaving industry. Gianyar is perhaps typical of Bali villages, each of which seems to foster its own seldom-exclusive specialty in the arts while staging markets that show a much broader range of wares. And, of course, almost every village carries out its own schedule of ceremonies and dances or drama.

In Candidasa on the east coast a whole new resort area is growing by leaps and bounds, supported by legions of visitors who shun the beaten track of south Bali hotel accommodations. It certainly is more peaceful and isolated here, compared to all but the insular resorts of the south, and the prices lean toward the Kuta Beach range.

Inland from Candidasa, another isolated village, Tenganan, bypassed by the wave of Hindu conversions hundreds of years ago, retains a lifestyle that dates back to year one. Only recently have outsiders been permitted through its walls and the reception is ambiguous. With less than a thousand residents, Tenganan has set up shops to greet the visitors and they purvey a supposedly magical *geringsing* fabric, believed to prevent harm from befalling the wearer. The villagers have their own dances and rituals, but many seem uneasy about the changes that outsiders are causing.

Ujung and Amlapura, not far away, are more accustomed to visitors coming to see the relatively new water palaces created by the 20th-century king of Karangasem.

North Coast

The whole north coast of Bali, which historically has felt the first impact of seafaring visitors and conquerors from all over the globe, today is the most neglected by tourists, largely due to problems of access, but this is changing . . . not the access, but the neglect.

Uncrowded, different, inexpensive. These are the reasons why tourists go to the north coast. There is a black sand beach, water sports, pools, waterfalls and a growing hotel industry, not yet spoiled by the numbers that throng on the southern beaches.

The capital of the north, Singaraja, maintains an old colonial charm to some degree, but its days as the chief port city seem to be numbered because of the lack of protection from the sea. A newer port in a small bay at Celukanbawang, to the west, gets more cargo vessels today, and the ocean liners go around to the southeast, at Padang Bay. Meanwhile, the favored recreational beaches, around Lovina, also represent a shift to the west.

At the pier in Celukanbawang, old Bugi schooners often tie up. These ancient sailing vessels, still carrying inter-island cargo as they did a hundred years ago, are handmade and sailed by mariners with a fearsome history of South China Sea piracy that some say has not been completely abandoned. Yet sometimes the vessels take on passengers for short hauls; the facilities are spare.

South of Singaraja it's only about a half-hour's drive to the mountain lake area near Bedugul which features an eighteen-hole golf course, waterskiing and views that have an almost mystical quality. Lake Bratan's popularity as an escape from the heat of the lowlands keeps growing, for in a way it provides a microcosm of Bali, affording outdoor sports amid great scenery.

Some three dozen villages close to the northern coast boast temples of varying interest, the most popular being at Kubutambahan and Jagaraga, adorned with modernistic reliefs with a sense of humor, automobiles, airplanes and other contemporary vehicles mixing with the usual monsters.

Sawan, inland several miles, produces the traditional gamelan musical instruments and gongs on a small scale. Also along this coast, there are waterfalls cascading into cool pools, a fine Buddhist monastery, a national park (including the untrammeled island Palau Menjangan, popular with divers), and Yeh Sanih at the east end offers all around excellence in general beauty. In the west lies the ferry port of Gilimanuk for the short trip to Java.

Altogether the north coast presents a more leisurely aspect of Bali. The temples, the arts, the mountains, the seashore, all are here but there seems to be more space, less hurry, fewer travelers, than in the southern part of the island.

THE GAMELAN

The native orchestra of Java and Bali is the *gamelan*, a unique collection of percussion instruments, strings and reeds that produce an ancient and other-worldly sound which distinguishes the music of these islands from that of other parts of the world.

One of the most famous reviews of the gamelan calls it "the sound of moonlight."

Often accompanying the dances and puppetry so popular in Indonesia, the gamelan usually includes drums and gongs, cymbals, bamboo flutes of varying size, the two-stringed *rebab*, the 26-string *celempung* and its smaller version, the *sitar*, and the *gender*, which resembles a xylophone.

Male and female vocalists often take part in gamelan performances, which can be seen everywhere in Java and Bali, with noticeable regional differences.

The venerable age of this traditional music is shown by stone carvings throughout the islands, some of them a thousand years old, depicting the gamelan instruments being played.

Getting Around Bali

Some will come to Bali just to lie on the beach, some to climb mountains or engage in the sports that abundant and varied waters afford. Some will come to Bali to visit its off-shore islands, and especially popular among these are the three off the southeast coast, Nusa Penida, Nusa Lembongan and Nusa Ceningan. Skindiving enthusiasts will find no shortage of special facilities on these islands and the one in the north, Palau Menjangan.

With artists and artisans everywhere, temples and volcanoes, dancing and playlets, there is an endless array of attractions for the visitor, beyond the scenic bliss of sand and sea. Too much, some will say. With all that there is to see and do, the senses go into overload.

How does one reach so many far-flung destinations in so brief a time as is usually allotted to a vacation trip? This can be easy, inexpensive, and also quite comfortable, which is important.

For example, just about everything on the island is within a day's journey by vehicle. Adequate bus service, mostly originating in Denpasar, is available, and cheaply so, but the crowds turn away most visitors from this means of transportation. Try one bus ride over a short haul. Sit down (if you can get a seat) next to a Bali resident carrying fish from the market, or a live chicken, or a coat of volcanic ash. Unless you are on an extremely skimpy budget, you'll soon be pondering other, more comfortable rides.

There are vehicles to rent in Denpasar, Kuta, Sanur and Nusa Dua, and if you are going to be using them in certain uncrowded areas of the island they can be ideal. Not a great bargain, but certainly the most flexible means of transport. Still, before one grasps at this mode of getting around, some research into happy motoring on Bali should be disclosed. Look before you jeep.

First of all, the average good road in Bali is paved approximately fifteen feet wide. Operators drive on the left side of the road, or sometimes the center, or wherever. A study shows that territorial rights and divisions of this fifteen-foot space have been carefully allotted as follows in the unwritten rules of the road:

The average pedestrian being no more than two feet wide, foot traffic has been granted, informally, eighteen inches of space at the very edge of the pavement, a right which is subject to random revocation, without notice, upon the whim of any operator of anything on wheels.

Bicycles also are allotted eighteen inches of space, but this is the same eighteen inches at the edge of the pavement that pedestrians use. However, if a bicycle is laden with banana stalks, baskets, logs or bales of market goods exceeding its cubic mass or wider than five feet, then the bicycle must enter motorcycle territory.

Motorcycles take three feet of pavement immediately adjoining the bicycle and pedestrian traffic, or, in practice, any other space that seems to be open.

Three- and four-wheel passenger vehicles, bemos, becaps, horse-drawn carts, busses, and trucks up to a width of eight feet are given the major portion of the roadway, an eight-foot strip located directly in front of the vehicle in question.

Simple addition shows that this accounts for less than thirteen of the fifteen feet usually available, which allows plenty of room for everybody. It does not, however, make any provision for traffic coming from the opposite direction, which it does, and which logic tells us also takes about thirteen of the available fifteen feet of space.

Meanwhile, U-turns, cross traffic and unsignaled stops are performed on impulse. Speed limits are established only by the existence, absence or distance of obstacles in the path of the operator. Bali has an island-wide policy of issuing unrestricted driver's licenses to all homicidal maniacs, by the way.

If these complications don't bother you, if you love adventure, have already lived a full life and are well insured anyway, refer to the list of auto rental agencies included in this chapter.

There are some areas in which traffic chaos is not a major

problem. Such places are away from the congested track of day-to-day tourism, however. The same applies to bicycles and motorbikes in the hands of island visitors; there are places where they can be safely used.

But to recommend that you rent a bicycle or motorbike in high traffic areas could be tantamount to conspiring to create an accident. If you choose to rent such a vehicle, be sure to carefully assess beforehand the value you place on the very thing you would place on that bicycle seat, not to mention the con-commitant peace of mind.

Tour and taxi agents, or the front desk of your hotel, are the recommended contacts for getting around Bali. When one re-members that a good air conditioned taxi with an English-speaking driver can be hired in Bali for less than five dollars an hour, and that coach tours are even less expensive, these bargain rates, the reduction of stress and maximized mobility, override all other considerations.

The logic is inescapable. The choice is between a taxi, which can transport three or four people comfortably, allowing them to determine destination, the duration of stops, the length of the tour and the selection of restaurants for lunch; or decision-free trips on small, package tour buses, predestined, one might say, with traveling companions provided.

Of course, it could be argued that one rides on the same roads by taxi or tour bus as one does in a rental vehicle, but this point is spurious. Indonesians are accustomed to driving under these conditions. Visitors are not, and there is no safe manner of learning. As a passenger one does not have to look at the road ahead and thus, besides enjoying the view, avoids many a shud-der. One's life does not flash before one's eyes, just the scenery.

Most hotels of any size have connections with taxi and tour services, or can recommend a half dozen.

As an example, what follows are the taxi rates for typical itineraries as suggested through the Bali Mandira Cottages at Kuta Beach. For comparison, the rates on similar package mini-bus tours also are given.

Tours By Taxi

Volcano Tour: 41,000 rupiah or approximately $24 U.S. per taxi. You are taken to Batubulan to watch a *barong* and *kris* dance, to Celuk to see their gold and silver work; to Mas to view wood-carving techniques and products; to Ubud for the Museum of Paintings and shopping; to the Elephant Cave near Bedulu; to the holy springs and Water Temple at Tampaksiring and to Mount Batur, the volcano at Kintamani.

Besakih Tour: 44,000 rupiah or approximately $26 U.S. per taxi. This tour proceeds first to Celuk for gold and silver crafts, then to Batuan's hand weaving center, to a sarong-making factory at Gianyar, to the Court of Justice at Klungkung, and, enroute to Besakih, the mother temple, views overlooking terraced rice fields and other scenic wonders.

Bedugul tour: 44,000 rupiah per taxi. This tour first takes in the sacred monkey forest at Sangeh, then the royal family temple of Taman Ayun, and ends up in the mountains at Bedugul, the resort on the shores of Lake Bratan, including visits to their flower market and country club.

All three tours above take the better part of a day, between five and seven hours in all, with lunch not included. Additionally, the taxi tour service lets the customer design his or her own tours and, of course, more than one destination can be wrapped into the same day's travel. Examples:

Singaraja: seven hours, 74,000 rupiah per taxi (about $40 U.S.).

Tanah Lot Temple: three hours, 26,500 rupiah per taxi (about $15 U.S.).

Sangeh Monkey Forest: two hours, 26,000 rupiah per taxi (about $15 U.S.).

Sanur Beach: two hours, 18,000 rupiah per taxi (about $10 U.S.).

Uluwatu Temple: three hours, 31,500 rupiah per taxi (about $17 U.S.).

Nusa Dua Beach: two hours, 19,500 rupiah per taxi (about $11 U.S.).

Denpasar City, two hours, 16,000 rupiah per taxi (about $9 U.S.).

Celuk Tour of Gold and Silver Craftspeople: three hours, 22,000 rupiah (about $13 U.S.).

Celuk, Mas and Ubud Craft Centers for silverwork, wood-carvings and paintings: five hours, 32,000 rupiah (about $17 U.S.).

Kuta Beach: one hour, 8,000 rupiah per taxi (about $4 U.S.).

Batubulan: two hours, 20,000 rupiah (about $11 U.S.).

Candidasa Beach Resort: seven hours, 62,000 rupiah (about $34 U.S.).

The above are sample asking prices for taxi tours in which passengers decide starting time, stops to be made and other choices enroute. Additional flexibility to extend your tour is provided with a flat rate of 7,000 rupiah (less than $4 U.S.) per hour over the initial time period agreed. These rates are negotiable and taxi agents will try to add 10 percent for air conditioning but, again, there is margin for bargaining.

Other Tours

Meanwhile, local tours and package trips are offered by approximately thirty different travel agents located in the Denpasar, Kuta Beach, Sanur Beach and Nasu Dua areas. All use Denpasar as their official starting and stopping points, but in practice there are free pickups at four major hotels on a regular daily schedule.

What follows is a list of generally available tours, varying in length from one hour to ten, and in cost from five dollars to about sixty. The longer tours are by bus, with a maximum of twenty reserved seats. Shorter tours use a mini-bus, with seats usually for no more than ten passengers.

Denpasar City Tour: three hours, city and suburbs, including the Sanur Art Gallery, Denpasar Museum, Art and Culture Center, handicrafts displays and open market area.

Kintamani Tour: eight hours, Denpasar to Celuk, Ubud, Tampaksiring, Kintamani, Bangli, and return to Denpasar, including gold and silver crafts, wood carvings, paintings, the museum at Ubud, springs, Lake Batur views, volcano.

Sangeh-Mengwi Tour: four hours, Denpasar-Sangeh-Mengwi-Denpasar, including the Bali Museum, an art shop, the monkey forest and the temple of Taman Ayun.

Besakih Temple Tour: seven hours, Denpasar-Klungkung-Besakih-Bukit Jambal-Denpasar, including Bali's Mother Temple, Mount Agung volcano, the ancient Court of Justice, the Bat Cave and spectacular views.

Kecak Dance Tour: one hour, hotel-Cultural Performance Center, including traditional Balinese dances.

Barong Dance Tour: one hour, hotel-Cultural Performance Center, including traditional Balinese dances.

Legong Dance Tour: one hour, hotel-Cultural Performance Center, including traditional Balinese dances.

Kintamani-Besakih Tour: ten hours, Denpasar to Celuk, Mas, Ubud, Tampaksiring, Kintamani, Bangli, Klungkung, Besakih and return to Denpasar, including handicraft and painting centers, holy springs, Mount Batur, Lake Batur, Konen Temple, Court of Justice and the Mother Temple of Bali.

Tanah Lot Tour: five to eight hours, Denpasar-Sangeh-Mengwi-Tanah Lot-Denpasar, including the monkey forest, temple Taman Ayun and sunset at Tanah Lot.

Ubud Tour: five hours, Denpasar-Ubud-Goa Gajah-Denpasar, including painting studios and galleries, the Ubud museum and the Elephant Cave.

Karangasem Tour: ten hours, Denpasar-Klungkung-Karangasem-Denpasar, including visits to many points in the eastern province of Karangasem, like the Court of Justice and areas devastated by the eruption of Mount Agung.

Turtle Island Tour: four to six hours, Denpasar-Serangan Island-Denpasar, including Sanur Beach, scenic vistas and a cruise to Turtle Island.

Trunyan Tour: ten hours, Denpasar-Kintamani-Penelokan-Trunyan-Tampaksiring-Ubud-Mas-Celuk-Denpasar,   including Lake Batur cruise, an ancient Bali village, and traditional handicrafts.

Bedugal Tour: six hours, Denpasar-Bedugul-Mengwi-Denpasar, including the volcanic mountain lake Bratan and Taman Ayun temple.

Rates differ according to two variables, the number of persons taking the tour and the travel agency itself, so, as with most things in Bali, it pays to shop. Keep in mind, however, that one tour operator's vehicles, guides and general standards may be superior to another's; in those matters a recommendation from a trustworthy source can be helpful. Prices stated below are an approximate, median figure varying by the number of persons:

TOUR PRICES PER PERSON (U.S. Dollars)

TOUR	GROUP SIZE				
	1	2	3	4 to 9	More
Denpasar City	16	9	7	6	5
Kintamani Tour	38	25	20	16	15
Sangeh-Mengwi Tour	25	15	11	10	8
Besakih Temple Tour	39	21	18	15	12
Dance Tours	15	10	8	8	8
Kintamani-Besakih Tour	50	27	24	21	18
Tanah Lot Tour	26	15	12	11	9
Ubud Tour	18	9	7	6	5
Karangasem Tour	45	26	19	15	12
Turtle Island Tour	36	25	19	15	15
Trunyan Tour	55	31	25	24	22
Bedugul Tour	36	22	20	16	13

It can be observed quite quickly that it pays to travel in groups on these tours. Many hotels post lists of recommended tours and organize their own sign-ups. Or travel agents can be contacted directly from the list of approved operators that follows. Usually one can sign for a tour as late as the day before, but, especially in high season, the earlier the better for making arrangements.

Names, addresses and phones of tour operators are:

Bali Indonesia Murni, P.O. Box 110 DPS, Denpasar. Phones 8464, 8434 and 8261.

Bali Lestari Indah, Jalan Raya Sanur 130, Denpasar. Phones 24000, 26099.

Balindo Star, Jalan W. R. Supratman 114X, Denpasar. Phones 25372, 22497, 28669.

Chandra Universal, Jalan Diponegoro 36, Denpasar. Phones 24305, 24756.

Celong Indonesia, Jalan Raya Sanur, P.O. Box 43, Denpasar. Phones 28227, 28325.

Carefree Bali Holidays, Jalan Bakungsari, Kuta. Phones 25056, 25160, 23782, 51261, 51262.

Easy Rider, Garden Hotel, Jalan Legion, Kuta. Phones 51746, 51672.

Kuta Bali, P.O. Box 192, Kuta. Phones 8142, 8143.

Golden Kuta Tours, Jalan Pantai, Kuta. Phone 51043.

Ida Dewi Saraswati, Jalan Pantai, Kuta. Phones 51205, 51934.

Jabato, Pertamina Cottages, Kuta. Phones 51151, 511216.

Jan's, Jalan Nusa Indah 62, Denpasar. Phones 24595, 23076.

Jatayu Mulya, Hotel Bali Beach, Sanur. Phone 8511 Ext. 115.

Natrabu, Jalan Kecubung 78, Denpasar. Phones 25448, 23452, 24925.

Nitour, Jalan Veteran 5, Denpasar. Phones 22593, 22849, 22707, 24233, 29278, 22791.

Nusa Dua Bali, Jalan Bypass, Gusti Ngurah Rai 1, Tuban. Phones 51223 Ext 415, 416.

Nusa Jaya Tour, Jalan Diponegoro 191, Denpasar. Phones 25232, 24636.

Pacto, Jalan Tanjung Sari, Sanur. Phones 8247, 8248, 8249.

Paradise Bali Indah, Jalan Setia Budi 39, Denpasar. Phone 22491.

Puri Astina Putra Ltd., Jalan Hayam Wuruk 8, Denpasar. Phones 23552, 23259, 23266.

Rama Witra Perdana, Jalan Raya Sanur 159, Denpasar. Phones 24972, 23285.

Satriavi, Jalan Veteran 7, Denpasar. Phones 24339, 24385, 27065.

Sunda Duta, Jalan Br. Batujimbar, Sanur. Phones 8498, 8764.

Trio Bali International, Jalan Pandu, Denpasar. Phones 26830, 25830, 23450.

Tunas Indonesia, Jalan Semawang, Sanur. Phones 8056, 8581, 8588, 8450.

Tejo Express, Jalan W. R. Supratman 24, Denpasar. Phones 28561, 28562.

Udaya, Jalan Raya Sanur, Denpasar. Phone 8564.

Vaya Tour, Jalan Hayam Wuruk 124A, Denpasar. Phones 24449, 23958, 23757.

Visata Express, Bali Beach Hotel Arcade, Sanur. Phone 8511 Ext. 579.

Tjampuhan Gunung Lebah, Jalan Nusa Indah 68, Denpasar. Phone 23953.

Most of these agencies also handle air bookings to other islands, and other transportation needs. Two of them, Natrabu and Tunas Indonesia, also specialize in wildlife safari adventure tours and marine sports excursions.

Vehicle Rentals

Those determined to rent their own transportation may contact the following agencies, or their hotel desks: Avis, phone 88271; Bali Happy, phone 51954; Bali Trip Rental, phone 52411;

Giri Putra Car Rental, phone 51349; GJ&K, phone 72055; Norman's Car Rental, phone 88830; Nusa Dua Rentacar, phone 71905; and Redjeki, phone 52411.

For an ambulance, phone 27911. The Army Hospital is at 28003 and a private hospital can be reached by phoning 25249. A private doctor is on call at 51315.

Hotels

Unless reservations have been made more than a month ahead, rooms will be hard to find in Bali from July to September, during the Christmas holidays and in early January, which generally are referred to as "high season."

The "high" seems to refer to prices. Some hotels do not even bother to advertise or otherwise promote themselves because they are over-booked with travel-agent packages and could not possibly handle more guests. Especially when traveling in high season, one should be sure to have confirmation in writing, or at the very least the name of the hotel official who made the confirmation.

If arrangements are made well in advance, whether through an agent (who often can get a better price than the individual tourist can) or personally by telephone, FAX or letter, there are thousands of rooms available and the rates—along with the accommodations—can vary in price from ten dollars or below to more than one hundred dollars per night.

The variety of accommodations requires a word or two. For thirty-five dollars or more per night (single or double) in the Kuta-Legian beach areas, for example, you can expect clean and comfortable air-conditioned rooms, private bath, usually your own refrigerator, good room service, a restaurant on the premises, a pool and a well-kept, sandy beach. But of course the levels of cleanliness and maintenance vary, as does the quality of everything else.

Bargain guest houses or *losemans*, also sometimes called "home-stays," will not be so complete. When you shop in the ten- or fifteen-dollar budget level, you still have a right to cleanliness, but being sure that you get it may depend on your own inspection, or evaluation of advance recommendations from others. All that you can reasonably expect at these prices is a good bed, a safe haven for your possessions, and access to a bath, either in the room or down the hall. Sometimes the bath will be a *mandi*, where you'll have to learn to throw water around effectively.

In a *mandi* you'll find a tiled area with a tap or a large receptacle of water, often big enough to climb into. Don't. You'll also find a ladle. Pretend that this ladle is a shower head. The proper procedure is this: One disrobes. One fills the ladle with cold water, pours it over oneself and screams. Repeat until soaked enough to soap up. Soap up. Then repeat step two to rinse off. If you have not splashed your towel and clothing in the process, you've done a good job.

(A word of caution repeated here from earlier sections: when traveling in Bali, as anywhere else in Indonesia, one must carry those little packets of tissues at all times, because public bathrooms are notoriously lacking in toilet tissue. This does not usually apply to your own private bath in your hotel room.)

Even at *loseman* prices, one should look for proximity to a beach, an overhead fan, or at least the promise of an ocean breeze. These are the variables in the lower price ranges. It's a competitive arena between ten and twenty-five dollars because so many young people flock to the budget hotels. At peak season there are more would-be roomers than rooms, and it is up to the buyer to bargain for the best for his or her money.

Of course, if you are prepared to pay sixty to one hundred dollars a night for your lodgings, luxury awaits. In this category, the quality and quantity of services multiplies, as it should. Sports and boat access, health clubs, a variety of activities and restaurants on the premises, all will be part of the package.

Good security is available at almost any hotel priced from about thirty dollars a night on upward, and if you are stolen from in a low-end-hotel room, chances are that your fellow traveler, not the islanders, are to blame.

Bargains in hotel accommodations will best be found in those months of the year with the least tourist traffic (which saves you money in all shopping arenas as well). If you are able to travel in May, June or October—just prior to, and after the big crush, yet reasonably clear of the rainy season, this could be considered optimal because the prices are down and the rains usually are not of deluge proportions.

Even in high season it rains a little, sometimes daily, but these are only showers, a relief rather than the kind of downpour that will cancel life on earth. A lightweight, foldable umbrella should be packed for any visit at any time of the year. It can come in handy.

It is said that with a little luck and a game spirit, you can take advantage of low season rates, generally February through May, with little inconvenience, but this depends on your interests. Not everyone needs total sunshine to survive and even in the monsoon season the rain tends to come in batches. It may rain four days out of seven. These odds are devastating if you only have a week to spend and want to hike, but if you have two weeks, three, or a month, you can count on enough clear weather to see and do the things you want to.

But the forests will be wet and their paths muddy. Ocean sports suffer, too. The waters become too rough for safe boating and the clouds too dense for much tanning. But life goes on in Bali, rain or shine.

By area, here are listings of hotels and room accommodations on Bali, preceded by a handy chart for figuring the low and high prices at each hotel. The minimum rate usually applies to low season, the maximum to high season, and hotels usually will quote the high rate first anyway, but upon request (if not over-booked) will quickly grant the lower rate. Hotels with three stars or more can be counted on to have air conditioning, attached bath, and telephones, usually a TV as well.

HOTEL PRICES (IN U.S. DOLLARS)

HOTEL RATING	SINGLE	DOUBLE	SUITE
Five-Star	$67–93	$72–122	$97–650
Four-Star	$58–64	$64–103	$103–272
Three-Star	$20–63	$25–63	$40–202
Two-Star	$10–58	$23–65	$40–120
One-Star	$7 –15	$15–25	

Denpasar

Bali Hotel, Jalan Veteran 3. Phones 25681, 25685. Telex 35166. Three-Star, 71 rooms.

Denpasar Hotel, Jalan Diponegoro 104. Phones, 26336, 26363. Two-Star, 78 rooms.

Pamecutan Hotel, Jalan Thamrin 2. Phone 23491. Two-Star, 44 rooms.

Adiyasa Hotel, Jalan Nakula 23. Phone 22679, One-Star, 20 rooms.

Damai Hotel, Jalan Diponegoro 117. Phone 22476. One-Star, 30 rooms.

Kuta-Legian

Pertamina Cottages, Kuta Beach, P.O. Box 121. Phone 51161. Telex 35131. Five-Star, 178 rooms.

Bali Oberoi, Kayu Aya Legion. Phones, 51061 to 51065. Telex 35125. Four-Star, 75 rooms.

Bali Mandira Cottages, Jalan Padma, Kuta. Phone 51381. Telex 35125. Three-Star, 110 rooms.

Bali Intan Cottages, Jalan Melasti 1, Phones 51770, 51891. Telex 35200. Two-Star, 105 rooms.

Karkita Plaza Beach Hotel, Jalan Karkita, Phones 51067 to 51069; Telex 35142. Two-Star, 120 rooms.

Kuta Beach Hotel, Jalan Pantai, Kuta. Phones 51361, 51362. Telex 35166. Two-Star, 40 rooms.

Kuta Beach Club, Jalan Bakungsari. Phones 51261, 51140. Telex 35138. Two-Star, 86 rooms.

Kuta Cottages, Jalan Bakungsari. Phone 51100. Telex 3542. Two-Star, 50 rooms.

Kuta Palace Hotel, Jalan Pura Bagus Taruna. Phones 51461, 51462. Telex 35234. Two-Star, 100 rooms.

Legian Beach Hotel, Jalan Melati. Phones 51711, 51715. Telex 35324. Two-Star, 110 rooms.

Ramayana Seaside Cottages, Jalan Bakungsari, Phone 25058. Telex 35491. One-Star, 60 rooms.

Nusa Dua Beach

Bali Sol, P.O. Box 1048. Phone 71510. Telex 35237. Five-Star, 500 rooms.

Nusa Dua Beach Hotel, P.O. Box 1028. Phones 71210, 71220. Telex 35206. Five-Star, 450 rooms.

Putri Bali, P.O. Box 1. Phones 71020, 71420. Telex 35247. Five-Star, 425 rooms.

Bualu Hotel, P.O. Box 217. Phones 71310, 71315. Telex 35231. One-Star, 50 rooms.

Sanur Beach

Bali Beach Intercontinental, P.O. Box 275. Phone 85117. Telex 35129. Five-Star, 605 rooms.

Bali Hyatt Hotel, P.O. Box 392. Phones 8271 to 8277. Telex 35127. Four-Star, 387 rooms.

Sanur Beach Hotel, P.O. Box 279. Phones 8011, 8015. Telex 35135. Four-Star, 320 rooms.

Segara Village, Jalan Segara Ayu. Phone 8407. Telex 35143. Three-Star, 110 rooms.

Sindhu Beach Hotel, P.O. Box 181. Phones 88351, 88352. Three-Star, 50 rooms.

Sanur Alit's Beach Hotel, Jalan Hang Tuah. Phone 8567. Telex 35165. Two-Star, 92 rooms.

Bali Sanur Bungalows, Jalan Raya Sanur. Phones 8421, 8422. Telex 35178. Two-Star, 175 rooms.

Besakig Beach Hotel, Jalan Tanjungsari. Phone 8424. Two-Star, 50 rooms.

Diwangkara Beach Hotel, Jalan Hang Tuah. Phones 8412, 8591. Two-Star, 40 rooms.

Gazebo Cottages, Jalan Tanjungsari. Phone 8300. Telex 35182. Two-Star, 62 rooms.

La Taverna Hotel, P.O. Box 40. Phones 8397, 8387. Telex 35163. Two-Star, 40 rooms.

Peneeda View Hotel, Jalan Tanjungsari. Phones 8425, 8426. Two-Star, 44 rooms.

Santrian Beach Hotel, Jalan Tanjungsari. Phones 8181, 8182. Two-Star, 137 rooms.

Tanjungsari Hotel, Jalan Tanjungsari. Phone 88441. Telex 35157. Two-Star, 25 rooms.

Irama Bungalows, Jalan Tanjungsari. Phone 28423. One-Star, 23 rooms.

Of course there are many fine hotels and guest houses, *losemans*, hostels, and other places to stay by other names that do not fit into the government rating system for one reason or another: Sometimes a hotel is new, or it doesn't supply TV to rooms and doesn't like the category it would thus be placed in, or it just doesn't bother to apply for a rating (and deal with the copious paperwork involved).

To name just a few, some of them worthy of five stars, some less, but all good places to stay:

Bali Padma Hotel, Jalan Padma No. 1, Legian. Phone 52111. FAX 52140. This is a splendid, new 400-room hotel.

Rama Palace Hotel, Jalan Pantai, Kuta. Phone 52063. FAX 53078. On the beach, with pool.

Kul Kul Beach Resort, Jalan Pantai, Kuta. Phones 52520, 52921.

Puri Wisata Bungalows, Legian. Phone 51637. Air-conditioned rooms, $25 and less.

Hotel Sanur Agung, Jalan Ngurah Rai 9, Sanur. Phones 88409, 88599. Pool, air-conditioned.

Bali Anggreh Inn, Kuta. Phones 51265, 51266. Telex 35256. Pool, air-conditioning, restaurant, TV, phones, etc.

Bali Resort Palace Hotel, Nusa Dua. Phone 72026. FAX 53094. 200 rooms, new.

Balisani Hotels, Nusa Dua, Kuta and Sanur. Phone 34143. FAX 34143. Fine-looking.

There's even a first class Club Med on Nusa Dua, one of the

chain's most popular locations and always booked well in advance. The reputation as Bali's most expensive hotel goes to the Amandari, which has villas from $175 to $500 a night, sequestered in the Ayung River Valley at Kedewatan, not far from Ubud.

The Ubud area is developing its own mini-hotel industry and other areas mentioned as growing in popularity include Candidasa and Singaraja, where people choose to stay as an alternative to the "touristy" southern bedroom headquarters. But tourist bureaus in the south remain the best contacts for identifying and choosing accommodations in these outlying areas.

Restaurants

Most good hotels in Bali have their own restaurants, and because they are prepared to serve visitors from many lands, their menus offer a choice of Indonesian, European or Chinese foods. Seafoods are especially good and abundant, and like most meals on Bali, quite inexpensive.

On the Kuta-Legian strip, restaurants and bars are everywhere. Fads rage and fade, often led by the latest wave of Australian revelers, so that the favored restaurant of one week will be empty the next, while another is suddenly jammed, relating little to the quality of food or other amusements.

A few favorites in the Kuta strip environs are the Bottoms Up restaurant and bar, with European, Indonesian, Japanese and Chinese foods, and music; BP Bar & Restaurant, with the same multinational menu, open 24 hours with take-out service; LG bar and restaurant, also multinational foods with Korean and seafoods a specialty; Monte Carlo bar and restaurant, which adds Italian and French cuisine to the list; Lenny's (no, not Denny's) which operates both in Kuta and Sanur; Kopi Pot on the strip, more like a coffee shop; and even a sushi bar at the Bali Garden Hotel. Alaski Garden and Asia restaurants also are good.

In Sanur there are the Janur Garden restaurant, Shindhu Corner, Arena (seafood and steakhouse), Canangsari, Kedaton, Poolside Tirta at the Sanur Beach Hotel, and the Trattoria Da Marco.

All of the major hotels in Nusa Dua have restaurants that are worth a visit. Plus, there is Ulam near the Putri Bali Hotel, specializing in Balinese cuisine, and the Diah Agustini Restaurant, among others.

One will have to go to Denpasar for Burger King but Swensen's Ice Cream has branches in both Denpasar and Sanur.

As one travels around the island on sightseeing and shopping tours, one will find that most tourist centers boast at least one outstanding restaurant: The Batur Garden in Kintamani, the Bali Handara Country Club in Bedugul, Mutiari in Gianyar, Bukit Jambul Garden in Klungkung, the Royal Garden in Mengwi. . . .

Shopping

Since much space already has been devoted to shopping in Bali, and since the whole island operates practically as one gigantic open market, it almost seems redundant to list shopping locations. However, some recommended souvenir and artshops in Denpasar are:

Arjuna Art Shop. Paintings, textiles, silver, leather. Jalan Gajah Mada 38.

Batik Karis Center. Batik articles and yard goods. Jalan Kartini 14.

Basakih Art Shop. Paintings, statues, carvings, textiles, silverwork. Jalan Surapati 20.

Hawaii. Paintings, statues, carvings, silverwork, puppets. Jalan Gajah Mada 1–3.

Pelangi Art Shop. Paintings, statues, carvings, textiles, baskets, etc. Jalan Gajah Mada 44.

Titiya Art Shop. Paintings, statues, baskets, batik, silverwork, garments. Jalan Arjuna 44.

Yudistira Art Shop. Paintings, statues, carvings, textiles, basketry, silverwork, coconut handicraft and dance wear. Jalan Gajah Mada 42.

Denpasar also boasts several department stores which carry just about everything: Dewata Ayu on Jalan Panglima Sudirman; Tiara Dewata on Jalan Majend Sutoyo; M'A on Jalan Diponegoro; Libi on Jalan Teuhu Uman; and Indra Plaza on Jalan Gajah Mada.

Nusa Dua's biggest department store is Tragia in the Ngurah Rai Shopping Center.

Kuta's shopping strip is something else. Just about anything a visitor could possibly want is for sale within a couple of blocks. Some examples: C. V. Diana garment showroom, Sherlin garments, Pelangi for leather and batik, Anatoma gold jewelers, Prince Leather, Bali Wood for art carvings, Mario International

for handcrafted silver, Target for clothing. Or just ask. Everything
is there, within walking distance.

Bali is called a paradise for many things, for its ubiquitous
beauty, for its scenic beaches and mountain temples, its placid
rice paddies, its pleasant populace. It just happens that Bali has
become a shopper's paradise, too.

CHAPTER 9

Other Islands

The few words offered in this broad general roundup of attractions beyond Java and Bali do not pretend to give more than a sampling of this multifaceted archipelago, and do not mean to dismiss any island, populated or not, as insignificant. But after all, there are some 17,000 islands sprawled from Malaysia, south to Australia, and hooking up again northward almost to the Philippines. To give specific islands the coverage they deserve would require volumes.

All of the 6,000 inhabited islands of Indonesia hold some attraction beyond the scenery, perhaps visiting primitive villages, or attending market days, when tribesmen and women emerge from the jungles bearing food and handicrafts. And since sultans once ruled most of the archipelago, all of which was swept by religious influences, it is a rare island which does not have its temple and palace as showplace or ruins.

But only the more adventurous travelers will visit the most isolated islands, proceeding by boat or small plane when other transportation is lacking, and making do with a variety of "substandard" accommodations: *losemans* or guest houses, village dwellings, tents or sleeping bags. Lombok is the closest.

Lombok

Only a short ferry ride to the east from Bali, across a strait churning with whirlpools and alive with sea creatures, lies the island of Lombok, similar in size and topography to Bali, but much less populated and much less developed.

The average visitor can sample the character of Lombok in a compact area of approximately twenty square miles, inland from the landing port of Lembar, and the road which circles the island puts bathers and skindivers within an hour's reach of many uncrowded beaches.

Lombok is the westernmost of what the Dutch called the Lesser Sundas, a chain of islands stretching eastward more than five hundred miles to Timor, the latter within a boomerang's throw of Australia's northern tip. Indonesia renamed the islands Nusa Tenggara, abandoning the derogatory "lesser."

But almost everything here—with the possible exception of a soaring volcanic mountain range—does seem on a lesser scale than the more favored islands to the west. Even the royal palace at Cakranegara, the former capital, is a mere bungalow, but interesting, nevertheless, for its combined Dutch and native influence.

Most visitors to Lombok come seeking a less-crowded, perhaps slower-paced version of Bali; or they come for the beaches and marine life. Some also come for the strenuous climb to the top of Mount Rinjani, at 12,300 feet the second highest mountain in Indonesia. The trek is only for the hardy: it is a two-day volcanic expedition without a Hilton in sight. But those who do undertake the journey say that the view from the top—revealing a crater lake and the panorama of eastern islands—is well worth the effort. You need a police permit, available in Mataram, a sleeping bag, food and water, and the climb can only be made in the dry season, April to October.

The modern capital, Mataram, and the neighboring coastal

village Ampenan, although picturesque, have few focal points for most tourists, who will find the marketplace, temples and shrines of Cakranegara, where a few reminders of its bloody history remain, more fascinating.

However, these towns, along with Sweta, the easternmost of the four, form a conglomerate in which the city boundaries are virtually indistinguishable.

The visitor will find good transportation, modest hotels and restaurants, bazaar shopping opportunities and even a tourist office.

Three pancake-like coral islands lying off the northwest coast of Lombok, the Gili Islands, are attracting an increasing number of snorkelers and beach lovers. Other "Gilis," spotted all around offshore Lombok, are numerous but harder to reach.

Sumbawa

From the air, Sumbawa at first looks like a collection of separate volcanoes, but these high points are linked by necks of land, and a road ties together the three distinct parts of the island.

Inhabited by less than a million fishermen and farmers, among them the most devout Muslims in all Indonesia, the island contains few accommodations or attractions for the traditional tourist, and not many visitors do make the trip.

Two principal towns, Sumbawa Besar and Bimi, and a dozen smaller villages dot the rather rugged landscape over which looms one of the deadliest volcanoes known on earth, one whose history of violence is said to exceed even Krakatau and Vesuvius. The volcano Tambora, now dormant, erupted in 1815 with an explosion that was heard all the way to Sumatra, a thousand miles west. The direct and indirect death toll was estimated as 92,000.

Tidal waves were only part of the secondary action. Neighboring Lombok, for example, was buried in a twenty-inch blanket of ash. Crop failure and starvation followed.

Indeed, the impact was even felt in Europe and America. Red sunsets were observed all over the globe as millions of tons of volcanic ash spread in the stratosphere, blotting out the sun and creating what was called "the year without a summer." It snowed in June in New England. A July cold wave froze well water in Maine, and wintry storms continued throughout the summer of 1916, killing virtually all crops. In August it snowed in London. Crop failures worldwide led to famine and epidemic disease.

It's possible for hikers to reach the desolate rim of this historic monster, the crater of which still hisses and roars, its vestigial steam vents emitting fumes of sulfur. The spectacle of nature's ravages is awesome and more than inspiring.

The scenery may be fantastic, but Sumbawa is off the beaten track except as a jumping-off point for Sulawesi and Komodo by ferry and flight, facilities which are better availiable elsewhere.

Sumba

Sumba, to the south of Sumbawa and almost its equal in size, also lies in the backwaters of traditional tourism, although people do test the irregular airline schedule (Merpati) to look over the local woven *ikat* textiles, the high-sloped roofs of the village Maru, and its festivals, which include non-Queensbury fist-fighting, horseback duels with lances, and animal sacrifice.

A few hotels are available in the capital city of Waingapu and in Waikalubak, but much of the island is undisturbed by regular visitors. Life here, in almost total isolation, is closer to old, unspoiled native ways. Leave your traveler's checks at home.

Komodo

Why do so many travelers seek out transportation to the desolate island of Komodo, where the only village contains merely five hundred natives?

Komodo Island and its poor neighbor Rinca, sandwiched between Sumbawa and Flores, are the only places in the world where dwells the endangered species *varanus Komodoensis*, popularly known as the Komodo dragon.

The Komodo dragon, which natives call *ora*, grows to ten feet in length and looks vaguely like a shrunken-nosed alligator on stilts. Theories hold that the legendary Chinese dragon originated from this fearful creature which fights with teeth, claws and a powerful, substantial tail. Basically, it's an overgrown monitor lizard.

There are only about two thousand of the now-protected species in existence. A couple of zoos on Java have the lizard on display, and the San Diego, California, zoo was scheduled to take possession of a pair in 1991. But this is the only native habitat.

It is a bleak island with a meager tourist camp offering the only accommodations. Visitors are warned not to wander off on their own, lest they whet the appetite of a dragon hiding in the bushes, step on a snake, or otherwise upset the local ecology. The usual routine is for visitors to pay villagers to attract the omnivorous, sun-loving, but shy Komodo dragon by sacrificing a goat, whose meat will bring out the reclusive creature for a photo session.

Organized tours are available through Bali travel agents, the cost running to approximately $400 a person, depending on the number in a group, but Komodo Island also can be reached by ferry or charter boat, from Sape on Sumbawa, or from the port of Labuhanbajo on the neighboring island to the east, Flores.

Flores

Although subjected to different waves of invasion by regional enemies as well as European conquerors through the centuries, Flores and the other islands to the east (forming the rest of Nusa Tenggara) have been linked to one another through history by common interests and trade.

Flores (meaning flower, a name bestowed by the Portuguese nearly five hundred years ago) demonstrates one native Indonesian characteristic perhaps better than any other island: the adaptability of the people.

As a result of the religio-commercial wars which outsiders conducted over the souls and products of the islands, Flores inhabitants are now mostly Catholic, but they practice the religion with a number of variations, still making offerings to their ancestors' spirits who reside in nature, still holding the once-worshiped snake in traditional high regard, and still, for example, purchasing their brides for a fair price of water buffalo, pigs and ivory. Thus ancient rituals survive, absorbed into daily life.

Rituals like the whip duels associated with the marriage ceremony, and the deer hunt, which is linked with fertility observances, complement the volcanoes and spectacular crater lakes which vary in color from red to green, as the major attractions for visitors.

Solor and Alor

East of Flores lies a chain of islands that includes Solor, location of a 16th-century Portuguese fort; Lembata, once a primitive whaling center; Pantar; and Alor, known for the ancient bronze drums called *mokos*, thousands of them, used by the natives.

These islands are not in the mainstream of tourism. They have rugged terrain with limited access, and spartan accommodations. But the islands—where head-hunting died out only after World War II and pearl diving remains part of the economy—reward the visitor with an insightful glimpse of things past.

Timor

Timor, the easternmost outpost of Nusa Tenggara, only recently opened up to tourism, because East Timor was involved in what might be called an ownership dispute. A takeover by staunchly anti-communist Indonesian forces, who claimed that the independent half-island was in danger of going red, seems to have settled the question, not without the presentation of arms.

Dili, the capital of the east sector, is said to be a fascinating place to visit, although Westerners are rare. Kupang, the west Timor capital, is the largest city in all Nusa Tenggara, with a population of about 100,000. It might be remembered as the landing place of *Bounty* captain Bligh after he was set adrift in the South Pacific by mutineers.

Kupang also is the gateway to the isolated Roti and Sawu islands, noted for producing *ikat* textiles, in which individual threads are dyed, and for the fact that natives subsist almost solely on the lontar palm. These are the southernmost of all Indonesian islands, only a brief hop from Darwin, Australia, and due to this proximity, the whole complex of Timor and its surrounding islands is experiencing a growing wave of adventurous Australian visitors.

The Malukus

The Malukus, a now-obscure chain of hundreds of islands, once were perhaps the most sought after territories on earth. These were the Spice Islands, the only place where Europe could find precious cloves, nutmeg and mace. Because of these spices and others, the islands were the object of hundreds of years of rivalry between covetous Europeans, principally the Portuguese and the Dutch.

Mentioned by Ptolemy, Pliny and Marco Polo, these islands, strewn across the sea north and west of Irian Jaya, were the real goals of Magellan and Columbus.

One other historical footnote: The Dutch, always shrewd bargainers, made a swap with the British in a 1667 treaty: Britain gave up its claim to the Bandas in Maluku and the Dutch ceded to them a useless little island across the Hudson River in the American colonies. It was called Manhattan.

Although politically stable today, the islands were rocked by the uprisings of independence-seeking natives until the 1960s, long after the Dutch had transported thousands of their own people back to the Netherlands, giving in to Indonesian rule.

Some remains of forts can still be seen on the islands, where visitors are few and accommodations are not first class. There are some active volcanoes. One, Mount Api, erupted in 1988, forcing evacuations. The islands are perhaps best known today among crossword puzzle fans: Ambon, Sula, Halmahera, Seram, Ternate, Bacan, Buru and Obi, to name a few of the thousand.

Relics of colonial days and some spectacular undersea gardens are the chief attractions of the Mulukus, which, like the spice trade, faded long ago.

En route to Irian Jaya, which formerly was the western half of New Guinea, one finds a scattering of islands with exotic names: Liti, Sermata, Babar, Tanimbar, Kai and the Aru islands. While a couple of these rival Bali or Lombok in size, there are little other grounds for comparison.

These are the southern Maluku Islands, which are reachable by plane and boat and have some attractions, such as the rare birds of paradise on the Arus. But accommodations for visitors are extremely limited, making an excursion more of an expedition than a tour. You travel by foot or boat, and not even many of the natives bother to penetrate too far inland, into the woods and mountains.

Irian Jaya

Irian Jaya is perhaps the wildest region on earth, largely comprised of impenetrable rain forest, swamps and mountains—at least one of which remains snow-capped year around, even in the tropics.

But thanks in large part to Garuda airlines, which carved out a refueling stop on the Irian Jaya island of Biak, where passengers are treated to native dancers during the stopover to Bali, curiosity has been aroused about this "last frontier." Many people now want to go there, perhaps just to say they've been to the wildest.

Natives here, believed to be related to the Australian aborigines, some of them just emerging from a Stone Age lifestyle, are still discovering the ruins of missing World War II fighter planes in the jungles, where General Douglas MacArthur made his campaign headquarters.

Although the government has undertaken an aggressive program of road-building, migration and development (mining, lumber and oil), many interior areas of Irian Jaya are restricted for travelers. The coastal cities, which have modest hotels, afford little attraction.

Nevertheless, the chance to visit the primitive tribes, such as the Dani, which cling to ways little changed since their discovery by the outside world in the 1930s, lures a number of hardy tourists to these parts.

The unspoiled wildlife, including tree kangaroos, cockatoos, cassowaries and crocodiles, can be found in such abundance as nowhere else on the planet. Indonesia's tallest mountain, Jaya, 17,875 feet high, dominates the rugged interior. There have been no confirmed reports of cannibalism since the mid-1970s.

Tours are available into such villages as Wamena in the Baleim Valley, where dances are performed for visitors. Tribesmen bearing spears, naked except for penis gourds, dwell within reach of coastal settlements that present a "boom town" atmosphere, and this wild setting holds intrigue for many an outsider who shuns the beaten path of tourism.

Sulawesi

Of all the islands beyond Java and Bali, Sulawesi, the great, orchid-shaped sprawl once known as Celebes, holds the greatest appeal to visitors, and tourism is rapidly becoming a major factor there.

In Sulawesi one finds the tall-masted *pinisi* schooners, the last remaining trade sailing fleets in the world, manned by the Bugi tribesmen who historically spread terror among the spice traders in centuries of piracy. All sailors carried home scary tales of the "Bugi man."

Another tribe of intrigue, in the interior, are the Torajans. In reverence for their dead, they display them in effigy on cliffsides in colorful, if bloody, rituals. The swooping, saddle-shaped roofs of their village houses recall the prows of the ships that their ancestors arrived in centuries ago. Also in Sulawesi, there are caves to explore, mighty waterfalls, scenic mountains and some relics of the former kingdom of Gowa, which dates back centuries before the first Europeans came here.

Ujung Pandang, the capital of South Sulawesi, which was called Makassar for hundreds of years can be reached by air on a good schedule, or by ship. Those seeking the Torajans face another short flight to Makale (or an eight-hour drive), all of which can be arranged in package tours. But during high season, July to September, the limited local facilities can become overtaxed, so plans must be made well in advance.

Fort Rotterdam, a reminder of Dutch colonial power which has been turned into museums and historic displays, today is surrounded by the port city Ujung Pandang. Close by are the tomb of a 1600s sultan, a mosque from the same era, Chinese temples, orchid gardens, and a monument to Prince Diponegoro, the heroic Javanese rebel captured by Dutch treachery and exiled in a dungeon at the fort.

The waterfalls and limestone caves, some with paintings said to be five thousand years old, are located within an hour's drive, near Maros, northeast of the capital. The center of boatbuilding by the Bugis and Makassarese will be found at Bantaeng, to the southeast. The largest cave, Goa Mampu, is near Wattampone on the east coast; visitors are warned that besides stalagmites and stalactites, the cave is full of bats. Arrangements for transportation to these and other points of interest can be made quite easily in Ujung Pandang.

Central, North and Southeast Sulawesi, each with its distinct peninsula and sandy beaches, are all accessible by boat and airplane, but these districts are not common traveler's destinations, even though they have a tourist office. Interestingly, the north is experiencing a baby gold rush near Kotamobagu.

The capital of the north province, Manado, may be the most "westernized" of all Indonesian cities. The dominant tribe, the Minikasans, are Christians, and the popular fashion among the young is T-shirts and jeans. Their music is more disco than drum, and to view more traditional native life requires a trek into the interior.

The north is probably the most interesting province, after South Sulawesi. Coral reefs, volcanoes, caves, pre-Christian rock tombs, copra plantations, sandy beaches, and lakes are among the most popular sites for visitors. The little islands which reach upward from Manado stretch to within a stone's throw of the Philippines.

Except for its north and south provinces, Sulawesi would seem to be in no danger of being overrun with tourists, but perhaps precisely because few people go there, it seems to attract the unconventional traveler, weary of sharing his or her experiences with a busload of casually disinterested strangers.

Kalimantan

Kalimantan shares one of the world's largest islands, Borneo, with two East Malaysian provinces and the oil-rich kingdom of Brunei. It is separated from them by steep mountain ranges that traverse the land mass two-thirds of the way north.

Oil, lumber, rubber and some mining interests prevail in Kalimantan, setting the atmosphere especially in the coastal cities; but tourism persists, attracted principally by the Dyak tribes of the interior, who wear heavy, deforming earrings, tattoo their bodies and dwell in traditional longhouses—all practices discouraged by the central government.

The orangutan and other jungle creatures, the gibbon, crocodiles, leopards, hornbills and fresh water dolphins also inhabit the interior, chased there, like the Dyak, by encroaching industry.

Visa problems may arise if one tries to combine a visit to Malaysian Sarawak, or otherwise detour from the established entry points at Pontianak in West Kalimantan or Balikpapan on the opposite coast, to which there are regular flights. Interior travel, for the most part, is restricted to the waterways, not by red tape but by the density of the jungle, coastal swamps, and the roughness of existing roads.

This is a frontier land but some safari-type tours can be arranged in advance, and some cities and villages are really worth seeing before they change completely. Among these are Merak for its orchid forest: Banjarmasin and Poutianak for their river and canal life; Singkawang for its dominant Chinese culture; Pauan Kembang and Palau Kaget for monkeys; Banjarbaru for its market; Cempaka for diamond and gold mines; and Panghalan Bun as the jumping-off point for Camp Leakey, an orangutan research facility in Tanjung Puting National Park.

None of these are luxurious resorts and in the few spots in Kalimantan where luxury can be had, the well-paid foreign oil and mining technicians working the area often have run the prices up and the availability down.

Sumatra

Although Java and Bali are the most popular islands of Indonesia, both with natives and visitors, Sumatra, off Java's western tip and extending north past Singapore, alongside mainland Malaysia, is fast becoming another major tourist attraction.

Geography has spelled the destiny of much of Indonesia, and Sumatra, stretched beside the key waterway, the Malakka Strait, sailed by seafarers for centuries, usually has been first to feel the influences brought from foreign shores.

Today, with the oil industry opening up new roads inland, with new international agreements for developing the offshore Riau islands and Batam in co-operation with neighbor Singapore, and with an overflow of tourists from Singapore, Malaysia and Thailand, more and more people are passing through Sumatra—and taking notice—on the way to and from Java.

A wild green region where loincloths and naked chests were only banned as recently as the mid-1950s, Sumatra, called the world's fifth largest island, spans a distance greater than that between New York and Chicago, or Madrid and Rome. To tourists it offers adventure in an unspoiled, relatively untrammeled land.

As a tourist destination on its own, Sumatra's biggest attraction is the Lake Toba district, which is included in every organized tour of the island. Aside from the spectacular beauty, this mountain lake wonderland in the north contains an island, Samosir, which is the center of the world for the Batak tribe, former headhunters and ritual cannibals who, until recently, were one of the most isolated tribes on earth.

Their native houses, sway-backed with twin peaks, are elevated on stilts, the better for defense, and traditionally entry was only through a trap door in the bottom. Some historians think that the Bataks are related to the Dayaks of Kalimantan and/or the Torojans of Sulawesi—all of them being in some way escapees from the invading hordes that swept down from Thailand and Burma centuries ago.

Curiously, the music and costumes of the Bataks bears an astounding resemblance to that of the Mexicans. When American visitors first see and hear Batak musicians in a hotel lounge, they often presume that the performers were for some reason imported from Mexico, so similar is the sound and clothing.

Package tours of Sumatra—available in 3-, 4-, 5-, 8-, and 13-day trips, usually include the city of Medan, an orangutan rehabilitation center, temples and ruins, rubber plantations, waterfalls, markets, and the highly unusual Minangkabau tribal villages.

Medan, the provincial capital of North Sumatra, shows an old elegance from its days as a colonial plantation headquarters city, despite crowding from its current million-plus population. Fifty years ago, in the pre-war era, Medan was known as "the most European city in the Indies."

In the highlands, a short distance away, is the cool mountain resort of Brastagi, once a playground of rich planters. Nearby is Lingga, a Batak village where traditional houses are still occupied by tribespeople. At Pematang, a two-hundred-year-old compound of Batak teak houses can be seen.

Prapat, on Lake Toba's northern shore, is the main attraction of most visitors to the area. The town has many hotels, restaurants and facilities for water sports, and is the departure point of regular ferries to Samosir Island in the middle of the lake, where Batak homes are clustered. The remains of an ancient court with stone chairs, where many a person's fate was decided, still stand. The lake itself, with sheer cliffs, and waterfalls nearby, is renowned as an unequalled scenic spot.

Sibolga, an ocean water sports center, is the district's principal port on the Indian Ocean and the point of departure for boats to Nias Island.

The Nias islanders, also a primitive tribe with a history of head-hunting and human sacrifice, have been traced back more than two thousand years. Their way of life scarcely changed until the 19th century, because of their isolation. The natives stage war dances for visitors and demonstrate their stone-jumping ritual, which originally was a coming-of-age challenge for would-be warriors, testing their ability to leap over a stone, or pile of stones, more than six feet high. The trip to Nias Island usually requires an overnight plan because the boat ride alone can take ten hours or more, one way.

Also in North Sumatra, visitors often make the trip two hours north of Medan for the Langkat Nature Reserve and its orang-utan rehabilitation center, where animals released from captivity are prepared to resume a jungle life. The reserve includes pro-tected areas for elephants, deer and a variety of other wildlife.

Little is said in most tourist books about the province of Aceh, which covers the northern tip of Sumatra and, like Yogyakarta, enjoys a good deal of autonomy. Perhaps this is for the best. Ask the average Indonesian on Java or Bali, and chances are they don't even know where Aceh is. This is odd because, in fact, Aceh was the first point of current-day Indonesia to encounter each of the influences which gradually spread throughout the archipelago: the influence of traders, invaders and religious con-versions.

Aceh today is almost completely unlike the rest of Indonesia; the people are closer to traditional, fundamental Muslims than anywhere else, for example. Periodic outbursts of political unrest occur and—again, unlike the general Indonesian scene—visitors should check carefully before planning to include Aceh in their tour. It's really too bad, because the province, with its capital Banda Aceh linked by daily Garuda flights, contains many of the outstanding features typical of Indonesia: jungle wilderness parks, sandy beaches, mountain resorts and a wealth of history.

More popular with visitors is the land of the Minangkabau tribes in West Sumatra. This rare society is matriarchal, that is, inheritance and family matters are dominated openly by the women.

Women own the property and inherit it, children become members of their mother's family group, and the mother's brothers assume most of the duties of the children's father. Thus, to the men, the children of their sisters are more theirs than their own. The Minangkaban men have become noted for wanderlust and an entrepreneural spirit which leads them to seek out their fortune elsewhere, but whether this resulted from the matriarchal system or gave rise to it, is not certain.

Padang and Bukittinggi are the most visited towns in the West Sumatra province, which is the "land of the Minang." Padang's museum and art center both enjoy good reputations, and nearby Bungus Bay attracts the sea-loving crowds. Bukittinggi, in the highlands a short distance north, can be reached by road, but the jungle train ride, across rivers, through mountain tunnels, and past high waterfalls, can evoke a sense of the wilderness akin to the River Kwai of the movies.

Overland tours of Sumatra by bus (Trans-Indonesia, Setia) depart from Jakarta and cross the Sunda Strait by ferry into South Sumatra, heading up to the provincial capital of Palembang, a river city with many older houses on stilts. Palembang has an interesting museum and other sites, but it is basically an oil town, like Jambi and Pekanbaru island to the north.

In the Lampung area, not far from the ferry landing point, visitors can see Sumatra tigers and elephants in the Way Kambas Reserve. Elephant rides can be arranged at a project where the animals are trained.

It can make an exciting, brief side trip out of Jakarta to ride the ferry across to Sumatra, view Krakatau volcano during the passage, and spend a day or more photographing wild animals at the Way Kambas Reserve.

Appendix

INDONESIA AT A GLANCE

REPUBLIC OF INDONESIA: A unitary republic with
    sovereignty vested in the people
PRESIDENT: Soeharto, reelected for his fifth term on March
    10, 1988
LOCATION: In Southeast Asia between continental Asia and
    Australia, the Pacific and Indian oceans.
GEOGRAPHY: World's largest archipelago: 17,508 islands;
    6,000 inhabited.
PROVINCES: 27
CLIMATE: Wet season November–April; dry season, May–
    October; average temperature: 91.4° Farenheit.
POPULATION: 185,000,000, the fifth largest country after
    U.S.A.
RELIGIONS: Islam, Christianity, Hinduism, and Buddhism.
CAPITAL: Jakarta, population: 8,000,000
NATIONAL DAY: August 17
NATIONAL MOTTO: *Bhinneka Tunggal Ila* (Unity in
    Diversity)
NATIONAL LANGUAGE: Bahasa Indonesia (Indonesian)

NATIONAL IDEOLOGY:
Pancasila: Five inseparable and mutually qualifying
    fundamental principles:
1. Belief in the One Supreme God
2. A just and civilized humanity
3. The unity of Indonesia
4. Democracy led by the wisdom of deliberations among
    representatives
5. Social justice for all the people of Indonesia
CURRENCY: Rupiah (Rp.); U.S. $1 = Rp. 1,830
NATIONAL LAW: 1945 Constitution

INSTANT *INDONESIAN*

By the time you finish reading this page, you will be able to
speak Bahasa Indonesia, the national language of Java and Bali
. . . at least a little.

In fact, you already know a few words. For example, want to
call a taxi? Shout, *"Taksi!"* You want to go to the station? Ask for
stasiun. In Indonesia bank is *bank*, apple is *apel*, coffee is *kopi*
and car is *mobil.* Can you say *"ya"*? That means yes.

A lot of Indonesian words translate phonetically into the same
or almost the same in English. But, of course, there are differences. No is *tidak.* Water equals *air,* and bus becomes *bis.*

The most useful words for visitors follow here. The letter "a"
usually is sounded like *ah*, while "ee" is as in *bed*, "u" is as in
put, "i" like in *feel*, "o" as in *all*; "r" is rolled a little; "c" is always
pronounced *ch*. There are no articles (the, a, an), no plurals, and
no strong stress.

How much/how many? . . . . *berapa*
What is? . . . . *apa*
This . . . . *ini*
That . . . . *itu*
Where is? . . . . *di mana ada*
Which way? . . . . *ke mana*

When?	*kapan*
What time?	*jam berapa*
Money	*uang (wang)*
I want to go to	*mau pergi ke*
I want to buy	*saya mau beli*
I	*saya*
You	*saudara*
He/She	*dia*
It	*ia*
We	*kita*
They	*mereka*
Sorry	*ma'af*
Excuse me	*permisi*
Thank you	*terima kasih*
Very much	*banyak*
Please	*tolong*
Big	*besar*
Small	*kecil*
Store	*toko*
Room	*kamar*
Bath	*mandi*
Ticket	*karci*
Train	*kereta api*
Airport	*bandar udara*
Drug store	*apotik*
Hospital	*rumah sakit*
Town	*kota*
Office	*kantor*
Post office	*kantor pos*
Entrance	*masuk*
Exit	*berang*
Here	*di sini*
Eat	*makan*
Drink	*minum*
Breakfast	*makan pagi*
Lunch	*makan siang*

Dinner . . . . *makan malam*
Hot. . . . . *panas*
Cold. . . . . *dingin*
Rice. . . . . *nasi*
Tea. . . . . *teh*
Sugar. . . . . *gula*
Salt. . . . . *garam*
Bread . . . . *roti*
Fish. . . . . *ikan*
Chicken. . . . . *ayam*
Pork. . . . . *babi*
Beef. . . . . *sapi*
Finished. . . . . *habis*
Check (bill). . . . . *rekening*

The all-purpose greeting word in Java and Bali is *selamat,* usually run together so it sounds like "slammet." You say *selamat pagi* for good morning until about 10 a.m., *selamat malam* for good night. In between there are *selamat siang* for good afternoon (confusingly, 10 a.m. to 3 p.m.) and *selamat sore,* which covers from 3 p.m. until dusk. If you are saying goodbye to someone, it's *selamat jalan. Selamat.*

Air, train and bus schedules and fares to help in planning travel in and around Java and Bali.

GARUDA DOMESTIC AIRFARES

TO \ FROM	JAKARTA	SURABAYA	DENPASAR	MEDAN
Ambon	267.000	232.000	186.000	–
Balikpapan	177.000	124.000	–	300.000
Banda Aceh	–	–	–	•
Bandar Lampung	39.000	–	–	–
Bandung	37.000	83.000	122.000	-·
Banjarmasin	138.000	82.000	–	–
B a t a m	131.000	–	223.000	123.000
Bengkulu	92.000	–	–	–
B i a k	382.000	343.000	300.000	–
Denpasar	125.000	51.000	–	261.000
D i l i	283.000	209.000	158.000	–
Jakarta	–	103.000	125.000	192.000
J a m b i	98.000	–	–	–
Jayapura	423.000	417.000	382.000	–
Kendari	239.000	161.000	–	–
Kupang	251.000	171.000	128.000	–
Manado	311.000	236.000	–	–
Mataram	143.000	66.000	–	–
M e d a n	192.000	–	261.000	–
Merauke	506.000	–	–	88.000
P a d a n g	138.000	–	–	–
P a l u	268.000	174.000	–	–
Palangkaraya	132.000	–	–	–
Palembang	75.000	152.000	145.000	–
Pangkalpinang	77.000	–	–	–
Pakanbaru	140.000	–	–	79.000
Pontianak	112.000	–	–	207.000
Semarang	64.000	40.000	89.000	–
S o l o	72.000	32.000	–	–
Sorong	307.000	289.000	246.000	–
Surabaya	103.000	–	51.000	–
Tanjung Pandan	68.000	–	–	–
Timika	420.000	–	320.000	–
Ujung Pandang	188.000	118.000	88.000	361.000
Yogyakarta	72.000	–	67.000	–

SEMPATI AIR FARES (Including Tax)

From – To	Fares
JAKARTA	
Pontianak	Rp. 127.300
Pangkal Pinang	Rp. 88.880
Tanjung Pinang	Rp. 141.680
Tanjung Pandan	Rp. 78.980
Singkep	Rp. 149.380
Pekan Baru	Rp. 158.180

MANDALA AIR FARES

From - to	Fares
JAKARTA	
Medan	Rp. 136.200
Padang	Rp. 117.300
Semarang	Rp. 54.400
Surabaya	Rp. 87.600
Ujung Pandang	Rp. 159.800
Ambon	Rp. 227.000
Manado	Rp. 264.400
SURABAYA	
Ambon	Rp. 197.200
Manado	Rp. 200.600
Ujung Pandang	Rp. 100.300
UJUNG PANDANG :	
Ambon	Rp. 108.800
Manado	Rp. 116.500

JOINT FARES GARUDA/MERPATI

TO - FROM		JAKARTA	SEMARANG
Manado	– Ternate	326.000	–
Balikpapan	– Samarinda	192.000	153.000
Balikpapan	– Tarakan	233.000	–
Manado	– Gorontalo	324.000	–
Ambon	– Ternate	316.000	–

SURABAYA	DENPASAR	UJUNG PANDANG
259.000	239.000	–
144.000	145.000	–
185.000	–	–
256.000	–	167.000
284.000	243.000	190.000

GARUDA SHUTTLE SERVICE AIR FARES

ROUTE	CLASS	ADULT	CHILD	INFANT
Jakarta – Surabaya	Y	118.000	61.000	12.000
	C	147.000	76.000	15.000
	F	163.000	84.000	17.000
Jakarta – Semarang	Y	75.000	40.000	8.000

MERPATI DOMESTIC ARIFARES

FROM	JAKARTA	SURABAYA	DENPASAR
Ambon	267.000	232.000	186.000
Balikpapan	177.000	124.000	125.000
Bandung	37.000	83.000	122.000
Banjarmasin	138.000	82.000	
B a t a m	131.000	–	223.000
Bengkulu	92.000	–	
Biak	382.000	343.000	300.000
Berau	–	–	–
Cilacap	75.000	–	–
Cirebon	47.000	–	–
Denpasar	125.000	51.000	–
Dumai	130.000	–	–
D i l i	–	209.000	158.000
J a m b i	98.000	–	–
Jayapura	423.000	417.000	382.000
Yogyakarta	72.000	–	67.000
K e n d a r i	239.000	161.000	–
Ketapang	129.000	–	–
Kupang	251.000	171.000	128.000
M a l a n g	103.000	–	51.000
M a n a d o	311.000	236.000	214.000
Manokwari	435.000	–	–
Mataram	143.000	66.000	33.000
Maumere	241.000	–	–
M e d a n	192.000	–	261.000
P a d a n g	138.000	–	–
Pakanbaru	140.000	–	–
Palembang	75.000	152.000	–
P a l u	268.000	174.000	–
Pangkalanbun	156.000	–	–
Pangkalpinang	77.000	–	–
Pontianak	112.000	–	–
Palangkaraya	–	–	–
R e n g a t	125.000	–	–
Ruteng	–	–	119.000
Samarinda	215.000	40.000	89.000
Semarang	64.000	40.000	89.000
Singkep	139.000	–	–
S o l o	72.000	32.000	83.000
Sorong	307.000	–	246.000
Surabaya	103.000	–	51.000
Sumbawa	–	–	53.000
Sumenep	–	–	52.000
Tanjung Pandan	68.000	–	–
Tanjung Pinang	125.000	–	–
Tarakan	241.000	–	–
Tambulaka	–	–	95.000
Timika	–	–	320.000
Ujung Pandang	188.000	–	88.000
Waingapu	228.000	–	103.000

BOURAQ AIR FARES

From/to	Class	
	Business	Economy
JAKARTA		
Balikpapan	Rp. 221.000	Rp 177.000
Bandung	Rp. 46.000	Rp. 37.000
Banjarmasin	Rp. 172.000	Rp. 138.000
Denpasar	Rp. 156.000	Rp. 125.000
Manado	Rp. 389.000	Rp. 311.000
P a l u	Rp. 335.000	Rp. 268.000
Pontianak	Rp. 140.000	Rp. 112.000
Semarang	Rp. 80.000	Rp. 64.000
Surabaya	Rp. 129.000	Rp. 103.000
Tarakan	Rp. –	Rp. 241.000
Yogyakarta	Rp. 90.000	Rp. 72.000
DENPASAR		
Bandung	Rp. 152.000	Rp. 122.000
Jakarta	Rp. 156.000	Rp 125.000
Kupang	Rp. 160.000	Rp. 128.000
Maumere	Rp. –	Rp. 116.000
Surabaya	Rp. 64.000	Rp. 51.000
Waingapu	Rp. –	Rp. 103.000
SURABAYA		
Balikpapan	Rp. 155.000	Rp. 124.000
Banjarmasin	Rp. 102.000	Rp. 82.000
Bandung	Rp. 104.000	Rp. 83.000
Denpasar	Rp. 64.000	Rp. 51.000
Jakarta	Rp. 129.000	Rp. 103.000
Kupang	Rp. 214.000	Rp. 171.000
Manado	Rp. 295.000	Rp. 236.000
Maumere	Rp. –	Rp. 149.000
P a l u	Rp. 217.000	Rp. 174.000
Tarakan	Rp. –	Rp. 145.000
Waingapu	Rp. –	Rp. 123.000
UJUNG PANDANG		
Balikpapan	Rp. 171.000	Rp. 137.000
Gorontalo	Rp. –	Rp. 135.000
Manado	Rp. 171.000	Rp. 137.000
P a l u	Rp. 100.000	Rp. 80.000

TRAIN SCHEDULES AND FARES

1. JAKARTA - CIREBON

Trains		Gunung Jati	Cirebon Expres	Cirebon Expres	Fares		
					Gunung Jati		Cirebon Expres
From To	Route No	118	114	116	II	III	III
Jakarta Kota	D	07.00	10.00	15.300	4.000.-	3.100.-	5.000.-
Pasar Senen	D	07.18	.	.			
Gambir	D	.	10.14	15.48			
Jatinegara	D	07.33	10.31	16.05			
Cirebon	A	11.01	13.24	18.18			

2. JAKARTA - MERAK

Trains		Cepat	Cepat			Fares
Route	Route No	220	224	226	222	
Jakarta Kota	D	.	08.30	15.30	16.30	Jakarta-Rangkas Bitung
Tanah Abang	D	06.00	09.05	16.05	17.00	Rp. 900.-
Rangkas Bitung	A	08.30	11.28	18.15	19.07	Jakarta - Merak
Merak	A	10.15	.	.	20.53	Rp. 1.300.-

3. SURABAYA - SEMARANG - CIREBON - JAKARTA ROUTE

TRAINS		Cepat Semarang	Mutiara Utara	SBM Utara	Senja Utama	Senja ekonomi
Route	Route No	203	3	7	35	43
Surabaya Pasarturi	D	.	16.30	17.30	.	.
Semarang	A		21.45	22.52	.	.
	D	07.00	22.00	23.00	20.00	20.50
Cirebon	A	12.03	02.29	03.36	00.32	01.24
	D	12.12	02.40	03.50	00.50	01.39
Jatinegara	A	16.49	05.51	07.01	04.11	04.50
Gambir	A	.	06.13	.	.	.
Pasar Senen	A	17.06	.	07.19	04.28	05.06
Jakarta Kota	A	.	06.20	.	.	.

4. SURABAYA - JEMBER - BANYUWANGI

TRAINS / Route	Route No	Mutiara Timur (Siang)	Argopuro	Mutiara Timur (malam)	Fares — Mutiara	Fares — Argopuro
Surabaya Kota	D	09.30	13.49	22.00	Surabaya Jember	Surabaya Jember
Surabaya Gubeng	D	09.40	13.56	22.10	II = Rp. 3.000,-	Rp. 2.200,-
Jember	A	13.37	18.30	02.07	III = Rp. 2.800,-	
Jember	D	13.54		02.24	Surabaya - Banyuwangi	
Banyuwangi	A	16.15		04.45	II = Rp. 3.500,-	
					III = Rp. 2.800,-	
					Surabaya - Denpasar	
					II = Rp. 5.900,-	
					III = Rp. 5.200,-	

I. Schedule I

5 JAKARTA - CIREBON - SEMARANG - SURABAYA.

Trains / From - To	Route No	Cepat 204	Mutiara Utara *) 4	Tegal Arum 120	GBM Utara 80	Senja Utama 36	Senja Ekonomi 44	
Jakarta Kota	D	.	16.30	16.41	.	.	.	*) Reclining seats and air condition
Tanjung Priok	D	08.00	.	.	.	.	.	
Pasar Senen	D	08.28	.	16.59	17.53	19.50	21.00	
Jatinegara	D	08.45	.	17.16	.	.	21.15	
Cirebon	A	12.44	19.57	20.41	21.13	23.10	00.47	
	D	13.00	20.10	20.57	21.35	23.21	00.55	
Semarang	A	18.00	00.13	(To Tegal)	01.57	03.30	05.25	
	D	.	00.30	.	02.15			
Surabaya Pasarturi	A	.	05.45	.	07.37			

II. Fares

From - To	Class III	I	III	III	I	II	III	
Jakarta - Cirebon	2.300,-	22.000,-	3.600,-	4.200,-	13.500,-	9.500,-	5.800,-	All the fares including insurance and station Charge
- Semarang	4.000,-	22.000,-	.	4.700,-	13.500,-	9.500,-	5.800,-	
- Surabaya	.	25.000,-	.	7.700,-	13.500,-	9.500,-	5.800,-	
Cirebon - Semarang	2.300,-	22.000,-	.	4.200,-	.	.	.	
- Surabaya	.	22.000,-	.	5.300,-	.	.	.	
Semarang - Surabaya	.	22.000,-	.	4.200,-	.	.	.	

6. JAKARTA - CIREBON - YOGYAKARTA - SOLO/SURAKARTA - MADIUN - SURABAYA

I. Schedule

Station		Fajar Utama	Cepat Solo	GBM Selatan	Bangun Karta	Matamaja	Bima	Senja Utama Solo	Senja Utama Yogya	Senja Ekonomi Yogya	Senja Ekonomi Solo
Route No.		44	202	10	16	14	2	32	34	40	38
Jakarta - Kota	D						16.00				
Tanjung Priok	D		07.05								
Gambir	D	06.20		12.10	13.15	14.15		17.35	19.20	20.00	
Pasar Senin	D		07.33								21.10
Tanah Abang	D									20.17	21.33
Jatinegara	D		07.50		13.31						
Cirebon	A	09.40	11.49	16.15	17.09	17.51	19.27	20.55	22.50	23.53	01.21
Cirebon	D	09.55	12.10	16.28	17.20	18.00	19.45	20.57	23.05	00.00	01.31
Yogyakarta	A	15.20	19.05	23.07	23.36	00.20	01.15	03.28	05.20	07.00	07.00
Yogyakarta	D		19.15	23.22	23.47	00.25	01.30	03.35			07.57
Solo Surakarta	A		21.12	00.40	01.00	01.38	02.43	04.52			09.31
Solo Surakarta	D			00.45	01.10	01.50	02.50				
Madiun	A			02.15	02.50	03.20	04.15				
Madiun	D			02.20	03.05	03.40	04.20				
					(To Jombang)	(To Kadiri)					
Surabaya - Subang	A			05.05			06.57				
Surabaya Kota	A			05.40			07.40				

II. Fares

Trains		Bima		Fajar Utama		Senja Utama Solo/Yogyakarta		Senja Ekonomi, Solo-Yogya, Bangun Karta Matamaja		GBM Selatan	Cepat Solo
Route	Class	I.	Sleeper	I	II	I	II	II	III	III	III
Jakarta - Cirebon		17.000,-	21.000,-	9.500,-	6.000,-	13.500,-	9.500,-	8.500,-	5.800,-	4.200,-	1.800,-
· Yogyakarta		17.000,-	21.000,-	10.500,-	7.000,-	14.000,-	10.000,-	9.500,-	6.100,-	6.100,-	4.500,-
· Solo		18.000,-	22.000,-	·	·	15.000,-	11.000,-	10.000,-	7.600,-	7.200,-	4.600,-
· Madiun		20.000,-	24.500,-	·	·	..	..	11.000,-	–	7.700,-	–
· Surabaya		22.500,-	27.000,-	·	·	..	..	..	–	7.700,-	..
Cirebon - Yogyakarta		17.000,-	21.000,-	9.500,-	6.000,-	13.500,-	9.500,-	8.500,-	5.800,-	4.200,-	2.500,-
· Solo		17.000,-	21.000,-	·	·	13.500,-	9.500,-	8.500,-	5.800,-	5.000,-	3.200,-
· Madiun		17.000,-	21.000,-	·	·	..	..	8.500,-	5.800,-	6.600,-	..
· Surabaya		20.000,-	23.500,-	·	·	..	..	..	–	6.600,-	..
Yogyakarta - Solo		17.000,-	21.000,-	9.500,-	6.000,-	13.500,-	9.500,-	8.500,-	5.800,-	4.200,-	1.800,-
· Madiun		17.000,-	21.000,-	·	·	..	..	8.500,-	5.800,-	4.200,-	..
· Surabaya		17.000,-	21.000,-	·	·	..	..	..	..	4.200,-	..
Solo - Madiun		17.000,-	21.000,-	·	·	..	..	8.500,-	5.800,-	4.200,-	..
· Surabaya		17.000,-	21.000,-	·	·	..	..	8.500,-	5.800,-	4.200,-	..

7. SURABAYA - MADIUN - SOLO/SURAKARTA - YOGYAKARTA - CIREBON - JAKARTA

Trains		Cepat Solo	Fajar Utama	Purbaya	Argopuro	Senja Ek Yogya	Senja Ut Yogya	Senja Ek Solo	Senja Ut Solo	Bangun karta	GBM Selatan	Bima	Martamaja
Route	Route No	201	45	209	211	39	33	37	31	15	9	1	13
Surabaya													
Subang	D	.	.	06.15	10.27	.	.	.	.	.	.	.	.
Madiun	A	.	.	10.59	13.12	.	.	.	.	.	14.15	16.10	.
	D	.	.	11.05	13.17	.	.	.	.	.	17.00	18.31	.
Solo	A	.	.	12.50	15.02	.	.	.	.	15.50	17.05	18.36	19.20
	D	05.10	.	12.54	15.08	.	.	.	.	17.36	18.36	20.01	20.50
Yogyakarta	A	06.44	.	14.27	16.50	.	.	16.35	18.10	17.41	18.50	20.09	21.00
	D	07.01	07.50			.	.	18.17	19.28	10.54	20.10	21.10	22.13
Cirebon	A	14.17	13.06			17.00	17.45	18.22	19.35	20.10	20.25	21.35	22.22
	D	14.35	13.28			23.27	23.50	18.23	01.29	00.57	02.37	02.56	04.04
Jatinegara	A	19.30	.	.	.	23.35	23.59	00.47	02.00	01.22	03.00	03.16	04.14
Pasar Senin	A	19.45	.	,		02.59	03.20	03.43	05.11	04.33	06.11	06.27	07.25
Gambir	A	.	16.45			03.15	03.36	.	.	.	.	.	.
T. Priok	A	.	.	.	.	.	.	.	05.27	04.49	06.32	06.54	07.42
Jakarta Kota	A	.	.	.	.	.	.	04.09	.	.	.	07.03	.

8. JAKARTA - BANDUNG

TRAINS		Parahyangan II	Cepat	Parahyangan IV	Parahyangan VI	Parahyangan VIII	Parahyangan X	Parahyangan XII	FARES
ROUTE	Route No.	102	206	104	106	108	110	112	
Jakarta-Kota	D	05.25	06.33	09.35	11.10	13.40	15.15	-	Parahyangan :
Gambir	D	05.39	00.44	09.49	11.24	13.53	15.29	18.50	Class I : 8000
Manggarai	D	-	08.54	-	-	-	-	-	Class II : 6000
Jatinegara	D	05.55	09.03	10.04	11.40	14.09	15.45	19.05	Cepat : 2.200
Bandung	A	08.38	12.40	12.55	14.23	17.00	18.28	21.40	

9. BANDUNG-JAKARTA

TRAINS		Parahyangan I	Parahyangan	Parahyangan V	Cepat	Parahyangan VII	Parahyangan IX	Parahyangan XI	
ROUTE	Route No.	101	103	105	207	107	109	III	
Bandung	D	05.00	06.15	09.10	10.18	10.45	14.50	18.15	
Jatinegara	A	07.43	09.06	11,53	14.20	13.28	17.33	20.53	
Manggarai	A	.	.	.	14.30	.	.	.	
Gambir	A	07.59	09.21	12.09	14.42	13.44	17.50	21.09	
Jakarta-Kota	A	08.12	09.33	12.22	14.55	13.57	.	21.22	

10. BANDUNG - YOGYAKARTA - SOLO - SURABAYA ROUTE

Trains / Route	Route No	Express Siang 12	Cepat Yogyakarta 206	Mutiara Selatan 6
Bandung	D	05.25	07.40	17.30.
Yogyakarta	A	13.47	16.59	01.50
	B	14.05	-	02.05
Solo	A	15.23	-	03.18
	D	15.38	-	03.25
Madiun	A	17.28	-	04.50
	D	17.38	-	04.54
Surabaya Gubeng	A	20.48	-	07.52
	D			
Surabaya Kota	A	21.00	-	08.15

11. SURABAYA - YOGYAKARTA - BANDUNG ROUTE

Trains / Route	Route No	Cepat Yogyakarta 205	Express Siang 11	Mutiara Selatan 5
Surabaya Kota	D		05.15	17.30
Surabaya Gubeng	D		05.26	17.50
Madiun	A		08.19	20.27
	D		08.25	20.32
Solo Balapan	A		09.56	22.03
	D		10.01	22.08
Yogyakarta	A		11.18	23.21
	D	08.10	11.27	23.37
Bandung	A	17.32	20.10	07.35

BANDUNG - YOGYAKARTA - SOLO - SURABAYA
Trains Fares

Trains / Route / Class	Mutiara Selatan		Express Siang		Cepat Yogya
	I	II	II	III	III
Bandung - Yogyakarta	13.500,-	9.000,-	5.000,-	3.800,-	3.500,-
- Solo	13.500,-	9.000,-	5.000,-	3.800,-	
- Madiun	15.000,-	10.000,-	7.500,-	5.200,-	
- Surabaya	17.000,-	12.000,-	8.500,-	6.100,-	
Yogyakarta - Solo	13.500,-	9.000,-	5.000,-	3.800,-	
- Madiun	13.500,-	9.000,-	5.000	3.800,-	
- Surabaya	13.500,-	9.000,-	5.000,-	3.800,-	
Solo - Madiun	13.500,-	9.000,-	5.000,-	3.800,-	
- Surabaya	13.500,-	9.000,-	5.000,-	3.800,-	

INTERCITY BUS FARES

I. JAVA

ROUTE	DISTANCE	ECONOMY	AC	AC + RS + TOILET
JAKARTA -				
SERANG	95	1.000	1.500	2.100
MERAK	125	1.300	1.900	2.800
LABUAN	160	1.700	2.500	3.500
CILEGON	111	1.200	1.700	2.500
ANYER	127	1.400	2.000	2.800
BOGOR (toll)	50	800	800	1.100
SUKABUMI (toll)	111	1.200	1.700	2.500
BANDUNG (via Sukabumi)	233	2.500	3.600	5.100
BANDUNG (via Puncak)	187	2.000	2.900	4.100
GARUT (via Sukabumi)	296	3.100	4.500	6.500
GARUT (via Cikampek)	246	2.600	3.800	5.400
TASIKMALAYA (via Puncak)	307	3.200	4.700	6.700
TASIKMALAYA (via Skbmi)	350	3.700	5.300	7.700
CIAMIS (via Skbmi)	370	3.900	5.600	8.100
BANJAR (via Puncak)	349	3.700	5.300	7.800
BANJAR (via Sukabumi)	390	4.100	5.900	8.600
PANGANDARAN (via Skbmi)	427	4.500	6.500	9.400
SUMEDANG (via Puncak)	232	2.400	3.500	7.100
KARAWANG	71	750	1.100	1.600
CIREBON	256	2.700	3.900	5.600
SUBANG	145	1.500	2.200	3.200
KUNINGAN	296	3.100	4.500	6.500
TEGAL	325	3.400	4.900	7.100
PEKALONGAN	392	4.100	6.000	8.600
PURWOKERTO	433	4.500	6.600	9.500
CILACAP	483	5.100	7.300	10.600
PURWOREJO (via Purwokerto)	554	5.800	8.400	12.200
SEMARANG	500	5.200	7.600	11.000
JEPARA	584	6.100	8.900	12.800
SOLO (via Semarang)	602	6.300	9.100	13.200
WONOGIRI	633	6.600	9.600	13.900
MAGELANG	576	6.000	8.700	12.600
YOGYAKARTA	618	6.500	9.400	13.500
MADIUN	714	7.500	10.800	15.600
KEDIRI	807	8.400	12.200	17.700
SURABAYA (via Tuban)	816	8.500	12.400	17.900
SURABAYA (via Solo)	878	9.200	13.300	19.200
MALANG	901	9.400	13.600	19.700

ROUTE	DISTANCE	ECONOMY	AC	AC + RS + T
BANDUNG -				
SEMARANG	368	3.900	5.600	8.100
TEGAL	203	2.100	3.100	4.500
YOGYAKARTA	486	5.100	7.400	10.700
SOLO	473	5.000	7.200	10.400
SURABAYA	684	7.200	10.400	15.000
MERAK	308	3.200	4.700	6.800
YOGYAKARTA -				
PURWOKERT	185	2.000	2.800	4.100
MAGELANG	45	500	700	1.000
SEMARANG	118	1.300	1.800	2.600
SOLO	65	700	1.000	1.500
CILACAP	210	2.200	3.200	4.600
GOMBONG	130	1.400	2.000	2.900
KEBUMEN	100	1.100	1.500	2.200
SURABAYA -				
SEMARANG (via Solo)	379	4.000	5.800	8.300
PURWOKERTO	526	5.500	8.000	11.500
MAGELANG	384	4.000	5.800	8.400
SEMARANG (via Tuban)	316	3.300	4.800	7.000
YOGYAKARTA	341	3.600	5.200	7.500
SOLO	278	2.900	4.200	6.100
MATARAM (W Nusateng-gara)	503	5.300	7.600	11.000
PADANG BAI	475	5.000	7.200	10.400
SINGARAJA	383	4.000	5.800	8.400
DENPASAR	411	4.300	6.300	9.000
DENPASAR -				
BANYUWANGI	129	1.400	2.000	2.900
SURABAYA	411	4.300	6.300	9.000
MALANG	418	4.400	6.400	9.200
YOGYAKARTA	752	7.900	11.400	16.500
MATARAM	85	900	1.300	1.900

BALI BUS LINES

NO	Destination	DENPASAR TERMINAL	VIA
1	AIR PORT	TEGAL	–
2	AIR SANIH	UBUNG	SINGARAJA
3	BESAKIH	KERENENG	KLUNGKUNG
4	BANJAR	UBUNG	SINGARAJA
5	BENOA VILLAGE	TEGAL	–
6	BENOA HARBOUR	SUCI	–
7	BEDUGUL	UBUNG	–
8	BEDULU	KERENENG	GIANYAR
9	BUKIT JAMBUL	KERENENG	KLUNGKUNG
10	BATU BULAN	KERENENG	–
11	CELUK	KERENENG	–
12	CANDIDASA	KERENENG	–
13	CANDI KUNING	UBUNG	–
14	G. KAWI	KERENENG	GIANYAR
15	GOA LAWAH	KERENENG	–
16	GOA GAJAH	KERENENG	GIANYAR
17	GILIMANUK	UBUNG	–
18	JATI LUWIH	UBUNG	TABANAN
19	KEHEN TEMPLE	KERENENG'	BANGLI
20	KERTAGOSA	KERENENG	–
21	KUSAMBA	KERENENG	–
22	KERAMBITAN	UBUNG	TABANAN
23	KUTA	TEGAL	–
24	LOVINA BEACH	UBUNG	SINGARAJA
25	MAS	KERENENG	–
26	MADEWI BEACH	UBUNG	–
27	MARGA	UBUNG	KEDIRI
28	MENGWI	UBUNG	–
29	MOUNT AGUNG	KERENENG	KLUNGKUNG
30	MOUNT BATUR	KERENENG	–
31	MOUNT BATUKARU	UBUNG	TABANAN
32	NUSA DUA	TEGAL	–
33	PELIATAN	KERENENG	–
34	P. BAI HARBOUR	KERENENG	–
35	PUTUNG	KERENENG	AMLAPURA
36	PENELOKAN	KERENENG	KLUNGKUNG
37	PENULISAN	KERENENG	–
38	PANCASARI	UBUNG	–
39	PULAKI	UBUNG	SINGARAJA
40	PEJENG	KERENENG	GIANYAR
41	RAMBUT SIWI	UBUNG	–
42	SUKAWATI	KERENENG	–
43	SANGEH	WANGAYA	–
44	SANGSIT	UBUNG	SINGARAJA
45	SANUR	KERENENG	–

NO	Destination	DENPASAR TERMINAL	VIA
46	TAMPAK SIRING	KERENENG	GIANYAR
47	TENGANAN	KERENENG	–
48	TIRTAGANGGA	KERENENG	AMLAPURA
49	TRUNYAN	KERENENG	
50	TOYA BUNGKAH	KERENENG	
51	TELUK TERIMA	UBUNG	SINGARAJA
52	TANAH LOT	UBUNG	KEDIRI
53	UBUD	KERENENG	–
54	ULUWATU	TEGAL	PECATU
55	AMLAPURA	KERENENG	–
56	BANGLI	KERENENG	–
57	GIANYAR	KERENENG	–
58	KLUNGKUNG	KERENENG	–
59	NEGARA	UBUNG	–
60	SINGARAJA	UBUNG	–
61	TABANAN	UBUNG	–

NO	Destination	DENPASAR TERMINAL	Crossby
1	SERANGAN	SUCI	BUWUNG
		(BY BEMO)	(BY BOAT)
2	NUSA PENIDA	KERENENG	BANUR
	NUSA LEMBONGAN	(BY BUS)	KUSAM
	NUSA CENINGAN		PADANG BAI
			(BY MOTOR OAT,
			SAILING OAT)
3	LOMBOK ISLAND	KERENENG	PADANG BAI
		(BY BUS)	(BY FERRY)
4	JAVA	UBUNG	GILIMANUK
		(BY BUS)	(BY FERRY)

Index

Aceh, 200
airlines, 32-33
airport, 40
Alor, 190
Ambarawa, 110
Ambon, 192
Anak Krakatau, 88-91
Anyer, 110
architecture, 41-42
arts and crafts, 141
art shops, 60
Atu, 192

Badui, 93
Bahasa Indonesia, 43, see
  Appendix
Bali, 129
Bandung, 81
Banten, 94
bargaining, 144-146
Baron, 109
Batak, 199
Batavia, 41, 56
Bat Cave, 156
batik, 62
Batubulan, 140
Batur Lake, 153

Batur, Mount, 158
bazaars, 59, 107
Bedugal, 160
Besakih, 151
Biak, 194
Bogor, 76
Borneo, 197
Borobudur Temple,
  100-102
botanic gardens, 76
Brastagi, 199
Bromo, Mount, 117,
  119-121
Bugis, 119, 160, 195
business hours, 34
bus tours, 31

Candi Dago, 122
Candidasa, 159
Candi Mendut, 102
Candi Pawan, 102
Candi Singosari, 122
Candi Suka, 105
Carita Beach, 88
caves, 80, 109, 156-157
Celebes, see Sulawesi
Celuk, 141-143

ceremonies, 149,150
Ciater Hot Springs, 79
Cibea, 91
Cilicap, 109
Cilegon,94
Cirebon, 82-83
clothing, 33-34
Conrad, Joseph, 117
construction, 39
currency, 33
customs, 34

dance 148-149
Danis, 194
Dayaks, 197
Debus, 93
Denpasar, 137-138
Dieng Plateau, 105
Diponegoro, 54, 195
Dutch, 44

East Java, 117
Elephant Cave, 156
erotic temple, 105

farming, 16
female equality,45
Flores, 189
food, 18-19, 63
forests, 80, 124

gamelan, 161
geography, 13-14
Gianyar, 159
Gilimanuk, 161
government, 16-17

Halmahera, 192
harbour, 55
history, 20-21
hotels, 68-71, 80, 83-85,
    95-97, 113-115,
    126-127, 172-178

income, 17
inoculations, 31
Irian Jaya, 194
Islam, 15
islands, number, 9-10
Istiquial Mosque, 55

Jakarta, 37
Jatijaja Cave 109
Java Man, 110
Jaya Ancol Park, 56
Jepara, 110

Kalimantan, 197
Karangasem, 138
Karangbolong, 109
Karek Bodo, 123
Kawi, Mount, 120
King Boko's Palace, 104
kingdoms, Majapahit,
    122; Mataram, 106
Klungkung, 158
Komodo, 188
Komodo Dragon, 188
Kota Gede, 108
Krakatau (Krakatoa),
    88-91
Kraton Ratubaka, 104
Kublai Khan, 117-118

Kuta Beach, 132–133

Labuan, 95
lakes, 77–80, 153, 158, 160
language, 43; *see* Appendix
Lembang, 79
Lombok, 184–185
Lovina Beach, 160

Madura, 117
Majapahit, Kingdom, 122
Malang, 122
malaria, 31
males, 45–46
Malioboro Street, 107
maps, 6-7, 38
Mas, 141–143
Mataram, Kingdom, 106
Mead Margaret, 11, 142
Medan, 199
Mengwi, 153
Merapi, Mount, 102
Merdeka Palace, 54
Minangkabau, 200–201
Monkey Forest, 154–155
Mount Batur, 158
Mount Bromo, 117, 119–120
Mount Galunggung, 82
Mount Kawi, 120
Mount Kelud, 119
Mount Merapi, 102, 122

National Monument, 54

National Museum, 54
national parks, 124
newspapers, 58
Nias, 199–200
Nusa Dua, 135–136

observatory, 79
oil, 17

Padang Bay, 160
palaces, Gianyar, 159; Klungkung, 158; Surakarta, 106; Yogyakarta, 106
Parangtritis Beach, 109
population, 15–16, 81
Prambanan, 103
Puncak Pass, 77

Raffles, T.S., 76, 101
Rangunan Zoo, 57
rate of exchange, 33
religion, 17–18
resorts, 78, 82, 109, 122–123
restaurants, 64–67, *see* city chapters
Roman Catholic Cathedral, 55

safety, 50–51
Sangeh, 154–155
Sangiran, 110
Sanur Beach, 134
Semarang, 110
Seram, 192

shopping, 59, 61, 181, *see* bargaining
Singaraja, 110
Slender Virgin, 103
Solo (Surakarta) 105
Solor, 190
Spice Islands, 14
sports, water, 139
springs, 77, 79
Sula, 192
Sulawesi, 195-196
Sumatra, 198-201
Sumba, 187
Sumbawa, 186
Sudanese, 81, 82
Sunda Strait, 88
Surabaya, 117
Surabaya Street, 59
Surakarta (Solo), 105

Taman Mini, 56
Taman Safari, 77
Taman Sari, 107
Tanah Lot, 151
taxis, 47-49
Teluga Warna, 77
temples, 147-148, 151-153
Tenggerese, 121
Ternate, 192

thefts, 50-51
Thousand Islands, 97-98
Timor, 191
tipping, 52-53
Torajans, 195
tour agencies, 72-73 85, 97, 169-170
Tretes, 122-123
Tuban, 123
Turtle Island, 157

Ubud, 142
Ujung Kulon, 91
Uluwatu, 152

Visit Indonesia Campaign, 10
volcanoes, 78-79, 81-82, 88-91, 117, 119-122, 158

Water Castle, 107
waterfalls, 77, 79, 123
wildlife, 71, 91, 124
women, 45, 81

Yogyakarta, 99

zoos, 57, 77, 81, 118

TRAVEL THE WORLD WITH HIPPOCRENE BOOKS!

HIPPOCRENE INSIDER'S GUIDES:
The series which takes you beyond the tourist track to give you an insider's view:

NEPAL
PRAKASH A. RAJ
0091 ISBN 0-87052-026-1 $9.95 paper

HUNGARY
NICHOLAS T. PARSONS
0921 ISBN 0-87052-976-5 $16.95 paper

ROME
FRANCES D'EMILIO
0520 ISBN 0-87052-027-X $14.95 paper

MOSCOW, LENINGRAD AND KIEV (Revised)
YURI FEDOSYUK
0024 ISBN 0-87052-881-5 $11.95 paper

PARIS
ELAINE KLEIN
0012 ISBN 0-87052-876-9 $14.95 paper

TAHITI (Revised)
VICKI POGGIOLI
0084 ISBN 0-87052-794-0 $9.95 paper

THE FRENCH ANTILLES (Revised)
ANDY GERALD GRAVETTE
The Caribbean islands of Guadeloupe, Martinique, St. Bartholomew, and St. Martin, and continental Guyane (French Guiana)
0085 ISBN 0-87052-105-5 $11.95 paper

By the same author:
THE NETHERLANDS ANTILLES:
A TRAVELER'S GUIDE
The Caribbean islands of Aruba, Bonaire, Curacao, St. Maarten, St. Eustatius, and Saba.
0240 ISBN 0-87052-581-6 $9.95 paper

HIPPOCRENE LANGUAGE AND TRAVEL GUIDES:
Because traveling is twice as much fun if you can meet new people as well as new places!

MEXICO
ILA WARNER
An inside look at verbal and non-verbal communication, with suggestions for sightseeing on and off the beaten track.
0503 ISBN 0-87052-622-7 $14.95 paper

HIPPOCRENE COMPANION GUIDES:
Written by American professors for North Americans who wish to enrich their travel experience with an understanding of local history and culture.

SOUTHERN INDIA
JACK ADLER
Covers the peninsular states of Tamil Nadu, Andhra Pradesh, and Karnataka, and highlights Goa, a natural gateway to the south.
0632 ISBN 0-87052-030-X $14.95 paper

AUSTRALIA
GRAEME and TAMSIN NEWMAN
0671 ISBN 0-87052-034-2 $16.95 paper

IRELAND
HENRY WEISSER
0348 ISBN 0-87052-633-2 $14.95 paper

PORTUGAL
T. J. KUBIAK
2305 ISBN 0-87052-739-8 $14.95 paper

TO PURCHASE HIPPOCRENE'S BOOKS contact your local bookstore, or write to Hippocrene Books, 171 Madison Avenue, New York, NY 10016. Please enclose a check or money order, adding $3 shipping (UPS) for the first book, and 50 cents for each of the others.

Write also for our full catalog of maps and foreign language dictionaries and phrasebooks.